### Fresh Brewed Murder

"Coffee lovers, this book is for you. A fresh take on the cozy mystery genre. This is a great debut!"

—*Criminal Element*

"Portland's beloved food carts provide a tantalizing backdrop for a new cozy mystery by Portland author Emmeline Duncan . . . A creative way to address both the quirkiness and the more dismaying aspects of life in contemporary Portland."

—*The Sunday Oregonian*

### Double Shot Death

"The possible killers and motives are well juggled, and Duncan's writing is fresh and realistic. Readers will look forward to more with Sage and her coffee cart friends and family."

—*First Clue*

"Solid prose, a well-crafted plot, and plenty of coffee lore draw the reader in. A socially liberal vibe—Bax happily mixes with his ex-wife, their young son, and her husband—sets this cozy apart."

—*Publishers Weekly*

### Flat White Fatality

"Tips on coffee and a touch of romance combine in a mystery with a strong West Coast vibe."

—*Kirkus Reviews*

Books by Emmeline Duncan

FRESH BREWED MURDER

DOUBLE SHOT DEATH

FLAT WHITE FATALITY

DEATH UNFILTERED

Published by Kensington Publishing Corp.

# DEATH UNFILTERED

## Emmeline Duncan

Kensington Publishing Corp.
www.kensingtonbooks.com

KENSINGTON BOOKS are published by

Kensington Publishing Corp.
119 West 40th Street
New York, NY 10018

All Kensington titles, imprints, and distributed lines are available at special quantity discounts for bulk purchases for sales promotion, premiums, fund-raising, educational, or institutional use.

This book is a work of fiction. Names, characters, businesses, organizations, places, events, and incidents either are the product of the author's imagination or are used fictitiously. Any resemblance to actual persons, living or dead, events, or locales is entirely coincidental.

To the extent that the image or images on the cover of this book depict a person or persons, such person or persons are merely models, and are not intended to portray any character or characters featured in the book.

Special book excerpts or customized printings can also be created to fit specific needs. For details, write or phone the office of the Kensington Sales Manager: Kensington Publishing Corp., 119 West 40th Street, New York, NY 10018. Attn. Sales Department. Phone: 1-800-221-2647.

KENSINGTON and the KENSINGTON COZIES teapot logo Reg. US Pat. & TM Off.

ISBN: 978-1-4967-4491-3 (ebook)

ISBN: 978-1-4967-4489-0

First Kensington Trade Paperback Printing: April 2024

10 9 8 7 6 5 4 3 2 1

Printed in the United States of America

*For my fellow Portlanders,
and especially those who inspired
the small, peak-Portland moments
in the Ground Rules series*

# Chapter 1

Sometimes, when you spend years planning and dreaming of something, reaching the end goal feels anticlimactic.

But I had faith this wouldn't be the case for me.

It was almost time: We were on the home stretch to open the Ground Rules brick-and-mortar store.

I wasn't the only one feeling the crunch. My business partner, Harley, was splitting her time between the roastery and the coffee cart. She'd even worked our second cart with one of our baristas at a festival last weekend. We were both looking forward to the grand opening. When the shop launched, our new employees would be trained, and we could settle into our new normal. And, hopefully, we could both take a weekend or two off. Maybe even take a week's vacation. Although not simultaneously, since at least one of us needed to be around to steer the coffee ship.

And, for me, when life slowed down, maybe it would be time to start wedding planning. But, even though my relationship with my fiancé, Bax, was a priority, planning a wedding had fallen down both of our to-do lists, as I had the shop to open. Meanwhile, he was on the home stretch of launching a new video game, which meant he frequently worked longer days than me. But we were solid.

I sometimes had to pinch myself because I was so close to the first

Ground Rules goal I'd made, back when the entire concept had been a dream: opening a real-life coffee shop. I loved our carts and wanted to keep them going as long as possible. But this shop felt more tangible, solid. Which contrasted with one of the first things I adored about opening a food cart: the idea that we could hitch Ground Rules up to a truck and move it wherever we wanted. Not that we'd wanted to move. Our main cart was still at the Rail Yard, aka one of my favorite food cart pods in Portland. The city's food cart scene was continually evolving, and the Rail Yard continued to be one of the prime spots.

With my two new hires for the shop, I was up to six baristas, plus Harley and me. Four of the baristas were pulling shifts at the carts while I trained the two newest, Nina and Colton, at the shop. But eventually, all of the baristas could work at any Ground Rules location. I suspected we'd need to hire two more baristas eventually, but I was waiting for the store to open first. The shop wasn't a finish line, exactly, just a pause to celebrate. Since I'd transition into managing a store alongside both carts.

As I looked at the two newest baristas, and remembered their backgrounds, I suspected the training would be easy. Nina had worked for the same coffee shop where Harley and I had met during our university days. The shop, Left Coast Grinds, used to be the gold standard of how to train baristas and even offered classes for shops that carried their coffee beans. Now, their owner, Mark Jeffries, had pretty much turned himself into a caped villain standing outside Ground Rules, saying he would've been the best coffee roaster in Portland if it wasn't for us obnoxious kids. He offered to buy our business at one point and hadn't wanted to take no for an answer until a cease-and-desist letter from my attorney told him to avoid the Rail Yard. To my surprise, it had worked.

Nina, now maybe twenty-six, had left Portland and worked for a fantastic coffee roaster in the Columbia River Gorge for a few years before returning to Portland when her husband accepted his dream job.

While Colton had moved to Portland a few weeks ago with bona fides from a roaster in Austin whom Harley adored. So far, he'd shown me he could pull a perfect shot of espresso and also craft a latte with a heart or tree in the foam. I needed to get Nina and Colton into the cart to work a few shifts to see them interact with actual customers, but I had a good feeling about both of them. Colton looked peak Portland with his undercut hair, fondness for flannel, Carhartt, corduroy, and a neatly tended beard.

Colton would fit seamlessly into the new shop, which also looked like a quintessential Portland coffee destination, but with a few extras that would make it feel like Ground Rules. The entire Button Building would feel special, and the thought of the food my fellow cafés would produce made me feel hungry.

The Button Building reminded me of a Bundt cake with one piece missing. Each shop is like an individual slice of an octagon, with one door opening on the street and the back door opening to a central, communal covered courtyard with skylights. Customers could order food from any of the micro-restaurants and have their food delivered directly to their seats in the communal seating area.

A shop-sized breezeway, aka the missing cake slice, connected the courtyard directly to an outdoor patio with a fire pit and several rows of picnic tables. In the summer, we could open the garage door between the courtyard and patio, and it would feel like one cohesive space. But with the door shut in the winter, it was a great spot to dine. We were set up to be a hip destination, perfect for grabbing food or drinks with friends who didn't have to agree on one café. One of the micro-restaurants, Déjà Brew, was a beer bar I'd known for a while since they also had an outpost in the Rail Yard alongside the first Ground Rules cart. They'd added cocktails to their Button Building lineup, and their liquor license included the whole facility. So people could buy a drink and take it anywhere on the property.

Fingers crossed, this venture would be a success. As a coffee shop, we planned to open earlier than most of our fellow micro-restaurants, who were generally focused on lunch and dinner.

But one restaurant would open in the morning alongside us: the Breakfast Bandits.

Aka the former food cart that had declared we were mortal enemies before I'd even had a chance to say hello.

And their owner, Bianca, glared at me as she walked past the Ground Rules order window that opened onto the street outside the shop. As a nod to our food cart roots, we'd built a walk-up window on the busy sidewalk outside, hoping to lure foot traffic into stopping. We'd already gotten a few questions from locals waiting to catch their bus.

I offered Bianca a big smile, and she scowled in response.

"What is her problem?" a peppy voice asked behind me. I knew the voice.

I turned to see Rose, true-crime podcaster and social media maven extraordinaire, standing at the counter.

"We're not open yet, Rose," I said.

Like always, Rose looked camera-ready. Her sweater and jeans were utterly on trend, with a studied casual vibe, and her makeup was on point. Her skill with eyeliner was impressive, and her skin looked dewy and glowing. Her chestnut brown hair framed her face in natural curls.

While Rose's focus was on her *Rose Investigates: Thorny Crimes & Intrepid Offshoots* podcast that dove into true crime, she also had an active social media presence. She posted short videos discussing weird facts related to her podcast, which had gone viral last year, and small snippets in her life. Even though my hair is stick-straight, I'd enjoyed watching her humorous video about how she uses the curly girl method to maintain her perfect spirals. Rose couldn't be more than nineteen, maybe twenty, and something told me she'd go far with her mix of tenacity, dedication, and sense of humor.

But Rose's current podcast series put her at odds with me on a fundamental level: She was researching my mother's crimes.

This made every interaction with Rose feel like a landmine. A perky, friendly landmine, but one filled with potential explosions.

Rose gave me a bubbly smile. "I know! I'm excited for your grand opening. I want to post about it, and I'd love to schedule an interview about the opening and your goals for the shop."

"Umm . . ." The last thing I wanted was for my shop to be known as the place owned by a famous con artist's daughter. It was already bad enough that we'd weathered a few suspicious deaths in our general surroundings, even if none had been our fault.

"I'm asking all of the owners to film one. Don't worry. These are all fun snippets. I'm trying to give my followers a sense of the Button Building. It'll tie in with my podcast, the owners, and my research here in Portland. I've found my viewers like these small behind-the-scenes looks into my life."

Owners? Businesses or building? My uncle Jimmy, technically my great-uncle, owned the Button Building and his company ran it. He mostly skirted on the right side of the law versus my mother's lifetime of grifts. She'd used me in scams a few times as a child, but I'd been a pawn.

I felt a sense of shame and guilt when I remembered my childhood, but I also knew it wasn't my fault.

"I'm even scheduled to interview Bianca in a few days, Sage," Rose said. "But I'm talking to Caleb today."

"As long as you keep the questions solely based on the coffee shop, I'll do it," I said.

Rose held up her pink backpack from the well-known Swedish brand. "Want to film now?"

"I'm not exactly camera-ready," I said. Granted, my teal Ground Rules T-shirt was clean, as I hadn't doused myself in coffee yet today, and my hair was in a neat enough ponytail.

Nina and Colton both watched us. Colton smiled, like he enjoyed observing this train wreck.

Rose nodded at them. "How about they work behind you as we talk, and the end of the video can linger on a coffee drink they just made? Maybe a twelve-ounce mocha?"

I smiled. "So you'd like a mocha?"

"I would love one. But no whipped cream, please." The podcaster reminded me of a flower in full bloom, fresh and vibrant, and something about her made me smile. I'm sure she'd have a Rose-like perfume if I stepped close enough to smell it.

"Okay."

Rose set up her phone on a tripod and filmed us standing side by side next to the ordering counter while my baristas bustled behind us. Rose asked me about Ground Rules, and I told her about how we roasted our own coffee beans and sold them at our shop and coffee carts.

Rose turned and faced the camera.

"I've been to the Ground Rules cart at the Rail Yard several times, and it's the bomb," Rose said. "Trust me, you're going to want to try their new shop early 'cause I know it's going to be packed."

As if on cue, Colton brought over the mocha, which he'd dusted with our house-made "magic dust."

Rose paused filming and recorded a close-up of the tree in the foam on top of the mocha, all sprinkled with our aforementioned magic dust. Then, after she'd filmed the drink to her satisfaction, Rose took her spot back in front of the camera and filmed herself sipping the mocha.

"Perfection," she said, then stopped recording with a small remote. "I think that's a wrap."

"That's a relief," I said.

"What? I don't bite," Rose said. She took another sip of the mocha.

Laura, the owner of Fowl Play, one of our neighboring restaurants, walked by the outside of our shop and waved. As I waved back, Rose spoke.

"You know her? Laura? She once had a hilarious fight in downtown Portland with Bianca. Let's just say there was an embarrassing amount of screaming."

"Really? How do you know about that?" I asked.

"The footage is still online. It went viral and was reposted all over the place. Some of the parodies are hilarious. Want a link?"

"That's okay. I do my best not to gossip." Although I sometimes fail.

Had Rose delved into the online drama around Ground Rules? So far, our name hadn't been directly linked to a murder in the news, although it'd been close. And our nemesis, Mark Jeffries, had alluded to it a few times on social media, although he'd stopped from any direct accusations. Although I suspected he was still watching our business closely, biding his time.

Or maybe the stress over the new shop was turning Mark into a pantomime villain in my head. He just needed a hipster mustache to twirl to look the part.

But I did make a mental note to do a deep dive into the Ground Rules online presence when I had a moment to breathe. It's always a good idea to keep an eye on our social media accounts and mentions, although I try to not take it personally. 'Cause some people are, simply, way too mean.

"And you know, we do need to talk about the elephant in the room," Rose said.

No, we didn't. "Did you know that some elephants like coffee? Or at least, there's a company in Thailand that sells coffee with the elephants performing the same role as civets in Kopi Luwak." I'd never tried either coffee, which are both considered delicacies, and both revolve around the coffee cherries passing unbroken through the digestive tract of the animals involved, only to be harvested intact from their waste.

"Umm, gross," Rose said. "Do people really drink poop coffee?"

"It's safe to drink, and supposedly, it's delicious. But if I talk about animals and the world's greatest beverage, I prefer the legend of goats discovering it. I also like knowing my coffee cherries were harvested by humans making fair wages."

Rose looked outside the coffee shop into the communal seating area, and I followed her gaze. Laura and Bianca were arguing near the entrance of the Breakfast Bandits. Had they really had a high-profile fight?

"Good job almost changing the subject. But you know what I'm talking about," Rose said. Her glance my way was knowing.

And she was right. I knew exactly what she was referring to.

Rumor had it my mother had died in a scam gone wrong. She'd been in a car chase in South America, and her car had gone off a cliff, killing her whole crew. Maybe her motto had been "live by the grift and die by it." She'd spent most of her life on the wrong side of the law without caring about the collateral damage it caused to the people around her, including me.

The whole situation made me feel sick, and I did my best not to think of it since I wasn't sure what to believe. I hadn't seen my mother in person since she'd dumped me in Portland when I was barely a teenager. She'd sent a few messages over the years and somehow managed to call me a handful of times even after I'd changed my phone number.

"I'm not going to talk about my mother," I finally said.

"That's a mistake. You should get your side of the story out and tell everyone your mother doesn't define you."

"Not being interviewed does the same thing. My mother isn't part of my life and vice versa. There's no reason to insert myself into the story." No more than I already, unwittingly, had been part. But those chapters were long finished and I was drafting my own narrative.

"Still, think about it, Sage. The first episode dropped yesterday. Listen to it; it might change your mind." Rose's tone was sympathetic, like she understood my stance, versus trying to wheedle me into doing what she wanted.

"We need to get back to work," I said, turning away from Rose. But a sight made me freeze.

Mark Jeffries. Here. In the unopened Button Building.

Mark had to be in his late forties or early fifties but looked younger. It wasn't just the artfully styled brown hair or the hip retro down jacket. If he wasn't dressed for a crisp late winter day, I'd have seen coffee-related tattoos adorning both arms, like a moka pot on one forearm. Even though I disliked him, I had to admit there was something vibrant about Mark that drew people to him. It's the same quality that causes devotees to rally around politicians.

Or charlatans.

I'd liked Mark when I'd first started working for him as a barista in my university days. But that was before I'd noticed the sketchy vein running through his charm.

And it was before he'd taken credit for Harley's award-winning work.

What was Mark doing here?

And more importantly, why was he talking with Bianca?

Bianca looked annoyed as she walked away from Mark toward the Breakfast Bandits–storefront-to-be. But she always looked like she'd smelled something gross. She reminded me of people telling me not to frown or my face would freeze that way as a child. Something annoying must have happened to Bianca once, and her face had frozen into that expression as a default.

Bianca paused by the entrance of her shop, and Rose walked up to her.

To my everlasting shock, Bianca smiled.

"That's a rare event," Abby Best, owner of Best Burgers, said as she walked up to me.

"You're on Bianca's bad side, too?"

"You think she has a good side?" Abby asked.

"Everyone does, I assume."

"Oh, don't get me started about Bianca. We were at the same food cart pod downtown for a while, and it was an absolute nightmare. Her breakfast burritos are good; I'll give you that."

"I've never tried her food."

"She's really creative. She has this cheesy mashed potato burrito with cauliflower that's clearly inspired by aloo gobi, given the spice profile. Plus, her traditional fare is excellent, like a pork verde that's unbelievably tender. She had a special for a while of a brioche French toast with some sort of pear compote that was, supposedly, to die for, given the long lines at her cart. And her bacon breakfast burrito is perfectly balanced."

"At least something about her shop is balanced," I muttered, then immediately felt guilty.

Abby laughed, which made me feel worse about my cattiness. "You know, Bianca was bragging earlier about how the owner of the Button Building called her and personally offered her a spot in this building."

"News to me." I didn't tell Abby that when I'd seen the list of applications, I'd asked my uncle Jimmy, the owner of the Button Building, to turn Bianca's application down.

But he'd never said he'd invited her, although he'd ignored my advice and leased her a spot.

Did my uncle and Bianca know each other, beyond their current landlord and tenant relationship? If yes, how? More importantly, how intimately?

I pushed the thought out of my mind. I had enough to worry about. After Abby and I finished chatting about the upcoming grand opening, she returned to her café. At the Rail Yard and the handful of farmers markets Ground Rules had set up at, there was always one food cart that took the lead in organizing the rest of us into a series of promotions or events, like the music series at the Rail Yard. So far, Abby was the driving social force of the Button Building.

I made a few notes in my phone about the upcoming grand opening, then forced myself to ignore Bianca and Mark, and focused on what I could control: getting the Ground Rules shop ready to make a splash on the Portland coffee scene.

When I arrived home, a small orange cat ran to me, chirping. He'd clearly had an eventful day and needed to tell me all about it.

"Hi, Kaldi," I said. I scooped him off the ground. He promptly snuggled onto my shoulder as I dumped my bag on the couch.

Kaldi had adopted me. I'd set up the second Ground Rules cart at a festival, and Kaldi started showing up like he was our newest and tiniest barista. After the festival, he came to live with Bax, since I was still renting a room from my brother, and his dog was terrified of cats. Kaldi had quickly settled in and added Bax to his inner circle of people and, in true cat fashion, hadn't blinked an eye when I'd moved in full-time.

As I prepared to cook dinner, I opened the first episode of Rose's investigation into Saffron Jones.

Aka my mother.

A few months ago, an FBI agent had contacted me and asked if I'd heard from her recently. I'd been honest: the last time I'd heard from my mother had been a text a few weeks after Ground Rules opened.

I'd laughed and told the special agent she wasn't exactly maternal.

I clicked play and started chopping vegetables for a stir-fry, letting Rose's voice fill my brain.

"Everyone, you all know that true-crime podcasts are my jam. And my fellow podcasters have done their best to bring justice for the victims of the crimes they profiled, but also, in some cases, justice for people falsely accused of crimes they didn't commit.

"But where does justice end? What about crimes that aren't murder, like fraud? Even small acts of crime or violence, like someone running into a parked car and not leaving a note, leave a lasting emotional ripple on the affected.

"Over the next few weeks, I want to explore the ripple crime has over the people surrounding a criminal event.

"How did it affect their lives? Their futures?

"I'm going to do this by looking into the life and times of notorious grifter Saffron Jones.

"You might have heard her name, but there's a good chance you haven't. Because she's never killed anyone.

"But that doesn't mean she hasn't ruined lives.

"What do you think when you hear the words 'Portland, Oregon'? Coffee? Hipsters? Political protests? Do you think of the deep forests of Oregon or the purposefully undeveloped beauty of the Oregon Coast?

"I'm in Portland now, and I've enjoyed learning about the dark underbelly of the city's history, like the historic Shanghai Tunnels. Although this could be an urban legend, people claim that sometimes men who drank at a tavern above the infamous tunnels would wake up to find themselves on a ship bound for Shanghai. They'd need to work their way back home.

"While it's easy to imagine what it would feel like to be one of those men, what about the devastation inflicted on the people they unintentionally left behind? A mother, a wife. Daughter. Son.

"Hopefully, their loved one returned to them, but imagine what it felt like if he didn't come home. Especially if they never knew what happened.

"You might wonder why I brought up Portland. And it's because this is where the story starts, although not where it ends.

"Is it a surprise that Saffron Jones was born in Portland? What was her early childhood like, and how did it prepare her to spend her adult years scamming her way across the world?

"Did it prepare her for her death? Because supposedly, Jones died a few months ago in South America.

"Her death won't bring closure to her victims.

"But a little light into her crimes might help.

"This is Rose of *Rose Investigates: Thorny Crimes & Intrepid Offshoots*. Throughout this season, we'll dive into the crimes of con artist Saffron Jones, but through the lens of the people she scammed.

"Catch me next week."

* * *

I pulled my headphones off, slid them back into their case, and tucked them into my bag so I wouldn't lose them.

Rose was right about one thing: crime does ripple over the lives of everyone affected. The bad things we experience, alongside the good, always have a lasting mark.

And the negative experiences leave deeper bruises that are harder to shake off.

But that didn't mean I wanted her to explore the subject by investigating my mother, especially since Rose wanted to interview me.

I looked at the positive side. Rose had a lovely voice for a podcast, both melodic and thoughtful. I wondered how long she spent writing her scripts or if she winged it. While her last series had done well, it hadn't hit the heights of its predecessors like *My Favorite Murder* or *Serial*, so it's not like the whole world would know my mother's name.

Given Rose's careful appearance, she must approach the podcast diligently, always putting her best foot forward. She clearly put a lot of prep work into each podcast, and, I decided, that had to include diligently writing them ahead of time. Hopefully, her research was also impeccable.

Steps entered the kitchen.

Bax. He must've come home while I was listening to the podcast. He wore slithery gray workout pants and a hoodie, so he must've hit the gym next to his office before heading home. Which was good 'cause he needs exercise to keep him balanced.

"Oh good, Coffee Angel, you're making extra," Bax said. He kissed my forehead before grabbing a glass and filling it with water.

"We can both use the leftovers for lunch. Good workout?"

"Pretty standard. Which is excellent since it means I actually got into the gym."

As Bax told me about *Falling Through the Shadows*'s status, also known as the video game development currently consuming his life, he grabbed a couple of plates and silverware.

"So, barring something horrific, we'll have the game ready on time next month. Pre-orders are strong, and I'm glad we won't let our fans down."

"Are you still going to launch at the comic con in Seattle?"

"Yep, so clear your calendar 'cause we want you to be part of the launch."

"As long as I don't have to wear a costume," I said. I'd done motion capture work for the video game, and the lead character was partially based on me. So I both dreaded and looked forward to seeing the game launch.

"Oh, you know you should dress up as the character," Bax teased. "It's just jeans and a leather jacket. Oh, and motorcycle boots."

"Totally my speed."

After a final stir, dinner was ready, and we plated our food and moved to the table while chatting about logistics.

The future looked so bright we clearly needed shades.

And a large iced coffee.

# Chapter 2

Two weeks later, it had finally arrived: the Button Building's grand opening. I ran through the opening day plans as I got dressed, choked down a piece of toast even though I was too excited to eat, and rolled my bicycle out from the garage.

The streets of Portland were dark as I made my way to the Button Building. I stopped myself from swinging by the Rail Yard to make sure Sophie, one of my baristas, was opening the coffee cart. I trusted she had everything in hand, including putting the sign advertising the shop's grand opening in the cart's order window.

We would be the first restaurant open at the Button Building this morning, and in honor of the grand opening, we'd leave the lights on and serve coffee until eight p.m. Normally we'd close at four.

Colton was waiting by the shop as I rolled my bicycle into one of the bike lockers outside Ground Rules's front door and secured it.

"Are you ready for the big show?" I asked him as I unlocked the door to the coffee shop.

"I was born ready," Colton answered as he followed me inside.

As we shed our coats and stashed them in the lockers in the small storage room at the back of the store, I noticed he'd worn a Ground Rules T-shirt. We didn't have a dress code for employees other than keep any body part you don't want potentially burned by coffee covered and don't wear anything that can't be improved by coffee stains. But it made me happy to see one of my employees wearing the T-shirt I'd given him during his work orientation.

Colton and I worked side by side as we prepped the store. By 6:30, our official opening time, the shop had received a delivery of pastries from my favorite bakery in Portland, and one of their marionberry and hazelnut muffins was calling my name. The espresso maker was calibrated, and our first carafe of house coffee had percolated, sending the rich aroma of our Puddle Jumper blend in the air. The tables were set up. Our order window on the sidewalk was ready. The order tablets were set up on their stands by both order counters.

The shop felt ready. It was time to fulfill Harley's and my brick-and-mortar dreams.

The custom Ground Rules music list I'd curated over the past few years gave us the perfect ambiance. The music was loud enough to be background noise but not too loud.

Now, we just needed customers.

Colton photographed me as I set up the Ground Rules sandwich board outside. We rushed back inside since it was too cold to stay out without a jacket. I quickly posted the photo to all of our social media accounts. I had several posts ready to go across multiple platforms in my social media management app, including a couple with discounts and two with prizes. I added the photo to the queue, then sent it out, announcing we were ready to fulfill everyone's caffeine needs.

The first customer wandered in about five minutes after we'd flipped the OPEN sign on. Colton and I glanced at each other, then I greeted the customer, took his order for a dry cappuccino, and Colton made it.

We high-fived as the customer wandered out, still looking half-asleep.

"I wanted to take a photo of him, but it would've been weird," I said.

"One of the other owners—I think her name is Abby—said that

the local newspaper is going to cover the grand opening later," Colton said. "It's too bad they weren't here to get a photo of the first Button Building customer."

"Abby told you?"

"Yeah, she chatted with me the other day."

Colton looked slightly pink, and I barely resisted the urge to tease him. I didn't know his romantic status; all I knew was that he'd been renting a room from friends since he moved here from Austin. Which made me assume he was single, but for all I knew he had a wife and four kids waiting to join him once he'd settled in.

We'd been open about an hour when Nina arrived, precisely two minutes before her shift started.

"I'll be ready in a tick!" Nina said. She ducked behind the counter and headed to her locker in the back.

A woman had followed Nina into the coffee shop. She held a notebook and showed me the voice recorder in her other hand. She identified herself as being from a local paper. "Can I interview you? I'm doing a piece about the Button Building opening for the food and dining section."

"Sure."

"Is it okay if I record? I always ask before starting."

"Of course."

"And I'd love to order a twelve-ounce oat milk latte. No syrup or anything."

The journalist clicked something on her voice recorder and put it on the counter between us. I instinctively switched into my public relations mode.

"Your shop used to be a food cart, correct?"

"We still have two coffee carts in addition to our brand-new shop." I explained our setup.

"Oh, I thought everyone here had switched from food carts. I'd like to ask your opinions about the future of food carts in Portland since many people have complained city regulations are making it harder for them to function."

"Part of being a business owner is keeping on top of the regula-tions affecting your niche, regardless of whether or not you think they're fair. Food carts are such an integral part of Portland's culinary and tourism scene that I'm sure everyone will figure out how to help them flourish."

"Do you think the city's regulations are unfair?" Her tone was strident.

"I think health and safety are important, and from what I've seen, my fellow food cart owners take those seriously. There's a reason why you have yet to hear about any serious food-borne illness out-breaks. But it's always worth seeing how we can improve things for all of us."

"Do you think the new regulations are actually making things better?"

"That's beyond my pay grade," I said. I was tempted to send the journalist to a few food cart owners I knew who'd happily rail against the regulations, which were tough to deal with when your business was already operating on long hours and razor-thin profit margins. This was one reason we'd worked to get Ground Rules products car-ried in grocery stores and other shops and had an active subscription service, so we didn't live and die by sales at the cart. Opening the shop should continue to firm up our profit margin and keep us on our path to world coffee domination.

Beside me, Colton had finished steaming the oat milk for the journalist's latte. He carefully crafted a tree in the foam as he com-bined the espresso and steamed milk. Truth be told, I suspected Colton's latte art was better than mine. He put the drink down in front of her, and she smiled.

"This looks lovely," the journalist said. "You roast your own beans, correct?"

"That's right. We have a roastery in Southeast Portland." I told her the usual Ground Rules spiel, feeling like I was repeating myself from earlier, and she wrote a few notes in addition to the ongoing voice recording.

She took a photo of Colton and me behind the counter, hope-fully looking perky in our Ground Rules aprons. Then she headed to the table near the front door with her coffee, looking at the street like she was watching for someone.

I took the orders for a handful of customers who trickled in. But my brain kept turning back to the interview. After the minefield of talking with Rose, hopefully, my skill to be interesting enough to be quoted without being controversial were in full force.

Although I suspected the journalist's motives. She seemed like she had a story she wanted to tell, versus asking questions to ferret out the stories she didn't know about the Button Building. An article about the grand opening sounded like a puff piece, but something about her reminded me of Rose's investigative side. But, I reminded myself, we're almost all viewing the world through preconceived no-tions.

I glimpsed Mark Jeffries, aka my nemesis, glancing inside our back door as he walked by carrying a box. I snuck over and saw him disappear inside the Breakfast Bandits.

Hmm.

After the journalist left, I saw Bianca and Phillip, her boyfriend, and I assumed Breakfast Bandits co-owner and partner in her quest to serve burritos to the world, walk into the communal seating area. It looked like they were arguing.

Nina slid into our work area while tying a Ground Rules apron behind her back. "I'm sorry I was so close to the wire," she said.

"Just don't make a habit of it."

Nina scrubbed her hands, preparing to pitch in and serve the short line of customers Colton and I were handling.

Nina looked the same as always. Dark leggings, long sweatshirt, today in a pine green, hair styled in a cute and slightly edgy pixie cut. Light makeup, including pink lipstick and silvery eyeliner. Very sim-ple, but it felt like Nina.

"Can you make me a cortado? I'm dying for coffee," Nina asked during our first lull after she started working. Nina sounded slightly overdramatic, which was also typical.

Colton obliged, which was also on-brand.

Time turned into a blur. My social worker friend Manny and several of his coworkers from Inner City Assistance all showed up, decked out in the bright orange T-shirts and hoodies they wore when working on the streets with the homeless.

"No, this is on me," I said as I hooked them up with house coffees.

"Are you going to come volunteer with me again now that you've opened the shop?" Manny asked. "We've missed you."

"For sure. Give me a week to ensure this is going, but then yeah. And let me know if you want to pick up some carafes of coffee for your rounds." I'd volunteered with Manny on and off for years. Once I'd started Ground Rules, I'd periodically donated containers of coffee on the go so Manny and his coworkers could hand out cups of hot coffee or cocoa to the population they served.

"Any chance we can get one for today? It's weirdly cold out there."

"For sure." The city opened warming shelters when it was freezing in the winter, although not everyone was willing to go to one. Offering someone a warm drink on a cold day was a great way to start the conversation and try to convince them to move indoors, at least temporarily.

Manny and his coworkers grabbed seats at a table. I brewed up a carafe of coffee and poured it into a cardboard coffee-to-go box with a foil liner inside that we picked up from our local restaurant supply store. Each container holds about twenty cups of coffee.

As I handed the container over to Manny, along with a bag of cups, sugar, and a container of cream, a woman waiting for her latte raised her eyebrows at me.

"Are those for sale? Like for business meetings?"

"Of course! If you ever want one but you're in a rush, call ahead and we can get it started while you're on your way here." I answered some of her questions, gave her one of the shop's business cards and a brochure, and then rejoined Colton and Nina.

But they were handling things, with Nina taking orders and Colton crafting drinks while joking with waiting customers. He multitasked like a champ. I collected a bin of coffee cups and set them up in the dishwasher to be cleaned and sterilized, then saw a customer walk up to the sidewalk window. I slid it open and took an order for a cold brew.

"Perfect weather for an iced drink," I joked as I handed the cold brew to the woman bundled up in a down coat and plaid scarf. Her Lab wore a matching buffalo plaid bandana, showing he was as much a hipster as anyone on the streets of Portland.

She laughed. "I drink iced coffee year-round. It tastes better than hot."

They continued their walk, pausing by the garbage can at the bus stop so the Lab could sniff the base. Everyone deserves their own treats, after all, even iced drinks on freezing days.

Harley dropped in midmorning. We took a few photos and squealed about opening the shop a few times, then she left to drop off bags of coffee beans at a local co-op who is one of our best wholesale customers.

"Back to the grindstone," I muttered to myself, appreciating the pun, as Harley paused and waved on the doorstep.

By lunchtime, we'd redeemed coupons for at least twenty free drinks, not to mention the paying customers who'd also dropped in. Colton had just returned from lunch, and I was about to send Nina on her break when Rose walked up to the counter.

"Two coffees, please."

Rose was dressed in a trendy blazer and jeans, with a perfectly made-up face. So I guessed she planned on being on camera today. Her deep red lipstick looked thick and flawless, like she somehow managed to glue it on.

Colton handed me two cups, and I filled them with coffee.

"It looks like you've been delightfully busy. I'm so glad," Rose said as I handed the cups over.

She took a sip of one. "Your coffee is just so good!" she said, and headed to the condiment station, which was stocked with carafes of oat milk, cream, sugar, sugar-free sweetener, honey, and more. Nina shifted to the side as she filled the sugar container so Rose had room to put her cups down. Rose added cream to both, and I turned to take an order from a man in a dapper business suit.

As Colton made the man's drink, I headed out to bus a few tables and collect the dirty dishes from the bus bin.

Rose put the coffee cups down on the table in the communal area and turned to talk with Laura from Fowl Play and Abby from Best Burgers. I looked down to rebalance a haphazard stack of ceramic cups, and when I looked up, Rose stood with Bianca.

They stood just outside Ground Rules in the communal seating area. Laura and Abby had retreated together to the side, whispering together. They looked like they were close, especially given the way Abby patted Laura's arm.

Rose's voice cut through the air.

"Just try it. I promise you're going to adore the coffee," Rose said.

Bianca begrudgingly took a sip.

Phillip walked up, blocking my view as he said something quietly to Bianca, then hustled away. She sipped coffee the whole time. Maybe she would become a Ground Rules convert, based on the lure of our perfectly balanced medium roast capable of breaking through her crusty exterior to the soft spot underneath she kept hidden from everyone.

"I only have a minute, so let's make this quick," Bianca said. She took another swig of coffee.

Rose clicked the remote in her hand, and her phone on its tripod started recording.

As Rose started talking, Bianca blinked hard, like she was trying to make the world come into focus.

"I'm here with Bianca Moore, owner of the Breakfast Bandits.

We're at the opening of the brand-new Button Building in Portland, Oregon. Bianca owns one of the micro-restaurants that, as of today, has a lean but mighty selection of breakfast burritos and sandwiches. They have a vegan option with avocado, so you know they've gotten my attention!" Rose said, looking straight into the camera.

If Rose decided podcasting wasn't for her, she'd be a natural on-air reporter for a local news station. She'd cover all manner of local events but with a focus on features showcasing the best of her community. Although, given her true-crime podcast, she had to think hard-hitting investigative journalism was her thing.

Rose turned to Bianca. "Congratulations on the big day! How did you decide to get into breakfast foods?"

"Everyone knows that if you want a good start to the day," Bianca said, but her voice trailed off into silence.

"And then what?"

"You need a good breakfast." Bianca rubbed her eyes and then blinked hard.

"You've worked around some of your fellow café owners before, right? Which is your favorite? You're drinking a cup of Ground Rules coffee now, and my followers know I'm a huge fangirl."

Bianca's eyes narrowed, and she lurched forward a few inches as she shifted, like she was going to fall, but caught herself. She swayed as she spit out, "Ground Rules? Why'd you bring them up? Let me tell you about them and how they're the . . ."

Bianca's voice trailed off again, and she put her hand on her chest.

And then Bianca collapsed to the floor. The dregs of her coffee cup spread from the cup she still clutched in her hand.

Rose screamed.

Laura and Abby rushed forward to help, and I pulled my phone out of my pocket and dialed 911.

Abby looked at me. "I can't find a pulse."

Rose staggered, and Colton rushed past me. He put his arm around Rose's waist and led her to a table.

Phillip rushed into the room and skidded to a halt. He stared at

Bianca with his mouth open. Caleb put his hand on Phillip's shoulder and they stood there, completely still, like statues.

Abby and Laura took turns doing CPR and mouth-to-mouth as I talked to the 911 operator. A fire truck pulled up, and the firefighters took over, followed by an ambulance and two straight-faced paramedics.

Laura, Abby, and I huddled together in the doorway to Ground Rules while Colton stayed with Rose, who bawled on his shoulder. Caleb and Phillip talked with one of the firefighters. Phillip gestured widely a few times and Caleb seemed to be focused on keeping him calm.

"She's not going to make it," Abby said, then burst into tears.

# Chapter 3

Colton, Nina, and I stood together in the Ground Rules shop. Everything felt surreal like we were starring in a farce but hadn't been given a script. Although I suspected I'd realize, emotionally, when reality set in, we'd discover we were part of a tragedy.

The police had wrapped caution tape around the communal seating area. My fellow micro-restaurant owners kept popping up behind the tape in their cafés like prairie dogs.

"Should we close?" Colton asked.

"We could serve people through the coffee window, maybe?" I asked.

I glanced into the communal seating area, where the police were doing their thing. Abby, Laura, and Caleb from Doughman Pizza stood just inside Fowl Play, watching the communal area. The look of concern on their faces reminded me of the worry roiling around inside me. Abby and Laura had done their best to help out Bianca, and we still didn't know if she'd made it.

Although it didn't look good.

Plus, we all had a lot invested in the Button Building. It wasn't just a new development but the culmination of many small dreams banding together to create something bigger.

Bianca's death could shatter all those dreams, leaving endless waves of devastation behind her. We were all invested in the success of the building and our businesses, both financially and emotionally.

Colton and Nina moved to the sidewalk order window, where a customer stood. I walked outside, shivering in the cold air as I made my way around the building to Fowl Play, and through their front door. The warm air felt like a toasty blanket. I noted the interior walls of the shop were painted a cheerful yellow with a painted graphic of a chicken. I walked to meet my fellow business owners still huddled together in the doorway to the communal area. I nodded at Laura's employee, who was doing amazing-smelling prep work that made my stomach grumble. I'd missed lunch, not that it mattered in the greater scheme of things.

"Should we close for the day?" Abby asked as I walked up.

"I have too much invested to close. I don't want all of the food I bought to spoil," Laura said.

Caleb looked grim. "I even have pre-orders," he said.

Which didn't surprise me. Caleb's pizza cart had long lines, and his customers following him to the Button Building felt like a given.

"Hopefully we can sell out of our restaurants even if part of the building is closed. We could just postpone the grand opening of the common area," I said. I wondered if my words were true or simply hope. And I felt guilty for planning how to continue everyday business as if a tragedy hadn't happened outside my door.

Phillip stalked up to us. His eyes were red, but I could practically see waves of anger rolling off him as he glared at me.

"You did this!" he yelled. "You killed Bianca."

"Wait," I said. "Killed?"

"Yes. Bianca's dead, and it's your fault."

Caleb took a deep breath beside me, and when I glanced over, he looked at the ground instead of making eye contact. Laura and Abby had turned to each other, and I could see grief in their mutual hunched shoulders.

Phillip took another angry step forward. Behind him, one of the uniformed officers stepped our way.

I held up my hands in a calming gesture. "Let's lower the temperature a bit, huh? I'm sorry for your loss."

Phillip's face reddened, and I wondered if we would have another health crisis. Because he looked like he was ready to explode. "You just couldn't allow us to be successful, but I wouldn't think you'd go this far to sabotage—"

Abby cut him off. "Chill, dude. Why would anyone kill your girlfriend? I'm sure it was a freaky health crisis."

Phillip turned his glare to Abby, who didn't flinch. His tone lowered to a threatening rumble. "You hated Bianca, too. You would've loved to see her fail."

"Grow up, Phillip. No one thought about you or Bianca when you weren't in sight." Abby crossed her arms over her chest.

Laura chimed in. "Just because no one got along with Bianca didn't mean we'd sabotage your business, let alone harm someone. I'm sorry for your loss, but getting angry at us is a mistake."

Phillip turned, glaring at us until his gaze settled on me. He pointed his index finger my direction. "You'll regret this," he said.

As he walked away, I realized two people were watching us. The police officer who'd noticed Phillip's rant and listened in, and a woman who had to be a detective. I glanced at her waist, where a badge was clipped to her belt.

"If I can have your attention, please," the woman said in a clear voice with a no-nonsense air. "We need you to clear the communal seating area. We're closing it down as we investigate what happened."

"Do we need to close down the individual restaurants?" I asked.

"Who are you, and why do you think you can order us around?" Abby said.

The woman half-smiled. "I'm Detective Leto with the Portland Police Bureau. If you have a problem with my decision, you can step outside of this area, and we can chat. And to answer the other question, we'll need access to all the restaurants, although we're especially interested in two."

I knew Ground Rules would be one of the two places to close.

"So I can continue to sell pizza?" Caleb's voice was hopeful.

"Yes, if you let one of our crime scene techs take a quick gander through your café before you start selling anything."

"Do they have time now?" Caleb had clearly gone the path of no resistance with the police, but he had the incentive to play nice. After all, he had pre-orders to fill for eager customers. And I couldn't see Caleb being involved with whatever had happened today.

I couldn't see anyone here trying to harm Bianca.

"Yes, we'll send someone over." Detective Leto said something quietly to the officer next to her, and he nodded.

"I'd like to be next after Caleb," Laura said.

"Wait in your restaurants, and someone will be by. For now, I'd like to talk to Sage Caplin."

I could practically feel Laura and Abby swivel to look at me. I forced an almost smile onto my face. "Do you want to talk here?"

"Let's head to your coffee shop."

She followed me around the perimeter of the communal area, and as I walked, my heart thudded in my ears.

I couldn't believe this was really happening.

As I stood facing the detective, Colton and Nina watched from the other side of the coffee counter. It almost felt like we should be acting in an improv, with my baristas as the audience.

Detective Leto was taller than me, but that wasn't saying much since she has that in common with almost everyone over the age of twelve. I'd guessed she was about 5'4", with curly dark brown hair pulled back into a ponytail. A few strands had escaped, and she'd tucked them behind her ear. The detective's eyes looked sharp like she didn't miss much, and I guessed she was in her late thirties. Her navy button-down shirt was tucked into gray dress pants, and she'd paired the outfit with shiny black three-hole Doc Martens. She looked like someone I could be friends with. But we were on opposite sides of a problem, meaning I should be careful about what I said.

In fact, I should call my older brother before speaking with her. My brother, Jackson, is a child advocacy attorney and spends part of his time in juvenile court. So if he knew I was talking to the police, he'd want to be here to manage the conversation.

"Caplin," Detective Leto said. "Your name is familiar."

"My father was a detective in the cold case unit but retired a few months ago."

She smiled. "Christopher, right? But he still volunteers with the cold case unit two days a week. He pulled some files for me a while back and was very helpful. He's great."

I nodded. Yep, that was my father. After serving in the army and spending over twenty years as a police officer in Portland, he'd retired. But he wasn't the sort to sit around, so he'd started volunteering with his old department alongside a fellow retired detective and a retired FBI agent. The three of them met up for dinner each week, discussing the cold cases they were working on and how the world had changed. And I suspected they helped each other through the transition into retirement. My father said once that the answers to all sorts of questions lie in the cold case files, but they don't know the right questions to ask.

But I respected what he did, and he seemed happier, like a weight had lifted off his shoulders. I asked my dad once what he did when he volunteered. That day at least, he'd reviewed a couple of requests from police departments in the Northwest who'd had cases that might be similar to past crimes in Portland. He'd pulled old files that could be relevant and analyzed them for similarities. He'd refused to say anything more about the individual cases, but I could tell at least one of them had been terrible based on the look that flashed through his eyes.

Detective Leto half-smiled as she glanced at the notepad in her hand, but her face was straight as she looked back up at me. Her eyes were light brown, almost like caramel. Something told me Rose would approve of the discreet copper eye shadow the detective wore, which brought out the golden flecks in her eyes. Rose had recommended slate gray to me to bring out the supposed stormy gray notes of my blue eyes or brown to make them pop with color.

"Can you talk me through your day leading up to the incident?" the detective asked.

"Sure," I said. I told her about how we'd prepared for the grand opening.

"So Rose bought two cups of coffee from you."

"Yes, Colton handed me the cups, and I filled them from the air pot. Then Rose took them to the condiment stand, and she was there momentarily before moving out into the communal seating area."

"Did you add anything poisonous to Bianca's cup?" the detective asked.

I shook my head and a few connections clicked together in my mind. But I still felt the complete picture of what happened was partially in shadow. "Just coffee. But there were people around Rose before she handed Bianca the coffee. Rose set the cups down before she talked to Laura and Abby, and Phillip also stood very close to Bianca when she was holding the cup. Any one of those people could've added something."

Did any of those three hate Bianca enough to harm her? Laura and Abby could've had multiple bad interactions with Bianca from their food cart days, as they'd all been on the scene for a while. And if Rose was right, Laura and Bianca's interactions had turned into a public flashpoint before.

But Phillip? Maybe his accusing me of murdering Bianca was a ruse. A way to throw suspicion off himself.

And onto me, someone who'd never had a cheerful interaction with his girlfriend. Although mild dislike of someone isn't the usual reason for murder.

But hatred? Love and hatred are flip sides of the same all-encompassing emotion.

The detective's voice interrupted my thoughts. "Had you met Bianca Moore before you both moved into this building?"

A slightly hysterical laugh wanted to escape from me, but I tamped it down like espresso, ready to make the perfect shot. I took a deep breath and let it out slowly, then spoke.

"Do you know the Campathon music festival?" I asked.

"Yeah, and you know what, I stopped by your cart several times at the festival last summer. That's why your logo seemed so familiar."

So the detective was a live music fan. Thankfully, our stint at last summer's Campathon had been less exciting than our first time as a vendor for the festival, when two people had died. We hadn't been sure the festival would survive, but it'd managed to pull through.

"We've been a vendor at Campathon for a few years now. Bianca and her cart were there, too. But I didn't talk with Bianca at the festival, although I saw her around." I'd avoided her cart on principle, but didn't need to bring that up now.

The detective's gaze studied me, making me feel slightly edgy, and I wondered if I made people feel the same way when I analyzed them.

"You didn't get along with her?"

I opted for the truth. "Bianca was abrasive and seemed to find Ground Rules's presence threatening on principle. Even though our carts were complementary since we didn't serve food at the festival, not even our usual pastries. It felt strange, to be honest, to be hated before I'd even said hello. And I know she had conflicts with other food carts at the festival. She wasn't known for playing nicely with others."

"Someone said you're related to the owner of this development. It's surprising you didn't complain about the Breakfast Bandits getting a spot here."

The detective didn't know how right she was. "Yes, my uncle owns this building, and he's also an investor in Ground Rules. But he negotiated the leases for the other restaurants without my input."

"Your uncle didn't run the other restaurants by you?"

"I saw the list and told my uncle about my experience with the Breakfast Bandits, but it didn't sway his decision. He said he'd talk to Bianca and remind her to play nice."

I'd been frustrated when my uncle Jimmy had downplayed my concerns about renting to Bianca. I'd long ago learned that, for example, hiring someone with the right values and attitude, even if they weren't experienced, would be a better business choice than hiring an experienced barista with impeccable skills but a lousy attitude.

But the Button Building was my uncle's project, not mine, so I knew I had to trust him.

And the only thing I could've done to protest was decline a spot in the building, which would've harmed Ground Rules.

"Can you give me the info for the building owner?"

I nodded again. "I have one of my uncle's business cards in my bag."

Detective Leto followed as I walked behind the counter and to our small storage room. I grabbed my messenger bag from the locker I'd left it in this morning. As I pulled out the pen case inside my bag, I told myself to take a deep breath and relax. The case included a stash of my Ground Rules cards, Harley's card, postcards about our mail-order bean program, and a second promo card for shops interested in carrying our products. I pulled out one of the Jimmy Jones Development cards tucked into the side of the case.

"That's very organized," the detective said.

"It makes life easier than to carry these around loose in my bag. Plus, they're less likely to get bent this way." I handed over my uncle's business card.

"Can I have one of yours as well?"

So I handed over one of my teal Ground Rules cards.

"Thanks."

As we walked back into the shop, I noticed that the detective's eyes took in everything. The shiny, top-of-the-line espresso machine; the burr grinders. The shelf of clean pour-over cones.

The dream coffeehouse I'd built now might turn into a nightmare.

A man waved at Detective Leto from the door leading to the communal area, and she headed to him.

"How are things?" Colton asked in a low voice.

"I have no idea," I said. But things clearly weren't good, and from the look Colton shot my way, he knew it.

Detective Leto came back in. "Okay, we need you to vacate your shop."

"Why?" Nina asked. A note in her voice struck me. It took me a moment to realize she sounded scared. I, meanwhile, just felt resigned, with sadness layered underneath.

"This is a potential crime scene." The detective had cracked out a no-nonsense tone like it wasn't worth arguing with her.

"So you're officially looking at Bianca's death as a murder?" I asked. But I'd known as soon as paramedics whisked Bianca away that this would happen. It'd felt inevitable, although I'd hoped she'd be okay.

Detective Leto made eye contact with me.

"Potentially. But we're still waiting on more data before making any official determination. It will be a while before we'll have the results of the victim's tox screens and other pertinent info. But if you've talked with your father about crime scenes, you'll know we just get one bite at the apple. This is our chance to investigate, so if you had nothing to do with this, you don't have anything to worry about. And the sooner we do this, the faster you'll get your shop back." Her words felt honest, and I hoped this would all work out quickly and not just for my sake. Bianca's family deserved a quick answer.

The detective watched as we collected our jackets and bags from the lockers. I waited behind Colton and Nina as a uniformed officer started to inspect Nina's fancy leather tote.

The officer pulled a pill bottle out of the tote and dropped it into a clear evidence bag.

Nina sounded panicked as she said, "I need that. I don't have more at home."

"Wait a minute, and I'll see what I can do," the police officer said. He motioned for Nina to shift to the side.

Nina huffed but stepped out of the way.

In true boy fashion, Colton carried everything in either the hip pocket of his burnt-orange cords or in the zipped pocket of his navy-blue barn coat.

But the police officer still checked out all the pockets in Colton's coat before handing it back and telling him he could go.

Nina shifted in annoyance to the side.

I handed over my messenger bag, glad I'd cleaned out the receipts and random items floating in the bottom of the bag over the weekend. After checking my pen case and bagging the small bottle of Advil tucked in one of the pockets, he returned it.

"Thank you," I said automatically. Even though I didn't really mean it.

The officer had turned to Nina before I'd walked out.

As I waited for Nina outside, I wound my striped scarf around my neck an extra time. The cold air had an unseasonal bite like winter had decided to overstay its welcome.

Rose walked down the street and changed direction slightly to intersect with me. Her eyes were still red.

"I can't believe Bianca died," Rose said. She looked crushed.

"It's surreal," I said. Sudden death always feels like a bad joke someone's trying to play as a slow feeling of "wait, this is really happening" filters through you, like a horror movie.

"We should talk later," Rose said.

"I'll be here when we're allowed to reopen."

Rose looked like she had something to say, but the door opened behind us, and Nina stepped out. Nina looked at me with a clenched jaw, and I hoped she'd kept her temper inside the shop.

"I can't believe they tried to take my . . ." Nina's voice trailed off as she clocked Rose.

"But you're okay now?" I asked.

"Yeah, I'm fine." Nina glanced at Rose a few times like she was uncomfortable with the podcaster being part of the conversation.

A quick glance at Rose told me she didn't particularly like Nina either. This surprised me since Rose seemed prepared to get along with everyone.

I mean, Rose had even gotten along with *Bianca*. Rose clearly had some sort of superpower hidden under her fashionable façade.

"I'll keep you posted about when we can reopen," I told Nina. She nodded and walked off toward the street parking behind the building. One nice thing about morning shifts: anyone who drives should be able to easily find parking nearby since we don't have a designated lot for the building. It'll be tougher to find rock-star parking when the building is in full swing.

"Make sure you eat something," I told Rose. "It's easy to forget to eat after a shock like this, and then your blood sugar drops, making you feel even worse."

"I don't feel like I'll ever be hungry again," Rose said. She glanced at me and started to say something.

But a late-model BMW SUV pulled into the empty parallel parking spot next to us. "Sage, do you want a ride home?" Nina asked.

"I have my bike."

"It'll fit on my bike rack."

"I guess I'll take the bus," Rose muttered, and slouched down the sidewalk to the bus stop.

Nina hopped out, and we put my bicycle on a rack bolted to the back of her SUV. "My husband's a big mountain biker."

"Do you go, too?"

"I've tried, but it's not really for me. Hiking is more my speed if I have to venture into the great outdoors."

I waved to Rose as Nina zoomed off. Her SUV had heated leather seats and a fancy sound system.

"Where to?"

"The roastery."

"Oh, I remember where that is." Nina slid into the center turn lane without using her signal and waited for a break in traffic. "What's the story with Rose, anyway?"

"I'm pretty sure she's what she seems: an enthusiastic podcaster and frequent social media oversharer."

"She seems sketch to me," Nina said.

"Why?"

"She's always so perfect. What's going on inside? And she's always hanging around despite not working for any of the businesses."

It sounded like Nina didn't know about my unfortunate connection to the main topic of Rose's podcast.

"I suspect she's lonely."

"She could've stayed at whatever university she's enrolled in and roomed with her friends," Nina grumbled. She pulled over in the loading zone alongside the Ground Rules roastery. "Here you go!"

Nina helped me unload my bicycle, said goodbye, and then zoomed away.

Did Nina have a point about Rose?

I told myself to think about that later.

# Chapter 4

When I rolled my bicycle into the roastery, Harley was playing her usual heavy metal through a small Bluetooth speaker, dancing as she measured out twelve-ounce bags of coffee beans for retail sales. Her glossy black ponytail swished against her long-sleeve thermal shirt. She was in her element in the roastery, ensuring our standard offerings were consistent, our single-origin specials were perfect, and our new blends were interesting. She'd never minded the grunt work of packaging beans and preparing them for transport.

Harley and I have been friends for years, and she seemed the happiest she'd ever been. Her role as a roaster played to her strengths, and she'd been focusing on improving her soft skills when dealing with the stores that carried our beans. I usually worked with the accounts first, and once they were set up and running smoothly, Harley took over the day-to-day management of them. It worked well since, while she struggles with small talk, Harley excels when talking about her passions, including which roasts a store should carry or what could be a fun offering for a coffee shop. Our accounts instinctively trusted Harley's enthusiasm. She was always willing to fill in at the coffee cart, but not dealing with customers day-to-day suited her better, even though she's a fantastic barista.

But Harley had told me once that dealing with people drains her, and knowing that she'll be able to retreat to the roastery once she's done pulling shots calms her.

These are the main reasons we'd partnered up. While I'm an excellent barista, I'll never have Harley's skills as a roaster. And while I have a better-than-average sense of taste and smell, helped by years of training from my time in coffee shops and with Harley at Ground Rules, I'll never have Harley's impeccable ability. But that's okay since she appreciates the skills I bring. I understand when to let Harley take the lead, and she knows to let me steer the ship through a sea of customers.

Harley's eyes widened in concern and she turned the music down. "Hey, Sage. Why aren't you at the shop?"

"Did you see my text?"

"Oh no. What happened?"

As I gave her the rundown of the day, she paused and leaned against the shelf where she was stacking bags of coffee beans.

"Do you know when we'll be able to reopen?" Harley asked. She started filling bags and measuring them on the scale again.

I started applying Puddle Jumper labels to the already-filled bags in need of good homes. "No idea, but I can't imagine it'll be too long."

Although flickers of fear kept trying to light inside me, as Bianca had been drinking a cup of Ground Rules coffee when she collapsed. But Rose had consumed coffee from the same batch and was fine. So maybe I was just paranoid.

"I only met her a few times, but Bianca sure was tense," Harley said.

"Very intense."

"No, tense. Like Bianca was filled with anxiety and wasn't sure how to handle it. She reminded me of me in a few specific ways," Harley said.

"The two of you were nothing alike," I said. I sometimes imagined Harley full of balls of nervous energy that she sometimes struggled to juggle. When anxious, Harley occasionally blurted out comments that didn't need to be said, but she was never mean.

"I wouldn't be surprised if Bianca has anxiety like me, though. I bet it's why she was mean to you. She was nervous, and that's how it spilled out. I can't imagine my life if I hadn't gotten diagnosed during my senior year of high school."

"If you don't mind me asking, what was it like to be diagnosed? Was it difficult for you?"

"My parents were hesitant to get help for me 'cause they don't believe mental illnesses are a thing. They thought I was just slacking off or seeking attention. But my older sister—"

"The doctor?"

"Yep, she was in college and knew I was struggling. She insisted. My parents didn't want me to take any medications, so the psychiatrist and therapist I worked with tried other therapies that worked well. Although I've tried a few medicines over the years," Harley said.

"Other therapies, like lifestyle changes? You were a kid."

"One thing my doctor suggested was to stop drinking coffee," Harley said.

"Umm . . ." I didn't even try to respond further.

"I took up running instead. It helps me, but it's not a solution for everyone."

"Just running?"

"I have a prescription for Xanax that I never use. And a few calming methods my therapist taught me. You know what's ironic? My parents were so proud of my sister for finishing med school, yet they acted like they didn't believe in medicine when it came to me. But they like to brag about their daughter, the doctor, and their daughter, the CPA."

"Their daughter, the coffee goddess, is way cooler," I said. Harley's sisters were an intriguing mix of scary smart and deeply kind the times I'd met them. They seemed fiercely protective of Harley, the odd duck out in the family.

And both of her sisters had been first in line to subscribe to our monthly bean program, which I'd seen as a measure of support for their baby sister.

As I talked with Harley, someone entered a code into our new keyless door lock system and walked in.

I smiled.

My dad.

When he heard we were overextended, he'd offered to work a few shifts each week in the roastery. He started off packaging up shipments for our coffee subscribers, who received bags of coffee each month, taking care to double-check the orders against our database. He seemed to enjoy it and Harley had slowly given him more to do.

"Hi, Chris," Harley called out, and she received an answering hello.

My dad shed his Columbia raincoat and neatly placed it over a chair on his way across the roastery.

"Pumpkin, I thought you'd be at the grand opening?" my dad asked me.

"You haven't told your dad about the drama yet?" Harley asked.

"You were my first port of call, Harley," I said. I told my father about my morning.

He made a good audience, clearly shocked and concerned at different moments.

After I finished talking, my father was silent for a few minutes. Given how the skin between his eyes furrowed, I could tell he was thinking.

"You know, if this was my case, the woman you sold the coffee to would be my first suspect, with you as number two," he said.

"Thanks for the support."

"So before talking with the police again, call your brother."

Of course he'd suggest that.

My father's always been fond of Jackson, even though they're not biologically related, and the respect was mutual. Jackson is technically my half brother, born when my mother was a high school student, and he was raised by his paternal grandparents. When I was a teenager and Jackson was in college and then law school, my dad had hired my brother to babysit me when my dad worked nights. Jackson took the job seriously, and we'd spent time studying together, watching movies, plus weekend hikes and adventures. I suspected Jackson had never wanted to relinquish that level of responsibility, and control, in my life. But it's born out of protectiveness, even if it sometimes chafes.

I decided switching topics would be the least frustrating for me. "You realize the woman I sold the coffee to is the podcaster investigating my mother, right?"

My father's lips flattened. While my mother wasn't a taboo topic, my father would never fully forgive her. Not that I blamed him since she married him to flee the USA and move to Germany, where he was stationed in the army. She then split with me as a toddler. He'd thought he was building a family, but the foundation was silt. But now we were good. He was one of my mother's victims, but different from the people Rose was interviewing.

"You haven't been interviewed on the podcast, have you?" he asked.

I shook my head. "I've avoided talking about anything serious with Rose."

"Real journalists are bad enough without amateurs running around," my dad said.

"Everyone has to start somewhere, and Rose's podcast is decent. She has talent."

"You've listened?"

I nodded.

My father glanced at the ceiling. "Well, we can't do anything now, so I might as well get to work."

I couldn't argue with him, but before I got stuck into a project, I knew I should make a quick stop. So as Harley and my dad started working, I headed out to the hallway that runs through the middle of our building.

We share the building with a seamstress specializing in bespoke clothing, a gym whose up-tempo music echoes through the hallway whenever they're open, and my destination. A place I loved, mainly because of who I'd find there.

The door to the Grumpy Sasquatch Studio was open, and I could almost feel the intensity of everyone with their nose to the grindstone, finishing up the final touches of the video game they were scheduled to launch.

I paused when I saw the life-sized cutout of the game's main character on display next to the couches in the entryway.

If the cutout was accurate, she was taller than me, about five feet eight. Slightly whiter blond hair, with the tips streaked in red. Motorcycle boots with a knife peeking out of one and a leather jacket over a black T-shirt. Brilliant blue eyes.

But she also looked like me, which made sense, as I'd been the character's inspiration and motion capture model. Looking at her was like viewing a distorted version of myself. Bustier while still being lean. Prettier, with bluer eyes.

"Are you visiting with your alternate self?" a voice asked. I turned to see Kat, one of my favorites amongst the Grumpy Sasquatches, standing in the doorway leading to her office.

Kat had added a charcoal wool cardigan to her usual flannel shirt and jeans look, with a navy beanie over her long brown hair, pulled into a tidy side braid. Plus, a pair of cheerful red Fair Isle hand warmers.

I nodded toward her hands. "Those hand warmers are legit."

"My sister knitted them for me for Christmas but just finished them last week. I thought I'd have to save them until next year, but it's cold."

I'd met Nadia, Kat's younger sister, who is part of a local group of cosplayers who dress up like dolls. Which was an interesting juxtaposition to Nadia's day job as a carpenter. The two hadn't had the easiest life, immigrating with their family to the USA when Kat was in high school. They both helped care for their mother with MS. But none of that stopped Kat from being one of the company's best programmers, with a subtle sense of humor.

"It's still so weird," I said. At least the character's costume wasn't over the top, and thankfully they hadn't gone with booty shorts or a skimpy dress. But costumes like that weren't the usual Grumpy Sasquatch style. So far, their offerings had been praised for their storytelling and "cerebral" elements. The studio's co-owner and half of their staff are female, which is subtly reflected in the games.

"*Falling Through the Shadows* is going to be amazing," Kat said. "The beta testers all raved about it, and the reviews have been excellent so far. People are going to love your character and her journey."

"Fingers crossed."

Kat left, and I headed down the hallway to Bax's office.

Bax had offered to let me beta-test the game, but I'd declined. Partially because I'd been too busy getting Ground Rules ready to launch the past few months. But I was also afraid to play it. What if I hated it? What if I couldn't handle seeing myself on-screen? What if I loved it too much, and it made me too cocky? Or obsessed, like Narcissus, so enamored with a reflected version of himself in a pool that he died alone, never able to get what he wanted because it was an illusion.

I understood the passion intermingled with obsession the sasquatches put into their games and the fans' feel while playing. It's on the same spectrum as the love and attention Harley puts into the beans she roasts before we release them to the world. It's why I make sure all of our baristas are trained with a focus on quality since we don't want to put a bad shot of espresso into a mocha and make a customer walk away unhappy.

But our drinks are gone once the purchaser finishes drinking it or uses up the last coffee beans in their bag. Video game fans will spend hours playing. From what the sasquatches had told me and based on Bax's intense outline the game had been based on, the choices a user made while playing *Falling Through the Shadows* would lead them to various outcomes. This would give enthusiasts a reason to play through the game multiple times and chart the different paths a player could take. Early kindness could ripple through into later situations.

It was like real life, with choices having consequences, except with a do-over. The user can always revert to an earlier saved version or start over fresh.

This could be another reason people love video games, or even books, even if we can't influence the journey unless we're reading a Choose Your Own Adventure book for children. We experience someone else's life and see things through their point of view.

It's similar to what Rose is doing with her podcast. Exploring questions by trying to look at different perspectives. And I had to admit, even if I sometimes didn't want to, that Rose was exploring an interesting perspective in her podcast. If she wanted, Rose could also explore the effect an event like Bianca's death had on a group of businesses like the Button Building.

But if Rose went that direction, I knew I still didn't want to be interviewed about Bianca. Even if it didn't hit as close to home as Rose's series about my mother.

Bax's door was open as usual, and he was focused on his monitor. When I knocked, his gaze snapped up, and his expression softened. "I didn't expect to see you here. Aren't you slammed with the grand opening?"

"About that." I plopped down on the couch in Bax's office.

Concern filled his face as he stood up, walked around his desk, and sat sideways, facing me on the couch. He rubbed my shoulder as I told him about the day.

"Unbelievable," he said.

"Is it really? Maybe Ground Rules is cursed."

"Or you've just been unlucky and close to a few crimes that weren't your fault."

Like this one. I wondered if the stress of Bianca's death would prematurely age me, then wondered how self-centered I was for the thought even crossing my mind.

"Maybe we should've sold Ground Rules." I referred to an offer we'd received from a local company a few months ago.

"It would've killed you to sell to Left Coast Grinds."

Bax and I both winced.

"I'm sorry, that was a horrific word choice. But my point still stands. You believe in Ground Rules and can get through this."

"But what if we can't recover from a death at the grand opening? Bianca was holding a cup of our coffee when she collapsed."

"Well, I believe in you. And when you open again, if you need me to, I'll be the first in line to order an Americano."

"Thanks, Bax."

"Anytime, Coffee Angel."

Just because I couldn't work in the new brick-and-mortar shop didn't mean I couldn't make myself useful, even though I was tempted to call today a bust and go home to nap. Since my dad and Harley were busy packaging beans to the thumping beat of yet more heavy metal, I headed to the small area by the seldom-used front door of the roastery. We'd set it up with a desk and couch-loveseat–coffee table so we could use it as a break area. It was a comfortable spot to sit with my feet up, alongside a cup of fresh coffee.

Today's task was one of my favorites: prepping our next monthly promotion. We send out regular emails with specials, including discounts on coffee blends. For April's newsletter, we would highlight one of the family-owned farms we source beans from in Guatemala. Nerding out over the details of our coffees is one of the best parts of working on Ground Rules marketing. These single-roast Gesha beans I planned to highlight were considered the best and usually the most expensive in the world. They originated in Ethiopia but take on a subtly different note when grown in the mountains of Guatemala. Striking the right balance of interesting and accurate details without overwhelming someone who enjoys a good cup of joe but doesn't need the nitty-gritty details is always challenging. But I love to read customer responses to our emails and appreciate it when the newsletter campaign leads to online orders.

As I worked on the newsletter, feeling myself settle into a comfortable groove after the stress of the morning, my phone dinged with a text from one of my baristas from the cart. I opened it.

She'd linked to one of Rose's posts with a single, one-word comment: sociopath.

I put my earbuds in and clicked play.

Rose was dressed in the same outfit as earlier, and she'd retouched her makeup. But I could still see touches of red in her eyes from crying.

"Guys, you won't believe it. Earlier today, while I was on the case for *Rose Investigates*, a woman died while I interviewed her."

Rose looked down briefly for a dramatic pause, then looked straight into the camera.

"But based on the questions the police asked me, this wasn't a natural death."

Rose paused dramatically. "She was murdered."

She stared straight into the camera. "Right beside me.

"I might need to put my Saffron Jones exploration aside because I have a new project. An immediate case to explore.

"I know that makes me sound unsympathetic.

"Trust me, I know a woman died. I feel awful about it, and it's hard to believe that, tomorrow, I won't be able to drop by and say hi to her in her restaurant. It's hard to believe she just blinked out of existence.

"Which is why I have to do something.

"So now, I've been on the ground floor, so to speak, of a murder.

"And I'm going to solve it.

"I'll bring justice to Bianca's family.

"And maybe bring comfort to everyone affected by this murder.

"Including me."

★   ★   ★

Rose pushing her nose into the investigation sounded like all shades of a bad idea, but I wasn't surprised. But I realized something: I needed a copy of Rose's footage, even though viewing it would make me feel macabre. Like I was seeking out a train wreck. But there might be something in the footage that could protect Ground Rules in case we got in trouble, either legally or even on social media. As the saying goes, knowledge is power.

Although ending up in a social media fight about how Ground Rules didn't murder people sounded like a battle that, if waged, would have no winners.

I wrote down a note in my trusty Moleskine notebook slash bullet journal to ask Rose for the footage. I texted back a thank-you to my barista and asked how things were going.

*Great! Busy, although I don't see why anyone is outside. It's cold!*

I responded, *The heater is working in the cart, right?*

*Yeah, it's nice and toasty. But it feels like winter out there. Later, boss, got more customers who don't have the sense to stay indoors.*

I laughed and got back to work.

But then my phone beeped again, and the text made me straighten up. My uncle asked if I could meet him in an hour. I quickly texted back yes.

My uncle Jimmy had always been a problem-solver; hopefully, he'd help us navigate this situation.

# Chapter 5

Since I only had an hour, I headed home and then caught a bus across the river. Normally, I'd bicycle over, but it was cold and promised to get chillier.

My uncle Jimmy had texted me to meet him at the Tav, and I walked in as happy hour started. A few customers were showing up for cheap well drinks and bar snacks. But the bartender, my cousin Miles, started pouring a lemonade before I said anything.

"Your usual," Miles said, and put the glass down in front of me. "Another death, huh, Bug?"

Hearing my childhood nickname made me feel like there was always hope, no matter what had happened.

Miles had managed the Tav as long as I remembered, and he was a jack-of-all-trades. In addition to bartending, he had handyman skills. My cousin—technically my mother's first cousin, but we've never been overly particular about labels—was a bit of an enigma, but he'd always seemed happy. And helpful. His employees all liked him, and amongst the many lessons I'd learned from Miles, one stood out: treat your employees with kindness and respect without being a pushover, pay them well, and have their backs, and they'll generally treat you fairly in exchange.

As we talked, I glimpsed one of my baristas, Sophie. She worked in the Ground Rules cart and, on my recommendation, had started picking up shifts at the Tav in addition to her graduate studies. I wondered when she slept, but she always seemed perky enough, and she's an adult, so clearly, I should trust her. But I was ready to help if she burned out.

Sophie beelined my way when she saw me.

"I heard there was drama at the shop today," she said. Her St. John's accent is melodic, and many people mistake her for being Irish versus Canadian. But the mistake makes sense, as the accent in Newfoundland evolved from the Irish immigrants who'd settled in the region.

"It's Sage, so you get three guesses as to what happened at Ground Rules today, except the first two don't count," Miles said.

"That's not fair," I said.

"I heard someone ended up in dramatic death throes inside the coffee shop," Sophie said. "Almost Shakespearean, in fact, if the rumors are true."

"Ding ding ding, we have a winner," Miles said. "The death part, anyway. The Shakespearean comparison sounds like a reach."

I felt sick when I remembered Bianca's death. "It wasn't dramatic, just tragic, and she died in the communal seating area. Not inside the shop."

"But still. Not the best grand opening," Sophie said. She bustled away when the kitchen called out an order. She quickly carried a tray of appetizers out to a table.

"It wasn't the grand opening I'd hoped for," I said. I looked at Miles.

He refilled my barely sipped lemonade like that would make everything right with the world. But then a large group walked up to the bar, most dressed in matching fleece jackets with CONQUER TS embroidered on the chest, and khakis that ranged from light to dark tan, like a work group hitting up happy hour together.

So I took my lemonade and retreated to the back of the bar,

where there was a line of booths. A few were occupied, but my uncle's favorite was empty, so I slid in. The Tav feels a bit like home, and this booth is basically the heart of the place for me. I'd had many conversations with my uncle and Miles in this exact spot.

I pulled up the local news sites on my phone as I waited. A quick scan showed me all the local news orgs mentioned the death at the Button Building. However, details were scarce, and just said the police were investigating a sudden death that may or may not be suspicious.

As much as I didn't want to call it a silver lining because it felt callous, if Bianca had died from natural causes, life would be easier for all of us. But I doubted she had, and not just because of the way I'd been questioned by the police. Something about the situation simply didn't feel right.

Uncle Jimmy slid into the booth across from me. He'd added a wool sweater to his usual button-down shirt, and his silver hair had been cut recently. But my uncle always looked the same, like he was a constant force in life that everyone else revolved around. But I also knew his smile lines were a bit deeper, and he walked a half step slower than he did a few years ago, which was still quicker than most. He was technically my mother's uncle, although he wasn't much older than her. While she'd been a young mother, producing Jackson as a teenager and me in her early twenties, he had to be over sixty and maybe in his seventies by now. Although he refused to specify his age, everyone stuck to a generic "another year around the sun" vibe at his annual family birthday party.

"How's it going, Bug?" my uncle asked.

"I'm fine, but I've had better days," I said.

"Don't get started without me." I didn't need to look to recognize the low voice with its notes of sarcasm that almost covered the underlying sense of concern.

Jackson. My older brother and self-appointed lawyer. He slid into the booth next to Uncle Jimmy. He'd clearly come from his law office and based on his dapper charcoal suit and blue striped tie, he'd visited court at some point today. The bulky parka over his arm didn't quite match his suit, but it made sense considering the freakishly cold weather.

So I told Jackson and my uncle about how everything had played out.

"You talked to the police without me? Without calling me first? Which you know was the wrong move, so don't give me that innocent look."

As Jackson geared up for his lecture, I sensed someone walk up behind me. When I caught a whiff of freesia with a spicy undertone of ginger, I knew who was there.

Rose.

I turned and looked at the podcaster slash social media superstar. "Did you follow me?"

But her eyes were focused on my uncle.

"Mr. Jones, I'd like to interview you for my podcast." Rose was still in her blazer and jeans from earlier, and she'd refreshed her makeup. She'd opted for a pink lipstick versus her dramatic red from earlier and it made her look softer.

If she left podcasting, something told me Rose could have a flourishing career as a makeup artist.

Or as a newsreader. She'd make an excellent evening news anchor.

"And you are?" My uncle eyed her, smart enough not to discount her out of hand but clearly skeptical. He'd make her prove she was worth his time.

"This is Rose, a podcaster. She also handed Bianca coffee right before she collapsed," I said.

Rose flinched at my words, and from beneath her assured façade, I saw a flinch of pain.

"As I told the police, why would I hurt Bianca? She was actually nice to me!" Rose said. She slid into my side of the booth, and something in her pink backpack clunked.

Uncle Jimmy held up his hand. "What podcast?"

"I'm the creative spark behind the true-crime podcast *Rose Investigates*, and I'm doing a series on Saffron Jones."

Creative spark? More like everything behind the podcast.

The sparkle in Uncle Jimmy's eyes faded. Jackson leaned back, and his face closed off.

Uncle Jimmy and my mother had been close at one point, and I've always wondered what he thinks, deep inside, in the thoughts he doesn't share with the world. No one is happy to be related to a notorious grifter. I bet everyone in the family had been interviewed by the FBI at least once. Plus, I suspected my mother was in sporadic contact with Uncle Jimmy, although I wasn't sure he welcomed it. She'd sent him photos of me during my childhood. When she'd dumped me in Portland at age thirteen, and I'd retreated into the Tav, both Miles and my uncle had recognized me before I said a word. I'd napped in this very booth under Miles's hoodie while Uncle Jimmy promptly called my father.

So it was oddly fitting that Rose had approached my uncle for an interview here. Although I was surprised she'd waited until now, as she'd already produced and released episodes of her podcast.

"Why would I want to be interviewed about my niece?" my uncle said. "She's forged her own path far away from me and my concerns. And far from Sage, for that matter."

I glanced at Jackson, whose eyes didn't flicker when our uncle left him out of the family tree. He clearly didn't mind being left out. For now, anyway.

"I'm examining how Saffron's actions have affected the people around her. I've interviewed several victims and I'd like to include the impact on her family. I'd love to learn more about her childhood and why she developed into the person she became before her recent death."

"There is no why, as far as I know. Saffron had a perfectly normal childhood, and none of her cousins are in trouble with the law."

Uncle Jimmy's words were careful. I got the sense there was something he wasn't saying, but also wanted to ask.

"You could provide such unique insight into her past. And I think I can offer both of you something in return." Rose turned her head, and her hazel eyes locked on mine.

"Oh yeah?" My uncle sounded skeptical.

Rose turned to face him. It felt like she was shifting between personas, trying to be the personable, enthusiastic, almost-friend she was with me versus a respectable journalist with my uncle.

Rose's tone was measured like she'd been thinking about this. "Sage and I are both suspects in Bianca's death. As Sage can confirm, I've been interviewing people around the Button Building for side videos I've been posting that are tangentially, at most, connected to my podcast. Some of the interviews are interesting. Meaning, exceptionally interesting. And they could shed light on the real killer."

"Or help your defense lawyer throw reasonable doubt on the situation," Jackson said.

Rose turned to my brother. He stared back with a level gaze that gave nothing away. Although it did give a glimpse of his RBF face, which I like to joke is resting brother face versus the usual definition.

Rose asked, "Who are you? I'm sorry, I never properly introduced myself."

"I'm Sage's attorney." Jackson maintained his deadpan look, and I couldn't blame him for not wanting to show his hand and let Rose know that he was part of the family. 'Cause if she found out, she'd ask to interview him, too. And while growing up, Jackson had had even less interaction with our mother than I did. Our mother and his father had been teens, and Jackson's paternal grandparents had stepped up and raised him. But, like me, our mother had randomly communicated with Jackson over the years.

It was creepy to have my mother suddenly contact me, usually knowing something personal enough that I wondered how she managed to keep tabs on me.

"So all of you agree that Sage is in legal trouble if you've hired a lawyer." Rose's tone suggested she'd just won the argument without realizing that no one had shown their hand.

Uncle Jimmy was thinking hard. "Okay," he finally said. "If you share all of your footage of the interviews you've done around the Button Building and also all of the footage you've recorded about Saffron, I'll let you interview me. Audio only."

"Wait, all of the interviews?" Rose blinked hard like it helped her think quickly.

Or she'd gotten a speck of dust caught in her eye.

"Yes, all. You can send the footage to Sage. She'll make sure everyone who needs to see it does. And remember what I said: all of the videos and footage, not just the ones you think are relevant."

They stared at each other, and Rose metaphorically blinked first.

"Okay, I'll get set up so we can record the podcast now."

"I'd like to talk to Sage privately," Jackson said. He stood up.

Rose let me out of our side of the booth and pulled a microphone and laptop out of her backpack. She'd come prepared. She laid a voice recorder between them on the table like a backup.

"Nice gear," my uncle said.

"This isn't just a hobby for me," Rose said.

Jackson sat at a table close to the booth, and I sat down next to him, so we both faced the interview.

"This is a terrible idea," Jackson said in a low voice.

"There might be something helpful in the footage, though. And you know Uncle Jimmy is cautious."

Rose was ready to record in a surprisingly short amount of time like she'd interviewed people on the fly before. Although I questioned how good the audio quality would be in the Tav given the crack of pool balls in the background and the occasional whoop or other bar noise.

"She's almost as annoying as you were at that age," Jackson said.

"Thanks."

"I said almost; you're still number one," he said. "Do you trust her?"

"Not really, but Rose seems authentic. I've listened to the first episode of her series on Saffron Jones, and she's good. But I don't know Rose well enough to rely on her if that's what you're asking." Or assume she wouldn't throw me under a bus, especially if it was to save herself.

"Send me a link to her podcast," Jackson said. "And forward on the footage she sends you."

"I already guessed you were on the list of people Uncle Jimmy expected me to send the footage to."

After a few tests, Rose was ready to record.

"I'll edit this to remove any umms and dead spaces," Rose said. "If you start answering and want to start over, say so and wait a few seconds, and I'll cut out the mistakes."

Jackson spoke into my ear. "Be sure to save the full unedited version of this interview in case she edits the footage to make it seem like Jimmy said something he didn't, so we have leverage."

"I'd say you have a fundamental lack of trust in human nature, but I know you're right."

"Let that be a lesson to ya."

"I was already planning on comparing the two." I couldn't let my brother think he was a step ahead of me. He shot an amused half smile my way, and his face settled back into its usual deadpan lines as he turned back to the interview.

"I'm here today with James Jones, Portland entrepreneur and business owner . . . and the uncle of Saffron Jones." Rose's podcast voice was smoother than her everyday tone, like she'd taken on the persona of a thoughtful investigator who never shied from exploring the tough questions. The fluffy side of her personality was shaved off. But that made sense to me; we all played parts during our lives, with different facets of our personalities coming out depending upon whom we're around.

And I'd seen a few different facets of Rose's personality tonight.

"Mr. Jones, what was your reaction when your niece became a notorious con artist?"

Uncle Jimmy stared at Rose for a half second, then said, "I was surprised, of course, and shocked."

"Were there any signs in her childhood that Saffron would join the FBI's most wanted list?"

"She was a good student. Better than good, actually; she was exceptionally bright and never in trouble."

But that didn't mean trouble hadn't followed her. Something told me my mother was the type to be the subtle ringleader who slid under her teacher's radar, covering up any bad behavior with a smile while shifting the blame onto her entourage without anyone noticing. How many people had fallen on their own swords to protect my mother over the years? Only to realize she'd moved on without a care, leaving others to deal with the aftermath.

"So you're saying it was all sock hops and SATs?" The sarcasm in Rose's voice surprised me.

The briefest of half smiles appeared on my uncle's face, and I realized he, too, was playing a part. He was fulfilling his commitment to be interviewed, but that didn't mean he'd say anything quotable.

"I'm saying that my niece seemed like a normal kid. Saffron wasn't perfect, but I was surprised when she took the route she did."

Rose asked a few more questions about my mother, and Uncle Jimmy gave a few more vague answers.

"Honestly, most of our family is boring. I mean, the rest of my nieces and nephews attended local universities and work in stable jobs."

Yes, that's us, salt of the earth, hold an annual secret Santa exchange on Christmas Eve, gather for low-key summer barbecues with the occasional vent session about the FBI dropping by for a chat.

"Do you have any favorite memories of Saffron?" Rose asked.

"There's not much I can say about my niece, but she somehow produced children whom I, and anyone, can be proud of."

"Children?" Rose said with a question in her voice. "I know her daughter."

"Exactly, her daughter is doing well in life, and she's nothing like her mother. She deserves her privacy and doesn't need anyone dragging her into this mess, as she's not responsible for any of it."

Relief that neither had said my name coursed through me.

Rose asked a few more questions, sounding increasingly frustrated by the vague answers. But if she wanted to make a career asking hard questions, she'd need to be ready for people skilled at not answering despite speaking eloquently. Especially if she ever interviewed politicians.

Something my uncle said struck me. Nothing like her mother. It was kind of my uncle to say so, but I had the skills to be a grifter if I wanted to be. I'd played around with cold reading customers at the cart, but never for money. If my mother hadn't dumped me in Portland when I was thirteen but had instead kept me alongside her, maybe I would've joined her as a wanted criminal.

Maybe I would've died alongside her.

But maybe she'd left me behind because she knew I wouldn't follow her anymore. I'd started asking her questions and demanded answers, and I was no longer the small child she could use as a prop.

Uncle Jimmy slid out of the booth. "Good luck with your podcast," he said.

"Thank you," Rose said. She'd resumed her aura of professionalism, but from the stiff way she packed up her equipment, I suspected she was still frustrated.

And I wondered what, if any, of the interview she'd use.

Jackson and Uncle Jimmy walked toward the manager's office in the back of the Tav.

"I'll upload all of the videos and interviews I've recorded and send you a link," Rose said.

I offered her one of my business cards, which included my email address.

"Nah, I already have one." She finished packing her gear into her backpack and turned to face me. Rose looked me straight in the eyes. "We should work together to solve this."

"That's a job for the police."

"Good to know, Oma," Rose said.

Oma. German for grandmother. I narrowed my eyes at Rose, but it was hard to feel too annoyed with her. Especially since I'd just watched my uncle talk rings around her.

Rose spoke again. "You know we have to be suspects one and two, and that's not fair to either of us."

I wondered which of us was suspect one and which was two on the detective's list. I hoped she had other names that would put Rose and me into the clear.

I knew I didn't want to be on the list. I didn't want the suspicion of Bianca's death to cast a shadow on my life and the new Ground Rules store.

"I'll tell you what," I said. "Let's see what we can come up with, but this is academic. Don't do anything stupid. Or illegal. We don't want to make this situation worse."

"Of course, Oma." Rose swung her backpack over her shoulder. "Expect the footage from me later tonight."

She left, and I watched her go. There was something I instinctively liked about Rose, even though I realized I didn't entirely trust her. I'd known her a few weeks and I don't let anyone into my inner circle too quickly.

Then I headed to the office in the back half of the Tav.

My uncle had a few questions to answer.


Jackson and Uncle Jimmy were in the private office in the Tav, and I found my spot along the wall, next to a file cabinet.

"Is the blogger gone?" my uncle asked.

"Rose, the podcaster, has left the building."

"On that note, I should go back to my office," Jackson said. He turned to me. "Call me before you talk to the police again, and I'll provide legal advice."

"You'll supervise me." My voice sounded resigned.

"There are worse things than having an attorney with you when talking to the police, as you know."

"Noted." I knew he was right.

Jackson left. I studied my uncle, who had a closed laptop on the desk in front of him.

"I have a question before I split," I said. "Why did you rent space to Bianca? I told you she didn't play nice with others, but you seemed to have a reason you wanted to rent to her. She was heard bragging you'd called her and personally offered her space in the building."

"You're right. I agreed to rent the space to Bianca on purpose, but she approached me. I didn't reach out to her." He motioned to the chair Jackson had vacated, so I sat down.

"I met Bianca's father about twenty years ago when he came looking for your mother," Uncle Jimmy said.

"Did she scam him?"

My uncle nodded. "Out of a decent chunk of change, including Bianca's college fund. Bianca's father owned some sort of business, and he never recovered from the financial hit. In the police investigation into your mom, his own misdeeds came to light. He faced criminal charges. He came here before he went on trial, trying to hunt Saffron down, but as far as I know, he never recovered any of the funds he'd lost. Then, when he was in prison, he was diagnosed with cancer, and while he pulled through, he was never the same. Bianca eventually moved here. It took her a while to get her footing, and her cart was successful, so I agreed to lease her the spot."

"You stayed in touch with her? With them?"

"There wasn't much I could do to help, but I felt obligated to do what I could for Bianca since she was an innocent party during her father's legal troubles. My sympathy was limited for her father. He didn't deserve to be scammed, but he also, let's say, dug his own hole that he wanted help climbing out of."

The guilt in Uncle Jimmy's voice spoke to the same sense of shame I carried around with me. Neither of us was responsible for my mother's actions, but it's hard to shake it off.

No wonder Bianca had hated me. Provided she knew I was related to my mother.

Wait, had Rose known about Bianca's family? Rose had always gotten along with Bianca; had she been buttering up Bianca so she would agree to be interviewed on the podcast? Because Bianca's life fit the theme Rose was exploring.

"Is that all? I don't mean to kick you out, but I have emails to respond to and numbers to run."

"Yeah, I should head home." I'd go to my snug house in Southeast Portland and let my uncle run his business empire from the back of a dive bar.

"Keep me posted."

"I'll let you know when we're allowed to reopen."

"Night, Bug."

"Night."

I dropped by the bar to say goodbye to Miles and Sophie before I bundled up, pulled my wool hat down over my ears, and headed out to the transit mall, where I'd catch a bus across the river and have a short walk home.

As I waited for my bus, a handful of people joined me, mostly dressed in business clothes. But a handful of street people also wandered past, some looking lost, others on a mission. I saw a bright orange Inner City Assistance truck roll by, which reminded me of seeing my friend Manny earlier today. But it felt like I'd seen him weeks ago instead of a matter of hours.

Manny. I smiled to myself. Even though he'd faced some tough challenges, Manny hadn't let them defeat him. He'd been homeless as a teen alongside his mother, and now he had a master's in social work and did his best to get others off the street. He was always full of hope intertwined with realism.

Like it or not, Bianca's death was the next challenge that Ground Rules, and I, needed to face. Whining about it, even in my own thoughts, wouldn't help.

And maybe there was something helpful in Rose's videos that I could send to the detective investigating. Something that would point at the guilty party.

# Chapter 6

The house was empty when I arrived home.

Well, mostly empty. Kaldi greeted me with a chirp. It took me a moment to find his perch on the mantel above the fireplace, sitting still like a petite orange lion statue.

"You're so weird," I told him before dumping my bag on the couch and stowing my jacket and scarf in the hall closet. I grabbed my laptop out of my bag and headed to the kitchen.

I double-checked my phone. Bax's last text still said he'd be working late and to eat without him, along with a crying emoji.

But I'd also gotten a new email.

True to her word, Rose sent me a link to a folder full of audio clips and video files. Despite my urge to order a pizza, I listened to the first clip as I assembled a quesadilla with leftover roasted bell peppers, cheddar cheese, and olives. Once I added salsa, it'd almost be like pizza.

If I pretended.

Okay, it was nothing like pizza, but it would still be tasty.

My phone dinged.

Jackson. *Can I come over?*

*Sure.*

*I'm outside.*

As I let my brother in, I asked if he wanted a quesadilla. He followed me back to the kitchen and settled in at the table. I put together dinner for both of us.

"No Bax?" Jackson sounded disappointed. While I hadn't looked for Jackson's approval when I started dating Bax, their bromance had been a good omen.

Kaldi jumped into my brother's lap while making a trilling noise like he was saying that even if Bax wasn't home, at least they could cuddle. Jackson pet Kaldi, who settled in with a few loud purrs that vibrated across the room.

"Bax is working late. Which is to be expected as they're close to their launch date. No Piper?"

"She's prepping for a trial that starts tomorrow." Jackson's fiancée, Piper, was a US district attorney who focused on white-collar crime.

"Did Rose send the videos over?" Jackson asked as I finished putting together an arugula salad, which I'd only added to the menu 'cause of my brother's presence. Like I wanted him to know, I still ate my vegetables even though we were no longer roommates.

"She did. I was about to start watching them."

"So you're saying I have excellent timing."

"If you say so."

I handed him a plate of quesadilla and salad and then sat down with my own dinner in the chair perpendicular to him. I adjusted my laptop so we could both see the screen. Jackson had a legal notepad and pen in front of him.

But my fingers kept hesitating before I clicked on the video I knew I should watch but dreaded.

The fateful video.

I finally clicked play.

Bianca looked stressed out and exhausted on-screen. Like she hadn't slept much in the lead-up to the grand opening. Her frizzy brown hair was pulled back into a low ponytail, and she had dark circles under her eyes. Her lips were chapped. Her long-sleeved T-shirt was several sizes too large and had the Burrito Bandits logo splashed across the chest in too-big letters.

Criticizing her shop's shirt made me feel petty.

Next to Bianca, Rose looked young and flawless, like a reporter who'd stepped into a disaster zone to interview someone who'd just gone through a hurricane and lost everything.

Although maybe I was projecting since I knew what was going to happen.

Rose had started recording before Phillip walked up. He partially blocked the camera as he handed something to Bianca. Rose glanced down at a note card in her hand.

"Don't forget, babe," was all Phillip said.

Rose tucked the card back into her blazer pocket as Phillip walked away. Bianca swallowed hard, and Rose nudged her lightly on the arm. Wait, had Bianca swallowed something? My eyes narrowed at the screen and I almost scrolled back to double-check.

"Try the coffee, Bianca. It won't kill you."

Bianca took a sip.

Jackson paused the video.

"You poured this coffee?"

I nodded. "Yes, Colton handed me the cups, and I filled them from the air pots. The police took the brewed coffee and some of our gear away for testing, but they won't find anything. Other people drank from that batch of coffee, including me."

"Who brewed the coffee you sold to Rose?"

"Me, I think."

"So Rose took the coffee to Bianca?"

"Yes, after stopping by the condiment station. I can show you footage from the security feed if you'd like to watch it step by step. I already saved it in case we'll need it."

After an incident at the Ground Rules Roastery, we opted to add a system that recorded the Ground Rules shop inside and out and stored the footage for two weeks before auto-deleting. We'd hoped we'd never need to use it.

We'd been painfully, tragically wrong.

I glanced back at the paused moment of Bianca drinking from a cup of Ground Rules coffee from Rose's video. The quesadilla set heavy against my stomach as we finished watching the video, including Bianca's tragic collapse and the aftermath.

I pulled up the shop's security footage and we watched it together. I couldn't see my face as Rose ordered the coffee, but I could see my hands as I accepted the cups from Colton and filled both from the air pot. I clearly didn't add anything. From Rose's smile after her sip, everything tasted normal.

Not that I thought the video would make me realize I'd slipped something into the coffee. But watching Colton pull the cups off the stack and hand them to me told me he also didn't have the chance to add anything. Rose carried them over to the condiment table, where Nina was cleaning up a spill with a sack of sugar beside her. Because of Nina, I couldn't see Rose's hands, nor could I see what Nina was doing. When Nina moved, I saw Rose put the creamer down and give both cups a final stir. She adjusted her bag over her shoulder before picking up the cups and walking into the communal seating area.

"From the video, you should be in the clear," Jackson said. He'd scrawled out a page of notes in his precise handwriting.

"Unless I have world-class sleight-of-hand skills."

"But Rose or Nina could've done something to the coffee."

His words made me feel sick again. "I can't believe either would want to kill Bianca."

"I'm just looking at who had the opportunity right now."

"Be sure to add Phillip to your list. He's already accused me of targeting Bianca." A sliver of anger slid through the sorrow weighing me down.

"I already noted that he was close enough to Bianca to add something to her coffee while also blocking the camera's view of him."

"Plus, Laura and Abby had the opportunity when they talked to Rose. They were close to the cups."

Could one of them have tried to poison Rose and gotten Bianca by mistake? But why would either of them want to harm the pod-caster?

They seemed close. Could they have been working together?

"Multiple suspects are good if the police keep investigating you," Jackson said. "It'll be easy to throw doubt."

Getting arrested for Bianca's murder and throwing mud on the people around me to save myself didn't sit right, even though I knew my brother was correct.

"I'd prefer we find the actual villain."

"Obviously that would be the best scenario." Jackson's tone held his trademark sarcastic note.

Instead of responding, I clicked back to the folder Rose had sent over.

"Rose has a video of Phillip and Mark?" I said. The file's metadata showed it was from a week ago.

"Is that a question?"

"Try surprise." I clicked on the link.

Phillip and Mark were standing in the communal seating near the doors that led outside.

"Can I do anything to help?" Phillip asked.

"I have everything handled for now, and I have an inside connection. But I'll let you know if I need you or access to the building."

"The sooner, the better, in my mind, so as I said, let me know. And be sure to bring by our order before the opening day, along with one of those 'we serve Left Coast Grinds' signs. I want everyone to know."

Mark's phone beeped, and he glanced down. "I gotta take this."

The video turned black like Rose put her phone face down on the table.

"What are you doing here, Rose?" Phillip's voice asked. The angry edge in his tone made me shiver.

"I'm waiting to interview Laura. I'm putting together a series of short videos about all the restaurants here for my socials. And this is a quiet place to work while I wait."

"Why? What are you trying to gain?" Phillip asked.

"Gain? Nothing, really, except some clips that I can add to my portfolio if they turn out well. I'm in school now, but I'll eventually need a job, although I'm hoping my podcast gets sponsored and I can turn that into a full-time gig. How about you? How's the setup going? Do you think you'll be ready for the grand opening?"

As they chatted, Rose's voice was its usual perky self. But I thought I heard a note underneath it, like she didn't trust Phillip.

But maybe I was reading into it 'cause something about Phillip made me instinctively keep him at arm's length. In the past, I'd temporarily left my coffee cart in the hands of my fellow cart owners when I'd rushed off for a quick bathroom break, trusting they'd watch the cash box and order tablet while telling potential customers I'd be right back. But I would never trust Phillip that much. While I'd instinctively trust Rose to watch the coffee shop for a brief moment as long as she promised not to touch anything.

And the Breakfast Bandits would offer to carry Left Coast Grinds in their shop? The audacity. It made me want to add breakfast burritos to our menu.

The video ended, still facing, I assumed, the top of a table.

"What else did Rose send over?" Jackson asked.

"There are a couple earlier interviews with Bianca and another with Phillip. Plus, she talked with the other owners at the Button Building."

We watched one of the videos of Rose and Bianca just outside the interior door to the Breakfast Bandits.

"Tell me about your new restaurant! Why'd you choose to offer breakfast and how did you come up with the name?"

Bianca kept pulling the sleeves of her baggy long-sleeved shirt down over her hands as she talked, then pulled them back up, revealing slender hands with a handful of scars and a healing burn.

"I knew I wanted to focus on the morning crowd and thought Breakfast Bandits rolled off the tongue. I would've gone with Brunch Bandits, though, if I'd known how slammed I'd be during lunch."

"Why did you decide to be a morning cart? Aren't most food carts lunch and dinner spots?"

"That's exactly why I chose breakfast. I saw an opening in downtown Portland and hoped to carve out my niche. Before we lost our spot due to the lot turning into an overpriced hotel, we were always hopping with customers."

"What happened to your old spot?"

"The city decided a useless luxury hotel made more sense than preserving a bunch of food carts." The bitterness in Bianca's voice was thick like it was choking her. "So we, like other carts, had to find new homes. We moved to an east-side food cart pod, but then that closed because the owners weren't organized. It didn't get morning traffic, so it was a terrible spot for us, so we needed to move. At least we got out without breaking our lease. So then we operated as a pop-up, opening at festivals and events. Those can be a pain because you have to apply and hope you get in. If you don't, you can end up with a hole in a prime weekend when you could earn money, but aren't, because you didn't want to double-book yourself."

"Will this be your first brick-and-mortar shop?"

"Yes, mostly. I ran a few pop-ups in a café only open for dinner. The pop-ups were a blast and packed, but the café didn't want someone using their space full-time, and only offered it in the future when they were on vacation. Even though I left the place cleaner than I found it, so they should've appreciated my efforts and wanted me around more."

Abby walked by, and Bianca glared at her. "Keep walking, Princess."

I couldn't see Abby as she responded, but her overexaggerated snort made me chuckle.

"Abby is almost as obnoxious as the coffee snobs. I wish everyone here would just focus on their own restaurants and chill with the drama," Bianca said.

I snorted out loud. Did Bianca hear herself?

"Umm, drama?" Rose's side-eye was perfect.

"You'd think we'd all be adults, but I keep finding the other owners standing around, gossiping. It's like dealing with the mean girls in high school all over again."

"Are you sure they're talking about you? Bianca, maybe they're just venting to each other." Rose's tone was compassionate again.

"You're so quick to think the best of everyone, Rose, but I know the truth. You'd be shocked by the dark pasts of some of the tenants here in the Button Building."

Wait, was Bianca talking about me? Or did she have dirt on my fellow owners?

"I should get back to work." Bianca sounded sad to stop talking with Rose.

Rose switched into full perky mode. "Thanks for talking to me today! As a reminder, I talked with Bianca Moore of the Breakfast Bandits. Her café is sure to become one of your favorite spots for a morning meal."

Bianca stomped off before Rose stopped recording.

I looked at my brother.

"Bianca seems pleasant," Jackson said.

But I'm also fluent in sarcasm so I understood him.

"As you can see, she was a ray of sunshine," I said. Guilt seeped through me. "I should be kind, but Bianca was tough to deal with. You know the people who take everything, even offhand comments intended to be kind, as insults? That was Bianca."

"She must've had a tough life."

We were quiet for a moment. Uncle Jimmy's comments about Bianca's dad flashed through my mind. I glanced at my brother, wondering again how his past had shaped his present. "Do you ever care that you were raised by your paternal grandparents?"

He shook his head but looked at me with raised eyebrows. "They were good to me. Why are you asking?"

"Are you in much contact with your dad?"

"We talk occasionally," Jackson said. "He's more like a distant relative. As you know, he moved out when he graduated high school and went to college on the East Coast. He never moved back and he clearly never wanted me to live with him."

"Did that bother you?" The undertone of my brother's words pointed to a soft spot in his sarcastic armor. If his biological dad were here, I'd happily tell him he'd been a jerk to Jackson.

"What do you think, Sage, that it made me happy? I talk more with your dad than my own. But my grandparents were my true parents. The weirdest part for me is having a couple of younger half siblings I've only met a handful of times. And I doubt I'll see them anytime soon, since my father no longer has a reason to visit."

The faint bitterness at the end of his words struck me. Jackson's grandparents had died a few years after he graduated law school, and he must've felt more lost than I'd realized.

"How old are your little brothers now?"

"Twelve and fourteen. From my father's second and third wives."

"Their loss." Jackson would've been a fantastic older brother for them, which I knew from experience. Part of me wondered, even though his grandparents had done their best, if Jackson's disconnect with his biological parents was one of the reasons he'd gone into child advocacy. He knew what it felt like to be lost and powerless.

Jackson would be an intriguing choice for Rose's podcast although there's no chance he'd agree to be interviewed. Provided I was right and our mother's actions, and his father's reactions, influenced my brother's path to help the voiceless stuck in situations they can't control.

But I also wouldn't mention this to Rose since I knew Jackson wouldn't like the attention.

We'd both wanted to separate ourselves from the idea of our mother and create our own lives. Yet the ripple of her actions kept upsetting the balance of our lives.

Although now, with her death in a car accident, at least we wouldn't have to hear about new victims.

But Rose was reopening old wounds, and Bianca's death had created new ones.

Was Bianca's death related to the past? Was there something that Abby, Laura, or Phillip didn't want to be known to the world? Could Bianca have known something worth killing over?

Bianca had her own tragic connection to my mother's past. Still, I couldn't see how that was connected to what happened, except for Rose's interview. Had someone seen the cup of coffee and known it was an opportunity? But that would mean they'd been carrying a drug, waiting for the right moment to slip it into the target's food.

Maybe Rose really was the intended victim. She was the one stirring everything up. If Rose had died, I would've been the perfect suspect with clear-cut motive.

Jackson's phone buzzed, and he read it. "Piper's on her way home, so I should split."

"Tell her hi from me." Jackson and Piper had dated in law school. When she'd taken a job on the East Coast and they'd broken up, he'd clearly pined for her and never fully moved on. I was glad she'd moved back to Oregon, and not just because she and Jackson had fallen back into their relationship.

I liked Piper. Someday, when I grew up, I hoped to be just like her.

And I liked how most of the sarcasm faded from Jackson's smile when she was around.

I walked Jackson to the front door, and he paused on the doorstep.

"Remember, call me if the police stop by again."

"Of course."

I locked the door behind Jackson and watched him walk down the front porch stairs and brick walkway to the sidewalk and street where he'd parked.

As much as his lecturing grated on my nerves, I knew I was lucky to have Jackson on my side. Not just in this situation but in life in general.

My history with my mother had led me to be careful with how I dealt with people and how far I let them in. I always tried to give equal to how much I received, if not more.

Maybe helping Bianca's friends and family receive justice would help with the debt I felt I owed, even if most of what I was atoning for, meaning my mother's acts, weren't my fault.

# Chapter 7

After I cleaned the kitchen, I settled on the couch with my computer, a cup of peppermint tea, and a purring cat. Kaldi kept trying to crawl under my laptop, like the space between it and my lap was the perfect spot to chill. He finally settled for nestling on my shoulder.

I clicked on one of Rose's "historical" videos in a separate subfolder. It was from two years ago.

In the video, Bianca and Laura were squared off. From the surroundings, I guessed it was from one of the old food cart pods downtown.

Laura, who had always seemed calm, with a Zen presence that made me wonder what was simmering under the surface, was practically spitting as she screamed at Bianca. A few people were watching, and the cell phone video was jerky as the filmer moved for a better view.

"You need to keep your stupid customers from stealing my napkins!" Bianca screamed.

Laura muttered, "Un burro sabe mas que tu," as she walked away from Bianca, walking within a foot or two of the person filming the encounter. She gritted her teeth, then disappeared from view.

The camera stayed on Bianca, who was breathing hard, and her face was red with anger. "You'll regret this!" she yelled in Laura's direction, then turned away and stomped toward her Breakfast Bandits cart. She climbed in and slammed the door, hitting it off the doorframe, so it rebounded open. People laughed.

"What a psycho," someone said.

"What exactly was that fight about? I missed the kickoff and only arrived for the final whistle."

"The breakfast cart is up to her usual tricks." The voice sounded familiar, but I couldn't quite place it. Male, most likely. A standard Pacific Northwest accent, from what I heard, which is close to General American. Which is a fancy way of saying the most neutral American accent, although no one actually speaks it since regionality creeps in with varying degrees. But it's the accent newscasters and anyone trying to slice off the regional notes in their speech revert to. I'd decided years ago the best way to tell if someone grew up in Oregon is to ask if they use an umbrella. Seeing an umbrella in Portland is the fastest way to identify a tourist or recent transplant.

But then the video ended, so I scrolled back and listened again. But I still couldn't place the face that matched the voice.

Maybe I was reading too much into the voice, and it was someone who sounded like a person I'd once met.

I searched online for Fowl Play and the Breakfast Bandits since Rose had mentioned this encounter had gone viral. The video had been posted on multiple sites, ranging from numerous social media apps to the local news.

Most of the comments were sexist and obnoxious, in the way social media can bring out the worst common denominators in people's souls when they post anonymously, or at least when they are several steps removed from the people being targeted.

Which didn't mean some of the roasts didn't make me laugh, like the person who said, "The breakfast chef is cracked like a boiled egg." But I also felt guilty about chuckling. It's one thing when someone who dishes garbage out gets roasted in return, but it's different when people argue on the street and a bystander records them. It's unfair, bordering on cruel. Although most of my sympathy was for Laura.

Rose had also recorded short interviews with Abby, Laura, and the rest of the micro-restaurant owners. Kaldi purred as I listened to them until he headbutted one of the earbuds out of my ear, causing the video to pause automatically.

"I guess this is the sign I should do something else," I said, reaching up and rubbing Kaldi's head. While the videos were interesting, none of them seemed relevant. I closed my laptop, swapped it out for a novel, and had a reading session with the cat.

Bax worked late, as he'd been the past few weeks when Niko, Bax's son, wasn't in residence. I decided to go for an early night, as I usually did since I had to wake up way too early to open Ground Rules. Someday, I'd become a morning person versus pretending to be one.

After getting ready to head to dreamland, Kaldi dive-bombed me as I slid into bed. He splayed across my chest and purred loudly as I stared at my phone. Scrolling through everyone's social media felt like arranging deck chairs on the *Titanic* when I really wanted to solve the problem. But there wasn't anything I could accomplish. Because I was a barista slash business owner.

And because it was night.

But instead of reading a book to unwind, I looked up Rose's social media.

Lots of short makeup tutorial videos, some of which I'd already viewed. I opened Rose's Instagram profile and scrolled back a year. I saw a mix of photos of Santa Cruz, California, where she went to school, and a few posts about starting her podcast. Like a photo of her podcasting gear artfully arranged on a table with the text "look at this new-to-me gear!"

She had a few promo posts for the first season of *Rose Investigates*, which was a six-part story of a recently solved cold case in a small California town. Rose had managed to score a couple of interviews with the family of Izzy, the victim, and her podcast had garnered quite a few listeners and social media buzz. Rose had managed to bring the victim to life, partially by getting her friends and family to tell stories about Izzy's childhood and teen years, leading up to the fatal night when she'd driven home from college for Christmas and disappeared. She'd left behind her favorite bomber jacket and purse in a local park, just blocks from her parents' house, only for her remains to be discovered two decades later. Making Izzy feel real, like someone the listener could've been friends with, gave the podcast a poignancy that stuck with you days after listening. Rose had barely focused on the man who'd eventually plead guilty to killing Izzy, supposedly on accident. She'd spent more time talking with the investigators, highlighting the work they'd done over twenty years to bring peace to Izzy's family, as well as the efforts of Izzy's loved ones to make sure no one forgot her. They'd even started a missing teen fund in Izzy's name and after the podcast, their fundraiser had quadrupled in support, leading them to publicly thank Rose.

Izzy's story reminded me of my father's current volunteer gig with cold cases, and his refusal to let victims be relegated to the past. Because as Rose was exploring in her podcast, each crime does have an effect that starts with the victim but ripples out.

How had Rose decided to delve into my mother's story? I'd asked her before, but she'd hedged instead of answering.

I put my phone down and looked at Kaldi. "If you were going to do a podcast, would you choose my mother as your subject?" I scratched his head.

He gave me a slight trill, and I guessed that was his only answer.

"You could also record one about the myth you're named after," I told him, and he trilled again. So I told him yet again the story of Kaldi, the goatherd, who supposedly discovered coffee after his goats ate from a strange bush and became energetic.

"But you know, I'm still amazed anyone discovered coffee. I mean, who figured out that the beans inside could be roasted, ground, and turned into the perfect drink? Tea makes more sense since it's just boiling leaves, even if there are important steps when designing the perfect tea blend. But if it was up to me, I would've been too chicken to try new berries or plants. Some of those are poisonous."

He trilled again, clearly focused on our conversation.

"You're right. We're both happier as house cats."

I turned off the light, and we went to sleep, only waking up when Bax apologized for waking both of us when he came home around midnight. The warm lump on my stomach left since Kaldi felt it essential to share his affection with both of us.

It was a lovely bit of normalcy in a world spinning in a weird direction.

# Chapter 8

I tried to sleep in the next day, as the Ground Rules brick-and-mortar shop was closed since it hadn't been released by the police, and my usual openers were at the cart. They didn't need me to get in the way of their regular routine just because I didn't have anything else to do.

But I couldn't stay in dreamland. Too many emotions kept pinging across my brain.

Would the coffee shop fail?

Was this one death too many for Ground Rules?

What if I had to lay off all of my employees? I'd never had to let anyone go before, and the idea of it felt painful.

More importantly, what had happened to Bianca? And would the police find the actual culprit or keep sniffing around me?

I gave up and dislodged Kaldi, who gave me a disgruntled meow before heading back under the covers. I gently patted the kitty-shaped lump under the duvet before heading to the shower.

After dressing in a thick wool sweater, my heaviest jeans, and my favorite everyday hiking boots, I biked to the Rail Yard. The air was biting cold, like it was midwinter instead of an early spring day.

When I pulled up to the cart, Kendall and Sophie had everything under control. Kendall worked the window with his usual easygoing charm while Sophie made a series of espresso drinks for customers. Both baristas were bundled up, but the space heater in the cart kept it warmer than outside. Although the open order window ensured a steady flow of cold air whipped through the cart.

I checked out the cart's supplies and made a note to restock the sugar-free hazelnut syrup, which we picked up from a local grocery supply store, and to bring a new batch of the bourbon vanilla syrup we make in-house. And by we, I mean I prepare it in the roastery's kitchen, along with a small lineup of seasonal syrups. Which reminded me that I should think of something for May. Maybe a lavender syrup to represent May flowers? The famed Mt. Hood lavender bloomed from May through August and my favorite spice distributor carried culinary lavender.

"You want a drink, boss?" Sophie asked as Kendall handed the last few drinks in line to waiting customers.

"I wouldn't say no to a cortado."

It was also a good day for my favorite La Bake marionberry muffin. So as Sophie made my drink, I used tongs to grab one from the pastry case and noted that I'd taken it so the numbers wouldn't be off at the end of the day. The wholesale cost of the muffin would come out of my paycheck.

"So, what do we need to know about yesterday at the coffee shop?" Kendall asked.

The dread I felt yesterday when Bianca collapsed came to mind as I told them about everything.

"Wait, that woman who glared at us at Campathon?" Kendall asked. He'd worked our events cart often, including the times we'd set up at the music festival. He'd managed the smaller one for a few farmers markets when they were in season.

"It must've been bad if you remember her," Sophie said.

"It was surreal," Kendall said. "Once, when Sage wasn't at the cart, Bianca walked up and stood two feet away from the order window and just glared at me."

"Wait, what? Why didn't you tell me about this?" I would've

done something to help Kendall, even if it had just been complaining to the festival.

"There was a lot else going on, and I chased her off easily enough. I wasn't scared of her, just confused by what she was trying to achieve. Although the guy she was with? He seemed like he was egging her on."

"What do you mean?" I asked.

"During our first year at the festival, when you were handling the cart, and I was picking up Hawaiian barbecue, I passed behind the Breakfast Bandits cart. They were talking, and he was amping her up. Saying that he'd heard 'the blonde from the coffee cart' and the 'chocolate cart' talking smack about them. He said their fellow cart owners were always two-faced and that they couldn't trust any of them."

"You really remember this and that you were going to get Hawaiian food?" Sophie folded her arms over her chest, her posture mirroring the skepticism in her voice.

"You'd remember the Hawaiian barbecue if you had it."

"Kendall's right. That cart was fantastic," I said.

But my thoughts were whirling. Had Phillip fed into Bianca's antagonism toward Ground Rules and me? Had he poisoned her relationships with the other food carts as well? But why? Was he equally paranoid, and they'd fueled each other's anxiety in a way that made it impossible for them to trust the world?

We talked for a while longer, and I headed to the roastery, happy that my staff had the cart under control. They didn't need me poking my managerial nose into their business even though I wanted to stay.

I spent most of the morning working in the roastery. I headed out for a taco lunch with Harley before she returned to the proverbial grindstone. I detoured to say hi to Bax. But he was clearly involved in a deep conversation with Lindsey, his co-owner and the technical genius of their operation, while he was the creative force. So I slipped out of the Grumpy Sasquatch Studio without anyone noticing.

As I was finishing a fresh batch of chai concentrate, my phone rang with good news: we'd gotten the okay to reopen Ground Rules the next afternoon. I texted Colton and Nina that, if they wanted to, they could come and help me clean up. But I told them they weren't obligated since I'd already called them off work.

Nina quickly replied. *Can't. I'm babysitting my sister's kids. But we'll be open tomorrow?*

*Yep! I'll see you at your scheduled shift.*

She responded with a series of coffee emojis.

But Colton waited when I parked my bicycle by the Ground Rules shop. He was bundled up in his usual coat, but he'd added a jaunty plaid scarf and knit orange beanie.

"Did you hear it's supposed to snow tomorrow?" Colton asked.

"Have you been waiting here all day?" I asked.

"Nah, I was playing video games at my friend's house nearby. It was time for me to do something that involved moving, so I headed this way."

Even though his words were nonchalant, I felt guilty for dragging Colton back to work. But I appreciated his help as we set the shop back to rights. The police had taken the air pots from the grand opening and the containers holding milk and sugar from the condiment table. I started an itemized list of everything they'd taken, hoping I'd be able to replace everything we needed by tomorrow.

We'd been forced to close before our usual afternoon cleanup. As I made my list, Colton put the chairs and stools in the shop on top of the tables and long counter so he could mop. I stacked the black mats behind the coffee bar so he could swing through with his mop, then focused on cleaning the espresso machine so it'd be primed for tomorrow. I ran dishes through the sanitizer. I also tossed out the stale pastries, which we give away if we don't sell them, but it was too late now.

"Do you think it'll snow at the Timbers game?" Colton asked as he made his way past me with a mop, leaving the lingering scent of bleach behind him.

"If it does, that'll be a first."

The Timbers Army regularly chanted, "Let it rain, let it pour, let the Timbers Army score," since quite a few games were played in a prototypical Pacific Northwest rain. But the snow was usually a visitor for maybe one to two days a winter, with the occasional ice storm. But in March? Virtually unheard-of.

We talked about the Timbers and their female counterparts, the Thorns, as we finished cleaning the shop and preparing for tomorrow.

Finally, we were done, and I let Colton out before locking the door behind us, leaving the shop ready.

"Be ready for snow tomorrow!" Colton called out as he walked down the sidewalk.

"It's not going to snow. It's March!" I called back.

On my way home, I swung by my favorite east-side taproom and coffeehouse, Hoptimal Pint, and locked my bicycle to the rack outside. Back when I'd had my first date with Bax here, they'd only offered beer. But they'd expanded their menu to be an all-day neighborhood hangout.

The place was about half-full, and I debated a pint of a farmhouse ale from one of my favorite local breweries. But I had an early morning tomorrow, with the shop reopening, so I opted for a naturally de-caffeinated rooibos tea with dried blackberries made by one of my favorite local tea makers before snagging a cozy booth for two in the corner.

Once again, I appreciated how the place was half beer heaven, half coffeehouse. Not everyone drinks alcohol, and it's nice to have joints that cater to everyone. Plus, they had excellent snacks, and to make it even better: they used Ground Rules coffee. Which was less impressive than it sounded as I had an in, as the owner was buddies with Bax. The owner had even hired Bax to design the Hoptimal Pint logo and branding, allowing Bax to stretch his illustration muscles.

A few minutes later, Rose arrived. She carried her usual pink backpack and looked flawless like always as she slid into the seat across from me. She put a large mocha in a printed yellow mug on the table between us.

"You know, when I was in college, I was a hot mess," I said. "If I remembered to put on ChapStick, I would've considered it a win."

"I doubt that," Rose said. Her smile made her real age shine out from the curated façade that, I guessed, would make a lot of people read her as older than around twenty, give or take a year. While people frequently read me as younger. So maybe I should take tips from Rose.

"Compared to you, I was. My wardrobe was pretty much flannels, hoodies, and jeans." Which wasn't that different from now, except I'd branched out into more sweaters and the occasional scarf. Although I rarely made it through a whole day with a scarf since it would inevitably get in the way.

"You know you can pick up surprising stuff at thrift shops, right? Especially if you have some basic sewing skills."

"Yes, I know the joys of thrifting. Although I can't sew." Harley knits, but my crafting skills ended at reading how-to guides.

"Seriously, Sage, I've picked up name-brand stuff and needed to hem the pants or nip the shirt in at the waist. We can go thrifting if you'd like, and I could help you alter everything. We could find you some fun stuff. Once, I bought this funky muumuu from the seventies and turned it into the best cocktail dress for a wedding. I still love that dress."

We chatted briefly about sewing, and Rose's eyes lit up as she talked about how she learned how to make a pillowcase at school when she was ten and kept on sewing, fueled by a home economics teacher willing to use part of her lunch to teach Rose and a few other classmates advanced skills.

"Home ec wasn't the cool class at my high school, but I took it anyway. My teacher encouraged me to apply to a fashion program, but I opted for journalism."

"How long do you have left in school?"

"About a year and a half. Although I'm doing everything distance this semester to focus on the podcast since my numbers are getting good. I decided to prioritize it in case it turns into something big. Plus, I can use it as an independent study course, so I only have three other classes to take virtually."

Rose leaned back with a gleam in her eye that I recognized. "You know, I've turned the room I'm renting into a pretty sweet recording studio. You should come over so I can record a better-quality interview with you."

"My opinion hasn't changed about being interviewed. It's still a hard no. But like I said, I'll look into this crime with you as long as we don't do anything illegal."

"Okay, Oma," Rose said. She tilted her head slightly as she looked at me.

Rose made me feel old, but not that old.

"Did you check out the footage I sent over?" Rose asked.

I nodded. "I've been working my way through it. After watching the video with Bianca's collapse and comparing it to the security footage, it looks like Abby, Laura, Phillip, and Nina all had opportunities to add something to the coffee."

"Security footage?"

"Yes, we have cameras in the shop. It's a bit Big Brother-ish, but it helps protect the business, so we have them."

"Can you send the footage to me?"

Rose's look my way was too wide-eyed and innocent. "As long as you promise you won't use it in your social media feeds, I'll send you the files so you can view them."

"I can agree to that." Rose made a note on her phone.

"I have a few questions after watching the footage you sent me. How did you get that video of Mark and Phillip talking?"

"Mark?"

"Dark-haired guy who was talking with Phillip. You filmed them but put your phone down on the table so the video went black, but you kept recording audio."

"Oh, him! I was writing a podcast script while waiting to interview Laura, and I heard them talking. What I heard sounded sketchy, so I recorded them on the down-low. I wish I could've gotten all their conversation since it sounds like they're up to something. From what I remember, the guy with the dark hair and the tattoos on his forearms hates you."

I could picture the moka pot and various coffee-related tattoos covering Mark's arms. "That's Mark Jeffries," I said, explaining who he was and how Harley and I had worked for him as undergraduates. "I did learn a ton about coffee from him, although I hated working for him."

"Was he a bad boss?"

"Not always, but he hit on female employees. Including me. But one of the worst things he did was claim Harley's award-winning coffee blend as his own."

I told Rose about how Harley had created a custom blend to enter in the regional Barista and Coffee Champions while working for Left Coast Grinds. When it won a gold medal, Mark claimed the roast as his own.

"There's a coffee championship?"

"Yes, it's huge. There are different categories regional coffee shops can compete in, and the winners can go to the national and even world championships. Mark won the barista part of the competition once, which is what made his name and helped him establish the roastery part of Left Coast Grinds, which had been a tiny shop before his national championship. He's good with coffee and would have shown that he was also an excellent mentor by celebrating Harley's blend. Instead, he used her award and the resulting attention to expand from multiple shops and build a significant distribution network. I used to see his coffee everywhere. But according to the local paper a while back, his business has been struggling, and he might have lost a contract to go national."

I told Rose more about the article, which had highlighted some of the smaller roasters, including Ground Rules, making waves in Portland.

"What, like he wanted to be the next mermaid coffee?"

"One of their competitors, for sure."

"I'll look into him more. I bet I can find something good." Rose tapped out more notes.

"He didn't have access to Bianca on the morning she died, and I can't see him killing anyone."

"But I've seen him talking to Phillip multiple times, and we know Phillip had access to Bianca. And honestly, there's something off about Phillip. He makes my skin crawl."

I nodded, remembering that Kendall had gotten bad vibes from Phillip, too, so it wasn't just Rose and me who thought he felt off.

Rose pursed her lips briefly, then said, "I can also look into Nina."

"She just moved back to Portland. I really can't see her harming Bianca. I doubt they knew each other."

"But I don't have a personal relationship with her, so I won't be blinded when I do a deep dive into researching her. And you said she had access, so she has to be on the suspect list." Rose tapped on her phone a few more times.

"You'll be wasting your time, but okay."

We discussed what happened for a few more minutes, then I left, dropping my empty teacup off in the dish bin on my way out. Rose stayed at the booth and pulled out her laptop, which she was now staring at intently.

I was thankful I'd packed a cowl in my bag, my usual gloves, and the thin but toasty beanie that fits under my bicycle helmet because it was cold, more like January than March. My body warmed up as I rode through the east side streets of Portland, but the bite in the air made me eager to get home.

And for the first time in a while, the lights in the bungalow were brightly lit when I arrived. I took care of my bike and then rushed to the front door.

"You're home!" I called out as I entered the house. The smell of roasting chicken permeated the air. I ditched my bag and layers on a chair before making my way to the heart of the home.

Bax greeted me in the kitchen and said, "I'm finally using that adobo spice mix I picked up. How was the taproom? You were meeting someone?"

I told him about my talk with Rose as he pulled a cast-iron skillet of roast chicken thighs on top of sliced potatoes from the oven and set it to rest. "But I would've skipped it if I'd known you'd be home early."

Kaldi watched from a kitchen chair and Bax gave him a warning look. "Don't even think of trying to steal our chicken."

Kaldi chirped, like how dare we accuse him of something he'd never do, as long as we were watching.

Bax also had a pot of tomato and orange soup simmering, with his favorite specialty cubes for freezing soup into perfect one-cup rectangles waiting on the counter. A couple of roasted beets cooled alongside carrots on a cooling rack. He'd already prepped bento boxes with quinoa to which he'd add the roast vegetables, a protein of some sort, and either a lemon vinaigrette or goddess dressing. The food was peak Bax, the recipes he'd perfected before he knew me. It was an added bonus that he always made plenty for me as well as him.

Plus, he cleaned as he cooked, proving he was a keeper.

"You've been a busy sasquatch," I said.

"You've been picking up the slack, and I wanted to do something to pull my weight. Plus, doing something that didn't involve looking at a screen sounded refreshing."

"I'm not complaining."

I helped Bax prep the series of bento boxes, and he let the soup cool as we ate dinner. Kaldi sat on a chair across from me at the table, sitting up straight like he expected us to put a plate in front of him.

"I have a new playable version of the new game if you want to try out *Falling Through the Shadows*," Bax offered as we ate.

"I'm still okay with waiting to play the game. Especially since you're taking the night off."

"And you have your own problem to solve. We can also create a video game flowchart if it would help you figure out what happened to Bianca."

"I appreciate the offer, but let's try to forget about all of that."

"We can try," Bax said.

And I understood what he didn't say. He was trying to let go of the stress of the game launch for the evening, but it was hovering in the back of his mind. Until it was solved, Bianca's death would haunt me, too.

I did my best to relax into an almost ordinary evening. Cleaning dishes while Bax finished the meal prep, including ladling soup into the waiting silicon soup trays and popping them in the freezer, and shredding leftover chicken for the roast vegetable and quinoa bento bowls. Tossing in a load of laundry and then streaming a British comedy together about a woman and her partner who inherit a manor house they want to turn into a B&B. But the house is full of ghosts, and she's the only living human they can talk to.

But nothing I did could silence my nerves and let me truly relax. I just had the sense something was going to happen.

Something I would despise.

But maybe Bianca's death had just made me too pessimistic.

# Chapter 9

March. Some years in Portland, it rains buckets. Other years, it's sunny and warm and fools everyone into thinking spring came early.

But as I stood on the front porch, I almost couldn't believe my eyes.

Snow.

And not just a gentle dusting, but at least an inch of powder giving the world a magical feel that would be perfect at Christmastime (which had been a series of rainy days).

Colton had been right about the weather.

And it was still snowing heavily, promising a winter wonderland. Or, considering what usually happens around here, my fellow Portlanders would treat this like a snowpocolypse. One of the times this happened, the local Fred Meyer quickly ran out of kale. Because what else do you need when you're stuck at home when schools and businesses close for the day, but bitter leafy vegetables?

"It will snow on your second reopening" hadn't been on my bingo card, but we'd make the best of it. Hopefully, customers would find us, drawn in by a cozy cup of coffee or other hot drink as a hedge against the still-falling snow.

The door opened behind me.

"If you're sure you want to open the shop, I'll drop you off."

Bax yawned behind me. He'd pulled his navy-and-red down coat over his pajamas and shoved his feet into a pair of the tall Bogs boots he usually reserved for yard work and, evidently, snow days. He tapped the purple-striped hat keeping my head warm. "I like this."

"Harley knit it for me." She'd even crafted a hole in the back for my ponytail and sewn a small coffee cup patch on the folding brim. I remembered my conversation with Harley about anxiety. Is knitting one of the ways she deals with it? I'd always thought she knit because she couldn't sit still while bingeing shows. But her reason could be deeper, showing there's always another layer to every story if you keep looking.

Kaldi watched us from the window like he wondered why we were venturing into the cold world when there was a toasty house we could lounge in, complete with tuna treats. I waved goodbye to him, and he stared back without blinking in peak cat behavior.

I stowed my messenger bag in the footwell of the passenger side of Bax's Subaru, but when I tried to help him scrape the windows, he waved me off. "I got this."

"You're doing me a favor. I should help."

"Why don't you make sure the seat warmers are on."

I really should help, but I let Bax do his thing. The seat warmers weren't on when I climbed into the car, so I flipped the switch for both front bucket seats. Modern cars have one significant advantage over bicycles: heated seats. Plus, air-conditioning in the summer.

And tunes. Although I sometimes heard cyclists blaring music as they crisscrossed the streets of Portland. I always smile when I remember hearing Marvin Gaye's "Let's Get It On" and seeing a man swaying side to side as he cycled down a bike boulevard, blaring his jam. I'd been impressed he hadn't crashed.

I usually forgo music on my rides, as I don't want to wear earbuds as they'd block out surrounding noise, and blasting music seemed unfair to everyone else in earshot.

So I also appreciated Bax flipping to his favorite alternative music station before he backed out of the driveway.

And I appreciated the man who'd dragged himself out of bed to ensure I got safely to work.

"Call me when you're about to leave, and I should be able to pick you up. I'm sure all of the sasquatches will work from home today, so my schedule will be flexible."

"They'll work from home even with the stress of the launch?"

"I'd much rather have employees working safely from home than getting in a car accident."

"Or stuck because someone else slid out." With the steep hills and snow that tended to be icy rather than powdery, snow in Portland always ground the city to a halt. The buses run slower than normal with chains, so it can take forever to get through town. Luckily the shop wasn't too far from Bax's house, and the route was flat. "I texted Kendall and Sophie that they don't need to open the cart this morning, but Kendall said he could be there to open up. Which is one of the advantages of his apartment only being two blocks away."

"I can't imagine how cold the cart will be."

"I told him that he can close it whenever it feels prudent. The cart's space heater does a better job than you'd think, but as always, safety first." And there's no reason to hang out if there aren't any customers.

"Still." Bax pulled up to the Button Building. "Keep me posted."

"Of course." After a goodbye kiss, I carefully stepped onto the sidewalk. My feet sunk into untouched snow, except for a series of footsteps made by the paws of an extra-large dog and, presumably, an owner in boots.

The shop felt still inside. Abnormally quiet. And clean, from Colton's and my efforts yesterday. I flipped the lights on, turned on the espresso machine so it'd warm up, filled the gooseneck kettle and set it to boil, and discarded my jacket in the back. To warm up, I started unstacking the chairs and stools, so they sat right side up under the tables and counter instead of being perched on top. My efforts also triggered the smart thermometer, which kicked in and slowly started pumping warm air into the shop.

I glanced at the door to the communal area, which was dark. No lights were on in the other shops, so I left that door shut and locked. If we got busy enough to need the seating overflow, I'd open it, but for now, people could use the main door to the street if they wanted to come inside. I doubted we'd get that busy.

I wasn't surprised that the Breakfast Bandits shop looked closed since I wasn't sure they'd ever be open again. Would Phillip want to continue on? Could he, without Bianca?

A fresh pang of sympathy flowed through me. Poor Phillip had lost both his business and life partner when they were on the cusp of fulfilling a dream. I couldn't bring myself to like Phillip, given how he'd treated me, but I couldn't imagine the depth of devastation he must feel.

The kettle finished boiling, so I made myself a Nicaraguan pour-over, taking a moment to enjoy the bloom of the coffee as the hot water from the gooseneck kettle flowed through it. Small moments like this, like standing with a hot cup of coffee in my hands while staring out at the brand-new coffee shop I created, are the sort of times I try to savor.

I glanced outside, reminding me of another favorite but rare activity: standing with a warm mug in my hands, watching snow bathe the world in white.

If the snow continued, today would be quiet. But I was still glad we were open.

My phone beeped with a text from Kendall. *The cart is a go. One of the neighborhoods nearby lost power, and we're one of the only places open. We have power, FYI.*

*How are you doing?*

*Fine, boss. Added bonus: someone showed up and shoveled the sidewalks and a path to the carts.*

Hmm, that was a surprise. I'd need to ask my uncle about the elusive snow shoveler.

Kendall followed up with a photo of the cart, which was lit up, including with the white holiday lights we'd left up after last December. He'd added a handwritten note to the order window. It said, *We're open!* in giant block letters in black sharpie, with *Please knock if we don't see you* in smaller text below.

The cart looked magical in the snow.

I popped open the app I used to manage the Ground Rules social media account and posted the photo to all our social media, along with a message. *Both the cart and our brand-new shop are open for your caffeine needs on this magically cold day! #StayWarmPortland #Snowpocalypse*

Someone knocked on the front door about fifteen minutes after I'd flipped the OPEN sign to on.

Colton.

I let him in.

"I'm sorry I'm late. I snowshoed over."

And I believed him since he held a pair of orange snowshoes in his gloved hands.

"I hadn't thought of you as a snow sport enthusiast." But it's not like I knew everything about my newest baristas.

"These belong to my roommate. I didn't need anything like this when I lived in Austin. If it snowed, or more likely got icy, I just didn't leave my house."

"Quite a few Portlanders follow the same ideology," I said. "It's not as bad on this side of the river since it's flatter. But the West Hills and the area around OHSU can get so icy which is a bad combination with steep roads."

Colton stored his gear in the back, then emerged while tying a Ground Rules apron around his waist. "No Nina?"

I shook my head. "And I haven't heard from her." I sent her a quick text.

"No pastries?" Colton sounded heartbroken.

"The bakery delivery hasn't shown up yet, but fingers crossed."

"Definitely, 'cause I'm starving after my long, arduous trek through the snowy streets of Portland."

"Well, I'll buy lunch if one of the other cafés opens. For the meanwhile, we have vegan energy bars."

"C'mon, Doughman, open today, please," Colton said. He then pulled himself a shot of espresso and drank it back. He closed his eyes, taking a moment to fully taste the espresso's notes.

His love of espresso is one of the many reasons Colton is a keeper regarding Ground Rules.

As I double-checked the OPEN sign, which I'd already turned on, I hoped it would gleam in the darkness like a beacon drawing people out from the dark for espresso. My phone beeped. Nina. *I'm stuck at home with the snow!*

I quickly replied. *That's fine. Colton and I have everything covered.*

She responded with a thumbs-up emoji.

A few minutes later, our first customer walked in.

"I need coffee immediately!" She was dressed in a utility-style snowsuit that reminded me of the younger brother in *A Christmas Story*, which was topped with two knit scarves and a trapper-style hat with earflaps that had long dangling cords. She pulled off her mittens to reveal a pair of gloves below like she was a human matryoshka doll. By the end, once she shed her layers, she'd probably be the size of a small child.

"We can help with that," I said.

"Let's go with an extra-large mocha. I need sugar to go with the caffeine, given the weather."

By the time Colton had slid over her mocha, she'd divested several layers and folded the snowsuit down to her waist, showing off a striped wool sweater with a turtleneck underneath. She was officially ready to survive the snowpocolypse.

I wasn't sure how she wasn't roasting, as I was toasty enough in my sweater and Harley-made hat. But in a city that wasn't used to snow, I'd long since accepted people either overreacted or didn't take it seriously enough, not realizing that icy snow in the mountainous Pacific Northwest is an entirely different experience in the much flatter Midwest.

A voice at the door caught my attention. "Guess who has pastries!"

"You made it!" I said. Our usual pastry supplier brought a bigger-than-usual collection of boxes to our counter. Her bakery wasn't far away, maybe half a mile. I could see her Subaru with a La Bake logo outside along the curb. It was already collecting snow on the windshield.

"You're one of my few customers open. Can I leave you extras, and if you sell them, you can pay me our usual rate, but if you don't, consider them freebies? They'll go to waste if I keep them."

"Sure." We wrote and signed a quick note, then I put the pastries in the case. Maybe the still-warm marionberry muffins, figgy scones, and other pastries, alongside a selection of cookies, all featuring as many locally sourced ingredients as possible, would lure customers into the shop.

"I also included a couple of baguette sandwiches for you and your staff," our baker said, and Colton showed up as if summoned.

"What's this about a sandwich?"

I laughed and pulled three butcher paper–wrapped sandwiches out of the side of the box. "Lunch is sorted," I said.

"They're ham and Swiss with fresh arugula and tomato jam on fresh demi-baguettes," the baker said.

"I feel like I should express undying love," Colton said.

"Just wait; you haven't tried it yet," the baker said. "Your love could be in vain."

"Be still my heart." Colton crossed his hands over his chest, and the baker laughed.

"I'll see you silly kids tomorrow since I bet my usual delivery driver will be stuck at home again."

She left, and Colton snagged his sandwich while I made a couple of hot cocoas for a man with two small kids and an old-school wooden sled with metal runners.

"Are you going sledding?"

"If you mean dogsledding with me filling in for the dog, then yes," he said. He handed the cocoas to his kids. "I don't trust these two on a hill."

"Have fun!"

They left. Once they were outside, I watched him settle the kids on the sled, and then he pulled them down the street. It looked like the sort of memory the kids would question later, wondering if it happened or was something they saw in a movie.

A while later, Colton nudged me and pointed outside, where a group of cross-skiers pulled up to the order window.

I gasped and opened the order window. "Is this the Stumptown Birkebeiner?"

"It is!" one of the skiers squealed back, and we chatted about their route. The loosely organized group holds a cross-country ski "race" together whenever there's enough snow in Portland to do so.

"This is the perfect snack break," the woman said as I handed a selection of drinks and pastries out to the skiers. She clutched a house-made chai in her gloved hands. "I'm so glad you're open 'cause I need this."

"I'm enjoying this bizarre snow day."

"It's an unexpected delight."

As much as I loved chatting with the cross-country skiers, I was happy to shut the order windows and warm my hands around an Americano that Colton thoughtfully made for me.

My phone beeped with my friend Manny, asking if we'd be up for donating carafes of coffee today to Inner City Assistance as they made the rounds.

*Of course. As many as you need from either the shop or the cart. Just text me, and I'll make sure they're ready to go.*

The door to the Ground Rules café opened. Rose slipped through, decked out in a jaunty knit beret with a matching scarf and mittens over a striped winter coat that reminded me of an eighties ski film. All of her look said vintage, and I bet they were thrift store finds. Rose headed straight my way.

"Can you believe this snow? I want to make a snowman. Or have a snowball fight." Rose twirled around.

"Someone doesn't need caffeine," Colton muttered behind me.

"Do you know what time it is?" Rose asked.

"Not time for more caffeine." Colton had officially joined the peanut gallery.

I smiled as I glanced at the clock on the wall and told Rose the time.

"Good!" She leaned toward me and whispered, "I'll be back for an appointment, but I have some sleuthing to do."

"Don't do anything illegal. I don't have funds to bail out podcasters in my operating budget."

"Thanks for the advice, Oma." Rose's smile told me she was trying to be teasing versus obnoxious, but it still annoyed me. "Can I leave my bag in here?"

"For today, yes, I can stash it behind the counter. But don't make a habit of it."

"Okay, Oma." Rose handed over her backpack, which was heavy enough that carrying it would count as a workout, and I slid it into an empty spot beneath the counter.

After Colton made her a cinnamon latte, which he offered to make decaf, and she laughingly refused, Rose exited through the doors to the communal seating area, which I'd unlocked a few minutes before when I saw signs of life from a few of the other cafés.

"Hey, look, the fire's lit," I said. Someone had prepped the seating area and lit the fire on the outdoor patio, which was underneath an awning that provided shade in the summer while protecting patrons from rain and, evidentially, snow.

Colton mock gasped. "Hopefully, Doughman is going to be open for lunch."

"Didn't you already eat a baguette and snag the third for later?" As long as Colton left a sandwich for me, I'd already said he could eat the other two.

"It's cold. I need the calories."

A few minutes later, a man in a wool overcoat and plaid scarf walked in.

"Is weather like this normal?" the man asked. He was older, maybe in his late sixties. Slightly older than my dad but younger than Uncle Jimmy.

Something about his voice caught my attention. It wasn't simply the accent that reminded me of London.

My heart started to pound, and a lump formed in my throat.

His voice brought back a memory of going to a soccer—or football, to use the local terminology—match and watching the crowd chant during the game. Of kicking a ball around in a park as it drizzled.

I'd known him once. In what felt like another lifetime.

I'd been young, maybe five? Six? He'd been one of my mother's marks, and she'd used child me to slither through his defenses. She conned people on her own, but as a single mother with a small child, she'd had a grifter fast track.

Colton's response was typically low-key like the man hadn't made his heart beat faster. Which made sense, as Colton most likely hadn't met this man before.

"No, this weather is unheard of. I'm assuming it's a sign of the apocalypse," Colton said.

I almost told him snowpocalypse, but I couldn't speak.

"I'm here to meet Rose. . . ." The man's voice trailed off when he clocked me. His eyebrows rose. "Sarah?"

"It's Sage, actually." But I'd gone by Sarah then. I'd thought it was a game. But I'd been wrong.

By all rights, this man should hate me.

But he didn't feel angry now as his clear brown eyes studied me. But I could sense a bit of understandable wariness.

"Are you visiting from England?" I asked. When I'd known him in a different lifetime, he'd lived in a flat somewhere in the bustle of London. Memories of walking down a street with redbrick buildings with white trim and turning to walk alongside a canal lined by colorful boats floated through my mind, but it felt nebulous.

"I'm here for a conference, and a young lady named Rose asked if I'd be interviewed for her podcast. But I never thought I'd run into you. You are Saffron Jones's daughter, correct?"

"I am." My heart was still beating too fast, making me feel shaky. He wasn't the first person who had seen me and automatically known who I was. Thank the genetics who'd made me a cookie-cutter image of my mother, at least physically. I hoped I'd taken after my father in the important areas.

How much digging had Rose done into my mother's past to find this man? I felt like a Band-Aid had been torn off my soul, revealing a wound I thought had scarred over that had, in fact, never healed.

His name emerged from the forgotten archives of my brain. "Are you Michael?" I asked. He'd been involved in, maybe owned, some sort of jewelry store. Something related to diamonds, too.

"That's correct."

Michael studied me again. From the corner of my eye, I saw Colton glance between us and then set about cleaning his work area. My barista had clearly picked up on the awkward vibes, but he wasn't the type to stick his nose in.

I reached up and tightened the ponytail sticking out of the back of my knit hat.

"May I look at your ring?" Michael asked, and nodded toward my hand. Even though I'd wanted to wear mittens, or at least my trusty hand warmers, I'd left them in a locker since they weren't sanitary for food handling. So my engagement ring was on display. I twisted it off my finger and handed it over.

Michael pulled a small magnifying glass out of his leather messenger bag and examined the ring, twisting it, so it was in the light of the coffee shop.

"That's a gorgeous star sapphire, and the setting is unusual," he said.

"My fiancé worked with a local designer." The band of the ring was twisted into an infinity symbol.

Michael handed the ring back. "The craftsmanship is excellent. Did you know some people refer to star sapphires as the stone of destiny? And others considered them to be a traveler's guide that protected the wearer from illness and bad omens. It's an appropriate choice for an engagement ring. Just be sure to clean it with warm soapy water and a soft cloth, and avoid harsh cleaners."

I slid the ring back onto my finger.

"Can I buy you a coffee or something?" I asked Michael.

He glanced at the menu again. "What, exactly, is a London Fog tea latte?"

I explained how we mixed extra-strong brewed tea, usually Earl Grey, with steamed milk and vanilla syrup. Although we can sub in a different black tea since not everyone likes bergamot.

"And people enjoy this drink?" Michael asked.

"It has devoted fans."

"Interesting. I'd like a dry cappuccino."

Michael slid his credit card out of his wallet, and I held up my hand with the palm out.

"It's on me," I said. It was the least I could do. As I made the cappuccino, I tried to parse the many reasons Michael's appearance unsettled me. My presence in his life had already borne a high cost, at least indirectly. I wasn't sure what my mother had stolen from Michael, but I knew it must have been significant. Michael being mostly normal with me versus angry was slightly shocking. It reminded me of the Maya Angelou quote. "People will forget what you said. People will forget what you did. But people will never forget how you made them feel."

My presence had to be both a visual and emotional connection to a terrible time, which would make most people feel unsettled. But Michael seemed too calm. Was he compartmentalizing his negative emotions? Could there be a reason he was acting friendly?

Or I was overthinking it. Maybe Michael was just the bigger person who couldn't bring himself to blame a small child for her mother's actions.

But I should research Michael. Was his showing up now truly a coincidence?

"Would you like a sprinkle of our magic dust on your cappuccino?" I asked.

"If it's magic, how could I say no?"

So I sprinkled the top of the drink with our in-house-made "magic dust" of cinnamon, sugar, and cocoa and handed it over, still feeling the ground could tilt under my feet at any moment.

A woman bundled up in a bright orange Inner City Assistance jacket and matching orange beanie walked in. She didn't even have to say anything, and I handed over a bag with cups, creamer, sugar, and two to-go coffee carafes. "Here you go," I said.

"Thanks. It's nasty out there today." She slid the bag's handles over her arm and picked a carafe in each hand. "You sure you don't want us to pay?"

"Nah, it's on the house, and let us know if you need more. Stay warm."

"Fingers crossed." She left, carrying the coffee and supplies, and returned to the frozen streets of Portland. The snow wasn't nearly as magical for her as it was for me.

I realized Michael was standing to the side, watching me. "The cappuccino is good."

"Thanks. It's a house specialty." While we carried a few house-made syrups for sweet drinks, plus a few bought sugar-free options, the classics are where Ground Rules shined. Anyone who recognized this received a gold star in my book. Although I can't begrudge anyone their favorite coffee drink, even if it's sweeter than a candy bar and doesn't taste like coffee.

Rose hustled into the store, an excited look on her face. "Sage, we need to talk! It's important," she said. Her eyes were bright, and she was practically vibrating with energy.

"Rose, this is Michael. I think he has an appointment with you?" I motioned to the Englishman.

Rose's eyes widened, and she straightened up. Her face smoothed over like she was pushing her excited energy into a mental box to release later.

"Hello, Mr. Fernsby. I'm Rose Trevino and thank you so much

for meeting with me. I see you have coffee, so let's go somewhere we can talk." Rose swept her hand toward the doorway.

"You, me, later," Rose mouthed at me before leading Michael toward the communal seating area. Michael followed, but to me, he looked skeptical. But politely so.

Whatever. Not my problem.

At least not yet.

# Chapter 10

A while after Rose had disappeared into the communal area with Michael, I realized it was the perfect time to check the dirty dish bins, giving me a reason to scope out the interior of the building.

The garage door to the seating area was down, which made sense, given the weather. A man and a woman sat by the lit fire outside. It looked like a scene from a romantic TV movie. She was probably an East Coast executive who'd had to fly home spur of the moment, leaving behind a high-powered executive fiancé. He was her childhood best friend with washboard abs and an emotionally fulfilling job running his family's Christmas tree farm, allowing him to bring the holiday spirit to the world.

Or I was overthinking things again. Although one of my good friends, Erin, is a professional photographer who pitches in at her family's Christmas tree farm every year, resulting in a love-hate relationship with the holiday season. She could've used the snow last December for beautiful family photos.

Rose talked intently with Michael at one of the tables, and something about his posture told me he was skeptical.

Then I paused.

Mark Jeffries walked out of the Breakfast Bandits carrying a bag.

He paused and turned, and Phillip walked up to him. They spoke again for a moment, then Mark left.

What was Mark doing here? Didn't he have his own shops to run?

Then I noticed the LEFT COAST GRINDS SERVED HERE sign on the Breakfast Bandits door and wanted to roll my eyes like an over-dramatic middle schooler.

Whatever. I turned back to my shop.

But the grinch in the back of my mind said that life would be easier for me if Phillip couldn't handle the Breakfast Bandits on his own and closed. But, I reminded myself, that was stating the obvious.

A steady flow of customers trickled, but not as many as we would see on a warmer day. But people seemed happy with their coffee, and part of the reason I co-founded Ground Rules was to make everyone's day a little bit brighter. So, today was a success.

We'd added a few drinks to the suspended order board, and a few had been claimed.

"Would you like me to look up the nearest warming center?" I asked as I handed a drink over to a man who clearly lived on the street. "I know the Convention Center is open, but there might be a closer option in a nearby church."

"I'm okay," he said, and left. I shut the window and watched, wishing I could do more to help.

I glanced at Colton.

"How much do you want to bet today is the day we call the Portland Street Response?" I asked him. The Portland Street Response is a city-sponsored program of social workers and paramedics sent out to deal with problems that, frequently, were medical or mental health emergencies with the homeless. They were urgent situations that weren't, hopefully, dangerous, but a police response would amp up, unintentionally or not. My friend Manny was a big fan of the program, and I made a mental note to see if there was something Ground Rules could do.

The front door jingled when a couple of customers walked in, and Rose bounced into the Ground Rules shop from the entrance to the communal area with a look of excited impatience on her face. She motioned for me to join her, and I held up a finger, telling her to wait as I took a couple of orders for coffee drinks and pastries. Once the customers were cared for, and Colton was crafting their drinks, I walked around the counter to the bus station. Rose joined me.

"You'll never guess what I found behind the counter in Breakfast Bandits," she whispered as I restacked the used dishes in the bin to safely carry them to be washed.

"What were you doing behind the counter?"

"Phillip is working solo and carried an order out. So I took the chance to look around. And there's a bottle of pills behind the counter. The bottle didn't have a label, so I took a photo of them to search for them online. And guess what?"

I resisted the urge to say "chicken butt." "What?"

"It's Xanax. See the markings? That's the manufacturer's mark so pharmacists can tell the difference between similar pills."

Rose showed me a photo from a drug database online, then toggled back to the photo she'd taken inside the Breakfast Bandits.

"How long did it take you to find it online?" Scanning through photos of drugs sounded like sorting out rice by type in a twisted purgatory.

"Not that long. Although, since I started with Valium, it took me longer than I hoped."

The importance of Rose's find was clear to me, although I still had questions about the process. "So Phillip or Bianca had access to Xanax."

"Yes, but where did he get them?" Rose asked. "There isn't a label on the bottle."

"Bianca or Phillip could have a prescription, and they brought a few pills to work in a different bottle. Or someone else could've left the bottle in the shop, and Phillip put it under the counter because he didn't want to leave it out or throw it away in case someone came back for it." I assumed the police had searched through Breakfast Bandits the same day they went through Ground Rules. I made a mental note to find out since it was a moot point if the bottle hadn't been around when Bianca collapsed. For all we knew, Phillip could've brought it in today.

"Yes, I can make up stories, too. But I'll see if I can question Phillip, maybe see if I can get him to give one of the pills to me. That'll show if he knows what the pills are."

"Don't do that. You're not an investigator, Rose, and you don't want to put yourself in danger. If Phillip killed Bianca, he won't want you sniffing around. And if he finds out you rummaged around in his café, he could accuse you of trespassing," I said. Although I wasn't positive if my trespassing claim was true. But I wanted Rose to think about her actions.

"I see myself as an investigative journalist, and trust me, I have the skills for this. He'll never suspect me. Hmm, I wonder if Phillip sells them? Could the café be a front for Phillip's drug trade? Or maybe they're just for his personal use. But I wonder if there's something deeper here." Rose looked excited as she chattered on.

A flash of understanding about how Jackson felt when I was involved, however unwillingly, in murders flowed through me. But at least I hadn't traipsed into the murder with visions of being the next Nancy Drew.

At least, I don't think I had. Maybe I owed Jackson an extra-nice birthday gift this year as an apology. As overbearing as he sometimes was, at least my brother was trying to save me from myself and my good intentions.

Sort of like how I felt about Rose right now.

"Just be careful. You don't want to get arrested."

"Okay, Oma."

I realized I'd put my hands on my hips and forced myself to relax. "You won't be able to solve the case if you're in jail."

"Don't worry, seriously."

"Change in subject. How'd you find the English guy for your podcast?"

"Michael Fernsby III? I caught a snippet in a case file online and found his contact info after some searching mojo."

In other words, Rose had googled his name, but I nodded.

"It was lucky he planned to visit the Pacific Northwest, although I offered to record our interview online. I record most interviews that way. It's easier than in-person, but I prefer the energy of sitting across from someone. Seeing their faces on my laptop screen just isn't the same. The chemistry's different, and when it's virtual, it's harder to tell when someone should be pushed for more information."

Rose looked at me. "Michael was resistant in an interview initially, but then I mentioned Saffron Jones's daughter was in Portland. He switched to interested pretty fast."

"Interesting." Or was it creepy? I was glad Rose hadn't been around to see our low-key reunion when Michael walked into Ground Rules.

Unless Rose had been hovering in the background, observing without me noticing.

"Today, we just reviewed the parameters of our interview, and what's off-topic to him. I'm going to record his interview tomorrow. Let me know if there's anything you want me to ask."

I nodded. "I'll text you if I think of something."

I remembered seeing Rose and Bianca together.

"Is that why you were befriending Bianca?" I asked Rose. "To get her on your podcast, too?"

"At first, she seemed the perfect person to profile on the podcast. Look at how her entire life changed after her dad was scammed. But the more I talked with her . . ." Rose's voice trailed off.

"The more what?"

"She clearly had a lot of issues, and it was hard to tell what problems in her life were a ripple effect of the crime and which were challenges she would've dealt with anyway. She was an awkward person, and I couldn't tell how much of that was due to the trauma she faced as a child and how much was her. I felt sorry for her, and I was going to profile her. But I wasn't sure how usable her footage would be given the chip on her shoulder."

We were quiet for a moment.

Rose's voice was more solemn than usual. "I really did feel sorry for her, you know? And she had her good moments. But she got in the way of herself if you know what I mean? She made it hard for people to like her."

"Some people are better at rolling with the punches," I said.

"She definitely struggled to make lemonade." Rose shot a grin my way, presumably over our shared appreciation of clichéd sentiments.

But they hinted at the truth, even if we didn't have the exact words to say what we wanted. What had Bianca been like amongst friends, away from the Breakfast Bandits? Away from Phillip? Was she always intense, or had the times I'd interacted with her, including the stressful time while setting up a brick-and-mortar shop, not shown her at her best? Maybe we would've been civil if I'd run into her at a party hosted by a friend of a friend.

As long as she didn't know who my mother was. That would've sunk any possible friendship. But maybe if she hadn't seen me, and Ground Rules, as some sort of threat, I could've sensed the person deep inside.

"I need to go write up some notes. I'll let you know if I discover anything else," Rose said. She hustled away.

Had Rose planned for Michael to see me? To see if he'd recognize me?

Could Michael showing up be some sort of revenge on me?

Being calm, even charming, today could've been his way to relax my defenses.

Bianca's death didn't just leave a shadow over my head. It also made me question my interactions, even trivial ones, with everyone.

To quote Yogi Berra, "That's too coincidental to be a coincidence."

# Chapter 11

Colton promised to watch the shop, so I took a few minutes to decompress. I decided to spend quality time with the ham baguette sandwich our baker had dropped off. In other words, take my lunch break.

As I ate, I told myself I should focus on something happier. But meeting Michael again still made me feel unsettled deep inside myself.

Since Rose had said his full name, it was easy for me to google the ghost from my past.

Michael Fernsby III. A few social media accounts popped up, mainly locked down to private, so I couldn't troll through his posts, which told me he was more cautious than most people I encountered. But I did find his jewelry store, which had been family-owned for generations and if you believed their marketing, was the place to buy the engagement ring of your dreams. They sold high-end estate jewelry, custom re-creations of vintage jewelry, and new designs made in-house. They highlighted pieces made with lab-created diamonds. This told me they were serious about alternatives to blood diamonds. And that was before I noticed their site had multiple posts extolling the value of lab-made diamonds instead of mined, praising the clarity and quality, and passionate arguments about why people should only buy conflict-free or lab-grown diamonds.

I also paused and perused their jewelry collection for children and tweens, which was adorable and, while not cheap, was less expensive than the offerings for adults. I fully believed their marketing claims that these pieces could become family heirlooms passed down from grandparent to parent to child. And I, presumably like most children, had been a bit of a magpie as a child, wanting to collect tiny treasures. I would've loved to receive something special like this. But I'd lived out of a carry-on-sized suitcase, so my mother hadn't let me keep much, moving through the world nimble and quick and leaving too many items behind.

I paused, remembering a heart necklace I'd gotten as a gift, which my mother had confiscated.

The necklace had to have been a gift from Michael. I'd cried since I'd loved it and had wanted to keep it. And I hadn't wanted to move again. I'd been happy.

But I hadn't had a choice, and she'd taken the necklace, and presumably sold it. And we'd flown to a country under a new name.

I made myself focus back on the task at hand.

So Michael's company had sound principles, at least on paper. And their social media feed showed a steady stream of gorgeous jewelry available for sale, along with occasional posts about fundraisers for local charities.

I wished I could look under the surface. Why, exactly, was Michael here? He'd mentioned a conference, so I googled local jewelry conventions.

Nothing.

So I expanded and searched Seattle as well, which is only a three-hour drive away.

Still nothing.

But when I searched for all conventions in Portland, a ballroom dancing convention popped up.

Could that be it? Michael looked like he was in decent shape. He reminded me of my dad, who ate a reasonably healthy diet and was more physically active than some of my friends.

It was also possible Michael had traveled with someone attending a convention. Like the urban planning one also being held in town. I smiled; the profession conference would have an up-close look at how the city had prepared for snow.

My friend Manny texted me. *You made the paper!*

He then sent a link to an article about the aborted grand opening celebration of the Button Building, complete with a photo of Colton and me behind the Ground Rules counter.

At least the photo was good. I clicked through the gallery and saw pictures outside the Button Building and close-ups of several signs from the various micro-restaurants. There was a photo of the interior of the Breakfast Bandits, with a blurry figure with dark brown hair ducking behind a rack. Like Bianca didn't want to be photographed.

Like she was already a wraith haunting the Button Building.

The article was light on facts about the crime but also avoided insinuation, just saying that the grand opening was curtailed due to an event being investigated.

I half smiled when I read one of the paragraphs. "When asked if a murder had been committed, the police spokesperson only said that they were investigating a death that may or may not be suspicious. According to one of the restaurants, who didn't want to speak on the record, one of the owners collapsed midmorning, and the police overreacted to what was clearly a fluke and unfortunate health issue."

All in all, not the worst coverage we could've received.

I texted Bax when I'd finished closing Ground Rules, and he texted back with an ETA. I locked up the shop, set the alarm, and exited through the communal door to check out the other micro-cafés without going outside. The communal area had a handful of customers with plates.

A man walked out of Fowl Play carrying a bag, and I saw several people waiting inside. Doughman Pizza also had a few patrons chowing down on pizza in their small seating area. I wondered if the heat from the pizza ovens made the restaurant feel like the Caribbean on a day like today.

Breakfast Bandits was closed, as was the bar, and I hadn't seen anyone from Déjà Brew around today, so I assumed they were staying closed. Had they even had the chance to open and make a single sale?

But hopefully, once the weather morphed into typical spring weather, they'd have a proper business launch. And I suspected they'd do well in the summer when patrons come to grab dinner with friends on the patio and enjoy the sunny weather.

Fingers crossed, we all make it until then.

Abby was standing outside her shop, holding a water bottle. She looked tired, like she hadn't been sleeping well.

"How's today been?" I asked.

"We're not hitting the numbers I'd like, but we've had a few mini-rushes."

I wanted to switch the subject to Bianca but couldn't just blurt it out. So I asked, "Did you see the article about the Button Building in the paper?"

"You lucked out and got a photo in the print edition and the main photo online. You have to click through to see a photo of my sign."

"Probably because I was one of the only places open when the journalist stopped by." I almost pointed out her sign was adorable, with a happy-looking burger with pickles for eyes.

Abby's grimace was almost a half smile. "Honestly, I wish the news hadn't covered us since I don't want people to associate the building with us being unlucky."

"Unlucky? Someone died."

"C'mon, there's no way anyone cared enough about Bianca to kill her. I feel sorry for her. She didn't seem to have many friends, but it was her fault for being so rude and insufferable all the time. But everyone reacted by avoiding her. No violence needed." Abby sipped her water bottle, looking like she was washing a bad taste out of her mouth.

"That's harsh."

"I've known her longer than you did. I'm just glad the journalist included my quote about the police overreacting. Although if it is murder, I know who my prime suspect is. You know the quote about it being a thin line between love and hate, right? And there's only one person here who fits that description."

So Abby was not on Team Phillip. I suspected the mailing list for that fan club didn't have many, if any, names.

"I wonder if Phillip will try to keep the Breakfast Bandits going?" I said.

Abby shook her head. "If he does, he's a fool. I'd love for us to get a different breakfast place here, or maybe just a sushi option because that would be awesome."

"Or sushi burritos." I regularly went through sushi burrito obsessions.

"Hopefully, the relaunch party will go better. Has anyone chatted about it with you yet?" Abby asked. "I propose we should hold an even bigger launch party than we'd planned last week."

"Works for me. What exactly are you thinking?" I asked.

"A giant raffle for one, with gift certificates to all restaurants," Abby said. She lit up, and we chatted about the new celebration until I needed to go outside to meet Bax.

As I walked away, I thought about how Abby was the unnamed source referenced in the news article. I wasn't surprised, but then I wondered: Was Abby trying to convince everyone it was an accident because she knew it wasn't? Or was she always this blunt?

Bax was pulled up to the curb outside Ground Rules, and as I opened the door, I realized he had a passenger.

His son, Niko, waved at me from the back seat. Niko was decked out in a striped beanie with matching mittens and a too-big red parka perfect for fluke snowstorms. He looks like a younger version of Bax, except he'd inherited his mother's green eyes.

"Laurel lost power at her house, so she came over with Niko and company for most of the day," Bax told me after I climbed in. "But they got power back, so I dropped them off on my way to pick you up."

Bax's ex, Laurel, had married a few years ago and had a small daughter. She didn't live far from Bax, and I'd picked Niko up from school on my bicycle before. Both Laurel and her husband held research professorships at a local university.

"And I wanted to say hi to you!" Niko said from the back seat.

I twisted around to look at Niko. "It's lovely to see you," I said.

"Kaldi helped me with my art project," Niko said, then proceeded to describe how the cat helped him design a poster about the life cycles of salmon in detail. "I think my drawings turned out awesome, and that's why Kaldi was obsessed with the fish sketches."

The main roads on the way home had been plowed, but the streets near the house were a mix of icy tire tracks and packed-down powder. Maybe half of the sidewalks had been shoveled, and I saw someone in snowshoes walking with a canvas grocery bag over her shoulder. We arrived home safely.

Bax had started dinner, and while it cooked, Niko and I made naturally gluten-free blondies from a recipe I'd been tweaking for a while. When they'd cooled off, I packed some up for Niko to take home to his mom and for Bax to take his coworker, Lindsey, who had celiac. Then the three of us and Kaldi settled in and watched a movie.

Almost a perfect snow day.

Except for the shadow Bianca's death continued to cast.

# Chapter 12

I was careful on my way to work the next morning. Just because the thermometer had snuck above freezing didn't miraculously melt the snow and slush on the streets. Nina texted that she couldn't make it in again, so Colton and I handled the shop.

And honestly, everything moved just fine with the two of us. Something told me three workers were too many, except when we were slammed. Maybe, once we'd been open for a while, I'd work the morning rush and then head to the office, leaving the shop in Colton's hands. Or I'd ask one of my long-standing baristas to take over as manager a few days a week. I could see both Kendall and Sophie working seamlessly with Colton, freeing up my time for other Ground Rules business.

I still had my doubts about Nina. She was a skilled barista; I also couldn't blame her for missing work because of the snow. Especially since she was babysitting due to the weather closing down the regular daycare her sister's children went to, while her sister pulled a nursing shift in the local ER. But something felt off. I wouldn't be surprised if she gave notice.

Or maybe I was overthinking her terse texts with the tacked-on excuse of babysitting.

Midmorning, I walked out into the communal area since I'd seen a group of customers head out that way with Ground Rules mugs, so I needed to check the dish return. And sure enough, they'd left their cups in the bins. I loaded the dirty dishes into the bin I'd brought with me.

There were a handful of metal plates, like the sort you take camping, in the bins as well. One held a barely touched burrito. The second had what could charitably be called a deconstructed breakfast sandwich, with a few bites taken out of one slice of the bread, most of a runny egg, and an inch of bacon left.

I glanced at them a second time before walking away with my mugs. Had the breakfast really been that bad? It looked like the egg had runny whites, which is an automatic no in my book.

And someone had left bacon behind. That's a travesty.

"Are you stealing my dishes?" a strident voice asked behind me.

I turned around, telling myself to remain calm. I kept my voice level when I responded, "Of course not."

Phillip stepped a little too close to me. "Then what are you doing out here?"

"Picking up Ground Rules's cups from the *communal seating area.*" I pushed the bin of dirty coffee mugs into the space between us, forcing Phillip to retreat a few inches.

"Are you sure you're not sniffing around, putting your nose in where it doesn't belong?" Phillip asked.

"What, did I wake up in a film noir? Get out of my way. I have a business to run."

Phillip stepped out of my way. But he said, "For now," as I marched past.

I was tempted to turn and argue with him, but I told myself it wasn't worth it. That fighting with Phillip would be like the meme of playing chess with a pigeon. The pigeon would knock the pieces over, make a mess on the board, and strut around like it won.

Except the meme uses slightly saltier language. And if I stayed around Phillip, my speech would turn equally salty.

As I reached the door to Ground Rules, I heard Phillip speak again, sounding even angrier.

"You're still here? Are you still trying to claim Bianca was a drug user?"

I paused, turned, and watched Phillip square off against Detective Leto.

The detective's expression was calculating. But Phillip caught sight of me rubbernecking. Before she said anything, Phillip pointed my way.

"There's the one you should be talking to. I bet her pathetic coffee poisoned Bianca. She hates us."

I almost said my coffee isn't pathetic but awesome. Instead, I just turned and marched into my shop.

"Don't play chess with pigeons," I said.

"What was that, boss?" Colton asked.

"Nothing important." I carried the bin around the counter to load the mugs into our sterilizer.

But then Colton cleared his throat, and I followed his gaze.

Detective Leto had followed me in.

"Can I help you with something?" I asked. "If you're in the hunt for coffee, we're doing a single-origin pour-over of a bean from Costa Rica that's pretty fantastic."

"I would adore a pour-over, but I think I'd rather have your house blend," Detective Leto said. "I'd also like to talk to you."

"I can make that pour-over and handle the dishes," Colton said.

The detective paid for her coffee, and as Colton made it, we moved over to the far wall. I told myself I should call Jackson. But I didn't.

"I heard Phillip. Bianca was poisoned?"

"Ms. Moore died of a drug interaction."

"Poor Bianca." How unlucky.

Or meticulously planned. I shivered.

"Do you have access to ketamine?" Detective Leto asked.

My gaze snapped up to her. Her eyes analyzed me like she was looking for cracks in the façade of my face.

Ketamine. I flipped through the databases inside my brain. Even as a student, I'd never been into the drug scene, even casually. Partially 'cause it would've let my father down. But also because I didn't like to lose control. But I'd known a few people who'd partaken in shrooms and harder drugs.

"Ketamine is basically cat Valium, right?" I asked.

"It's primarily used in veterinary clinics, but it's a popular club drug," the detective said. "Do you have access to Xanax? Or anything similar?"

I thought for a moment, wondering how to best answer this. Give me a few phone calls to old friends and classmates, and I bet I could find almost anything, even if it wasn't my scene. But I'd never bought drugs, so I went for simplicity.

"I don't have Xanax or ketamine, nor would I drug someone with them. And I'd never add them to my coffee." Ground Rules was my baby, and the last thing I would do is potentially ruin a cup of coffee. Or hurt someone. "Wait, how could Bianca not notice her coffee was drugged? Wouldn't the ketamine make it taste weird?"

The detective shook her head. "It can be flavorless. It's sometimes used as a date-rape drug because it doesn't leave a taste in a drink and it's sadly effective in the wrong hands."

"So it wouldn't be noticeable mixed in coffee." I felt sick but also annoyed. Who had managed to slip drugs into Bianca's cup between me handing it to Rose and Rose giving it to Bianca?

There were a limited number of people on the list.

And I knew all of them, which didn't make me feel any better.

"As you heard a few minutes ago, Phillip is adamant that Bianca wouldn't have taken ketamine."

Harley's comments about anxiety flashed through my mind. "Did he say the same thing about Xanax? Because Bianca always seemed wound up tightly, like she had a deeper struggle going on. I could see her having a prescription."

The detective clearly wasn't going to answer that question. Instead, she glanced down at her phone for a moment, swiped it a few times, and then showed me the screen of her phone. "Do you recognize this man?"

The detective showed me a mug shot of a guy. Maybe late twenties. Closely shorn dark brown hair, thick eyebrows, and jade-green eyes that'd be appropriate for the hero of a romance novel. He wasn't smiling at the camera, but he wasn't glaring, either. If anything, he looked bored, and he didn't make danger signals immediately scream in my head. He also wouldn't stand out in a crowd.

I studied the photo before shaking my head. "He's not ringing any bells. But I don't know every customer who has visited one of the carts. For all I know, he could be a regular I've never seen. Or someone who stopped by once, and I don't remember."

Not being sure who was and who wasn't currently a regular at the cart bugged me. Letting go of the daily Rail Yard operation to focus on the shop had been tough. It gave me a slight sense of loss that there could be a steady stream of regulars I'd never know. But I trusted Sophie and Kendall to represent us with style and impeccable customer service, with support from a handful of carefully trained baristas.

I knew I shouldn't offer to help, at least without talking to my brother first, but I said, "If you give me his name, I can try to search through our point-of-sale system. He might have signed up for our loyalty program or our newsletter. But if he paid cash, there won't be any trace of him."

"You have a newsletter?"

The detective's quizzical tone made me wonder if she was switching topics to keep me off-balance. Maybe if she confused me, I'd slip up and confess.

Or maybe she was just curious.

"Yep, it's monthly and an effective marketing tool. Our social media options rely on the algorithms of the various platforms we post on, which we don't control. But when people opt in to our newsletter, it creates a relationship we can curate. And at least we know we're contacting people who want to hear from us." Plus, it was a fun way to announce new blends, news, and offer an occasional coupon.

I told myself to quit prattling on about Ground Rules to the detective.

"Interesting. If you can search for his name, let's see what shows up."

I used the tablet by the walk-up window to search with the detective looking over my shoulder.

"What's his name?"

"Grantly Erikson." She spelled everything.

I scanned through the results and tapped on a couple. "It looks like someone with that name bought several cups of black coffee from us when we were set up at the Northside Farmers Market. We had our second, smaller coffee cart for there the past two years and plan to return when the market reopens in May."

"Hmm." The detective made a note to herself, then looked back at me with her sharp gaze.

I resisted the urge to point out that even the Portland drug dealers would support our farmers markets. Keep Portland Weird and all. And maybe he lived near the market, making it a convenient spot to stop for coffee, or a fresh loaf of sourdough from the beloved bakery that was a mainstay of the market, along with fresh produce and other local products.

"If we were up to something nefarious, I doubt we would've asked a drug dealer to pay with a traceable credit card. We don't have security cameras on that cart, but the farmers market does. In case you want to scroll through hours of footage."

Detective Leto half-smiled like she found me amusing. And hopefully, that was in an "I could be friends with this barista" and not an "I can't wait to arrest this punk" sort of way.

"If you discover that you do know Grantly Erickson, please tell me." Detective Leto pulled on her black raincoat as she left.

As I walked away, I wondered: Had the Breakfast Bandits ever set up at the Northside Farmers Market? Could Phillip have gotten to know Grantly then? I made a mental note to troll through the Breakfast Bandits's social media and see if they'd set up shop there. The market had a corner for food carts, and Harley had managed the cart the first year while Kendall had taken over for the second season. I should ask both of them.

But I'd talked to both about Bianca's death, and neither had mentioned the Northside Farmers Market. Either nothing had happened, or they hadn't thought it was important enough to share.

Rose finding Xanax in the Breakfast Bandits shop felt more significant now that I knew, somehow, the police had connected a drug dealer to Bianca's death. I wished I could've mentioned it to the detective. But then I'd have to basically tattletale about Rose snooping in the shop.

And if the drugs had been there when Bianca died, presumably the police would've found them when they searched the Breakfast Bandits. As the detective said, when they closed down Ground Rules, that was their one bite at the apple to find evidence. Anything found there now wasn't a clue, in a legal case.

The photo Detective Leto had shown me flashed through my brain again. Had Phillip bought the drugs that killed Bianca from Grantly? Had his accusation against me been an elaborate act to shift suspicion away from him and onto me, a convenient target? I'd always thought Phillip was calmer than Bianca, and he'd seemed to care about her. Love her. But maybe he was at the end of his proverbial rope and decided life solo was better than entangled with a shared life and business partner.

# Chapter 13

When it hit eleven o'clock, since we'd been open since seven a.m., Colton and I decided today should be a pizza day to celebrate both our busy day and the melting snow outside.

"Nina is going to be sad she missed out on the free sandwiches yesterday and the pizza today," Colton said as I grabbed my wallet to walk over to Doughman.

"Her loss."

The communal area was empty, but most of the cafés open at eleven, and it was barely a few minutes past.

Even though he'd only flipped his OPEN sign on a few minutes before, Caleb already had two people waiting in line. So I glanced around his micro-restaurant space, enjoying the warm shop. It was several degrees warmer in here than Ground Rules. While the heat was fantastic now, I wondered how it would feel during the dog days of summer. Most things, after all, have a cost and a reward.

Most of the space inside Doughman was dedicated to the kitchen, including a couple of powerful-looking pizza ovens. The only seating was a counter with a handful of stools along the windows and the far wall leading to the communal area. The walls and the divider separating the kitchen and order counter were painted an aggressively cheerful yellow, with cartoon square pizza slices painted on the wall.

Doughman is known for Detroit-style pizza, and the toppings are classic. Their lack of froufrou ingredients makes them almost aggressively hipster in a "we forsake arugula because we're going back to our roots" sort of way.

They also earned their hipster foodie credentials because their slow-rise dough and marinara were made in-house. The meats and produce were all as locally sourced as possible.

"You're seriously not letting me order a pepperoni and sausage with mushrooms and bell peppers?" The man ordering sounded whiny.

My eyes glanced at Doughman's menu board, which included one of Caleb's cardinal rules of pizza: you can only order three toppings per pizza, max, and only two can be meats.

"Yes." Caleb's voice was calm.

"But that's not what I want."

"There are other pizza places, but those are the rules if you want pizza here."

Behind him, in the kitchen, his employee didn't even look up as he sprinkled cheese on a pizza. Weirdly, there was a restaurant-sized bottle of olive oil on the back counter with a red ribbon tied in a bow looped around the neck.

I'd already decided to order a cheese pizza for myself since I'd fallen in love with one at his cart and wanted to repeat the experience. Its simplicity allowed the ingredients to shine, while Colton wanted pepperoni. We'd both have a few squares left over for later.

The annoyed customer finally ordered a pepperoni and mushroom pizza and stalked off to one of the chairs by the window. He pulled out his phone and started furiously texting. The woman in front of me ordered the Doughman's Default pizza off the menu (sausage, mushroom, and a drizzle of Mike's Hot Honey added once the pizza had been baked).

"How's it going, Sage?" Caleb asked when I was at the front of the line.

"Good. We've been busy, so we need some pizza to recover."

"I can't argue with that. What'll you have?"

After I ordered, I shifted down the counter as Caleb started stretching the dough out to fit in the special dark anodized pans he used for his Detroit-style pizza. The dough is wetter than New York style, leading to a thicker, chewier crust with crisp sides. The cheese and meats are layered on, and the tomato-based sauce is added last.

"Do you think Portland will be ranked best pizza in the nation again?" I said.

Caleb laughed. "If it is, it'll be fun to see everyone's head explode again. And I appreciated us getting the accolades since we do have a fun pizza scene."

Social media had gone into a tizzy when Portland was somehow ranked as the country's best pizza city. A magazine had highlighted the focus on quality regardless of a single style that defines the city, and Caleb's shop perfectly fits that criterion.

"You must be happy to have a full shop versus only baking in a cart," I said. "How did you manage all of the prep work?"

"Commissary kitchen. In a roundabout way, it's how I ended up here since I shared a commercial space with Abby and Laura. They told me about the Button Building and encouraged me to open here," Caleb said. "Those two have always been tight. Mess with one, and you'll mess with both of them."

"Were you in a food cart pod with them?"

"Nope, I opened in a bar's food cart pod over on Division. They were downtown and then out in North Portland."

"Oh, yeah, I dropped by your cart before. I love that bar."

Caleb layered cheese on top of the sausage of a Doughman's Default before adding three lines of house-made tomato sauce. "Thanks, I'm glad you enjoyed it. I opened here because it's a good business decision for higher-volume takeout. We'll see how managing a cart and this restaurant goes."

"Are you still renting commissary space?"

"Thankfully, no. I can prep everything for the cart here, so I won't miss paying for it. I'll almost miss sharing space since having people to talk to was nice. But now I won't have to worry about my olive oil disappearing or wondering what happened to part of my produce order."

"Someone was stealing from you?"

"Borrowing, since I'd usually find a few bucks stuck in my mixing bowl or replacements the next day. But it threw off my prep a few times."

"That sounds obnoxious."

"It's one thing if someone asks, although I most likely would've said no. I try to buy exactly what I need to reduce food waste."

"Hence the reason you frequently sell out," I said.

"Exactly. And people seeing my pizza as somewhat scarce helps. It makes it special."

Caleb's words triggered a connection in my brain. Could someone have stolen food from Bianca? If she'd threatened to call the police or try to get them kicked out of the building, maybe someone snapped.

Our conversation lagged as the pizzas baked and more customers walked in. Caleb took their orders and worked seamlessly with his kitchen staff to prepare them.

A few minutes later, Caleb handed over my pizzas. "I don't think Abby likes your little podcaster friend," he said.

"Rose?" Did everyone see Rose as my friend? Had she used me as access to the building?

"The one who is always filming and buzzing about here even before we opened," Caleb said.

"Rose is harmless," I said.

"Abby was afraid Rose was a culinary spy for a while, trying to parse out Abby's secret ingredients," Caleb said with a laugh. "Hint, it's garlic salt."

"That's it?"

"It is tasty, and her burgers are pretty decent. But yep, she relies on premade garlic salt for her burgers and seasoning salt for her fries."

"Thanks for the pizzas."

"I'll try to come by for a coffee. I'll need one before the dinner rush."

Caleb returned to work. I carried the pizzas away, the boxes warm in my hands, my stomach growling as the smell wafted up to me. As I walked out of Doughman, I saw Rose.

"I need to talk to you, but I must drop this off first," I told her. Colton was in desperate need of pizza, after all.

Rose and I had plenty to discuss, so her timing was good. I dropped Colton's lunch off, telling him it was okay to eat as long as he kept an eye on the counter and to call if he needed me, and walked back to the communal area, carrying my pizza. Rose was perched at one of the tables.

"So, what's up?" Rose asked as I sat down across from her.

"Detective Leto stopped by Ground Rules today." The smell of the pizza made my stomach grumble again, so I opened the box. The edges of the pizza were perfectly crispy, and I made myself slowly take a slice. It tasted like perfection.

"Is that really a surprise? She's investigating, right?"

I nodded and managed to say, "The detective told me that Bianca died from a drug interaction."

Rose's eyes widened. "Did she?"

"And the detective asked if I had access to Xanax."

"That's a useful clue 'cause, as I told you, there's Xanax in Bianca's restaurant."

"But I couldn't tell the detective about the drugs in the Breakfast Bandits because if I had, I would've had to tell how I'd known, especially since I've never been inside their café. I would've had to drop you into trouble." I carefully bit into my pizza, taking time to enjoy the experience.

Rose stole a slice of my pizza and closed her eyes as she took a bite. "This is so good."

"I didn't tell you to help yourself."

"What? It's not like you can eat all of this." Rose grinned at me, giving her the air of a mischievous twelve-year-old.

"About the police, Rose. You snooping in the restaurants could get you into trouble." If I told Uncle Jimmy, would he ban Rose from the building?

"It's okay, Oma. Even if you told the detective I'd found drugs in the Breakfast Bandits, it's not like they could prove I'd broken any laws. I've been inside their café loads of times, and I could've said I was just trying to check on Phillip."

"Lying isn't cool. Nor is sneaking around, even for the greater good."

"That's not lying, just putting a positive spin on the truth." She took another bite of my pizza.

I worked on my slice for a while, marveling at how Caleb took something simple and turned it into a culinary art form.

"You know who else sneaks around here? Abby," Rose said.

"Explain."

"I can do one better and show you." Rose opened her phone and scrolled through some videos. "Watch this, which I still need to up-load to the shared folder, so this is like a sneak peek, pun intended."

Rose's video showed Abby ducking into Doughman, looking a bit shifty, and walking out a moment later carrying a bottle of olive oil. Caleb walked out of the bathroom a moment later and returned to his shop.

"You just happened to record this?"

"I was getting my setup ready and thought Abby looked suspicious, so I started recording. After all, I could just delete it if it was boring."

Caleb had mentioned ingredients disappearing when he shared a commissary kitchen with Laura and Abby. Was swiping food typical of Abby? That could be why Caleb had a bottle of olive oil with a ribbon on his counter. I needed to talk to her about it and clarify that we'd have a serious problem if she stole from Ground Rules, even if she replaced it later.

I closed my pizza box, and Rose pushed her mouth out in a pout. "C'mon, just one more slice. I'm hungry."

I shook my head, then said, "Fine. Just one more."

After Rose grabbed a corner square, which are my favorite, I had one slice left, which I'd save for an afternoon snack and extend my pizza love into the afternoon. "I have to get back to work."

But on my way back, I paused by the doorway and glanced in the shop. A few people were drinking coffee, but no one stood at the register waiting for service. So I took a moment to google ketamine. Some results claimed it tasted bitter, while others claimed it was flavorless, like the detective said. If it was bitter, would the taste of coffee hide it? Or would the coffee taste over-extracted, which would bring out bitter notes?

So maybe the coffee hadn't entirely hidden the taste and made Bianca think it was the worst cup of joc she'd ever tasted.

I read up a bit on ketamine and found that when used in clinics, it's a liquid, but it's also sold on the street as a powder and infrequently as tablets. Some people even snort it.

All of this made me feel even more confused.

So I returned to work and focused on the parts of life I could understand: coffee.

# Chapter 14

The next day, Harley dropped by a few minutes after opening with a restock of our house coffee, Puddle Jumper, and a crate full of single-origin beans for the retail shelf in the shop.

"Is this the new Guatemalan?" I asked as I picked up one of the bags.

"It is!"

Harley and I nerded out over coffee for a bit, and I realized Colton was laughing at us.

"Don't you have anything better to do?" I asked him in a joking tone.

"Is it okay if I take a quick break?"

I glanced at the clock. "Go for it. I can cover the shop."

Colton left his apron on a hook and headed outside, passing by an incoming customer like ships in the night. I stepped up to the front counter to take their order while Harley took a moment to drink a cup of house coffee.

Colton came back mid-rush and helped out. When we were done, I turned back to Harley.

"I've been meaning to ask you something," I said. "When you were at the Northside Farmers Market, did you interact with the Breakfast Bandits?"

"Why, what did you hear?" Harley asked.

"Nothing. I'm just curious."

"The first day we were at the market, the Breakfast Bandits were a couple of carts away from me. But the guy from the cart—Phil?"

"Phillip."

"—got into a huge fight with the owner of the bagel cart. The next week, the Breakfast Bandits were on the other side of the market, away from the other food vendors."

"That sounds on-brand."

"Supposedly, the Breakfast Bandits were on a final warning with the farmers market. I heard Bianca complaining to one of the organizers that being hidden in the corner away from the other food carts made their revenues plummet. Which I could believe since we were slammed, but she was over next to the craft vendors."

"It must have made Bianca feel like an afterthought." I'd be annoyed if I'd been moved away from the other food vendors. But then, I would've played nice with my fellow food carts from the start.

"It gets better," Harley said. "The bagel cart was vandalized one day toward the end of the festival. Someone cut their power cord midday."

"Really?"

Harley nodded. "One of the other carts claimed they saw Phillip skulking away suspiciously. I don't know what happened, except the Breakfast Bandits weren't at the farmers market anymore for the last two weeks."

"Dang."

"I think some other food cart vendors had a toast in celebration."

"Champagne?"

"Orange juice in tiny plastic glasses."

I laughed. "It's the shot that counts."

Harley shook her head at me in mock disapproval, like she didn't secretly love puns.

"Did you ever meet a guy named Grantly Erikson at the Northside Farmers Market?"

Harley scrunched her nose for a moment. "Grantly? That's not ringing any bells."

"It was a shot in the dark. Long story."

We chatted briefly about the shop, and then Harley left to deliver more coffee bean shipments around town.

Nina rushed in about ten minutes after her shift was scheduled to start, apologizing profusely. She looked paler than normal and I didn't say anything as she headed to the back to grab an apron.

A while later, after a few mini-rushes, I arranged the single-origin beans on the shelf by the end of the counter, interspersing them with our collection of Ground Rules cups and thermoses when Michael Fernsby III walked in. Seeing him made a few nerves flutter in my stomach again, but I squared my shoulders.

"Hi, Michael."

"Hi, Sarah, I mean Sage," he said.

The name Sarah was like a pinprick to my heart. But I soldiered on. "Back for another cappuccino?"

Or meeting with Rose? But I had yet to see the podcaster today.

"Actually, I want to try that weird tea drink on your menu."

I picked up the now empty crate and moved back behind the counter. Colton looked up from unloading a batch of freshly cleaned mugs. I shook my head at him, meaning "I got this."

"You can go on your break when you're done," I told Colton, and he returned to his task.

"The London Fog?" I asked Michael.

"That's it. It's an odd name."

As I pulled down a tin of loose-leaf Earl Grey tea and added a teaspoon to a tea infuser that reminded me of an immersion brewer for coffee, I said, "The London Fog originated in Vancouver, British Columbia. Supposedly, a pregnant woman who couldn't drink coffee still wanted a drink that reminded her of her favorite latte, and this drink was born. The name came about because once the drink is put together, it looks like a foggy afternoon in London."

"Sounds appetizing."

I laughed at Michael's deadpan tone. "I like it, but if you don't like it, I will happily make you something else."

I poured water into the infuser and set the timer next to the tea to brew for four minutes since I didn't want to over-steep the tea and make it bitter. Although I used slightly less water than I would for a cup of tea to make it stronger to hold up in the drink.

Michael watched as I steamed milk. When the timer beeped, I did one of my favorite things: I put the infuser on top of a mug and watched it drain into the mug, then put it by the sink so we could wash it for the next batch. I kept the tea on the counter next to the steamed milk.

"We make the vanilla syrup in-house," I told Michael.

"Is it hard?"

"Not at all. It's actually the easiest syrup we make. It's just sugar, water, and vanilla extract." I measured the syrup into the tea, stirred it, and added the steamed milk.

"Voilà!" I handed the mug over to Michael.

He took a cautious sip, then a second. "It's not too bad. I don't usually add sugar to my tea, but the sweetness isn't overpowering."

I approved of his palate. "I see it as a good drink on a cold day when it's raining. Although it's also good iced during the summer."

We chatted for a moment. It was a slow time, with just five people sitting at a table in a group, all staring intently at their laptops.

"Have you traveled much?" Michael asked.

"Not as much as I did as a small child. Once I graduated from Portland Trinity—that's a local university—I worked for a nonprofit for a while and barely traveled. I did spend six months volunteering in Indonesia, and of course, I'd love to explore the world more."

"You must be busy here."

"Yep. Although I managed to make it to Trinidad and Tobago for a week when my boyfriend, well, fiancé now, and I took his son there to see his mom. She was doing research there for six months. It really ignited the travel bug for me."

"If you make it to London, let me know, and I'll take you to the best coffee in the city. It's at the flower market. I think the founder won a big award, like a world championship?"

"The World Barista Championship? Winning that competition is living the dream."

"The founder might have moved on. Time goes by so fast, and when I blink, everything has changed, even if some things feel the same. Regardless, I still love the cart and their cappuccinos are perfect."

Something told me Michael was talking about more than the London coffee cart when he mentioned time. "Anyone trained by him is probably amazing, as they took his lessons to heart."

Michael pushed up his sleeve and glanced at his shiny silver watch. "Thanks again for the weird tea drink."

"Anytime."

"I'll probably stick to coffee." He smiled as he nodded at me, pulled his wool coat on, and left.

I glanced around the coffee shop. The group in the corner was still silently working. Although one woman was gesturing at her laptop like it wasn't cooperating with her. Colton came back from his official break with a smile on his face.

Nina sidled up to me. "So, who was that? You clearly knew him."

"It's a long story," I said. "In a nutshell, someone I knew as a child."

Colton grabbed an apron and headed to the hand-wash station.

"Did you know him well? He seemed nice," Nina asked.

"My mother has history with him, but it's not something I like to talk about." As my mother was a bit sketchy.

A bit sketchy. More like hella sketchy.

"Did he call you Sarah?"

Nina was starting to seriously annoy me.

But Colton spoke first. "If it's not something Sage wants to discuss, let it go."

I glanced at Colton. "I can fight my own battles. But Colton's right. I don't want to talk about it. Although I will say, he has good taste. And Nina, if you want to take your break, this would be a good time." Even though she'd only been here for an hour and a half. But we'd pick up again closer to lunch.

"I'd love to go to London," Nina said. She walked toward the communal area. A couple customers came in.

After the customers had departed with their mochas, I glanced at Colton. "Thanks for the help with Nina, but I could've handled it."

"I'm sorry, it's just habit. I hate it when people ignore obvious conversational boundaries. It's my biggest pet peeve."

I half-smiled when I saw the journalist who'd written a profile on the Button Building hold the door open for Rose. A woman in a gray jacket walked in behind them.

"I saw the article," I told the journalist.

"When you have another formal reopening, I'll try to cover it. But no promises," the journalist said. "Do you have any comments about the death of Bianca Moore?"

"Nope, not a single one."

Rose was eyeing the journalist, and I couldn't quite read her expression. Envy? Curiosity? A mix? Maybe a touch of jealousy?

The journalist smiled. "That's fine. A sixteen-ounce oat milk latte with an extra shot and a muffin, please."

"It's a caffè latte. If you order a latte, you're just saying you want hot milk," the woman in the gray jacket said.

"That's true in Italy, but we've taken the coffee vernacular and run with it in our way," I said. "Don't get me started on the word 'macchiato' and customer expectations."

The journalist laughed, and the woman in the gray coat looked annoyed.

I looked at the journalist. "Pear-ginger or marionberry muffin?"

"Tough decision. Marionberry."

She paid for her order on the tablet while I put the muffin on a plate, then moved down the counter while Colton made her drink.

Rose ordered her usual mocha but looked distracted and kept glancing at the journalist.

"Caffè latte, please," the woman in the gray coat said. She'd removed her coat and wore a gray cabled sweater beneath it.

"You got it."

Rose tried to chat with the journalist, who took her coffee from Colton. The journalist headed to a table with her drink, leaving an annoyed-looking Rose behind.

"Hey!" Rose said.

"I'm off the clock and want to give my brain a break. Email me if you want to schedule a time to ask questions about my job. Maybe we'll schedule an informational interview. If I'm feeling generous."

Rose took her mocha and stomped out to the communal area.

I glanced at Colton.

"Oh, to be young," he said, and prepped for the woman in gray's drink.

A few more customers came in, and I remembered how, when I was in college, every moment felt monumentally important. Like life would pass me by if I took a moment to stop. FOMO, I told myself. Fear of missing out. That the party you don't go to will be life-changing instead of just another Friday night.

"Here's your latte," Colton told the woman in gray.

"Caffè latte," she grumbled, and took her drink to a table.

Colton looked at me, and I shrugged. "She's not wrong." But that didn't mean she wasn't pretentious.

As I worked, I glanced periodically at the woman in gray, who rotated between checking her phone, half-heartedly reading a novel, and almost jumping up each time the door opened before sitting back down, looking sad.

It was time for my lunch break since Nina and Colton had everything in control in the shop. As I sat down at a table in the corner with my container of homemade lunch of quinoa salad with grilled chicken, I read a message Rose had sent me.

*The audio file with Michael hasn't been edited yet, so expect an occasional "aah" or "umm" or one of us starting to say something, then stopping and starting over. It's the sort of moment I edit out of the final podcast. But you might appreciate hearing this now versus after I have time to edit. I'll send over the closed captioning script once it's done.*

Of all the interviews I knew about, this was the one I wanted to listen to but was also terrified to hear.

There's no time like the present. I wedged my headphones into my ears and hit play.

Rose's smooth voice said, "Hi, everyone. Thank you for tuning in to *Rose Investigates: Thorny Crimes and Intrepid Offshoots.* I'm Rose, your host, and I'm here today with Michael Fernsby III. How are you doing today, Michael?"

Michael sounded wry. "I'm doing well, thank you for asking."

Rose continued, "As you know, this series delves into the life and crimes of Saffron Jones, a notorious grifter. While none of Saffron's crimes have been violent, that doesn't mean she hasn't left a path of devastation in her wake. I'm digging into the aftereffects of these crimes and how they've rippled through the lives of the people she harmed.

"Michael is one of the victims. Michael, can you tell me about your interactions with Saffron Jones?"

Michael took a deep breath, and the pause felt palpable like it was upping the suspense. His voice fell into an even keel as he settled into his story. "Well, I met Saffron over twenty years ago in London, although she used a different name. Sophie James, in fact. I'd lost my pregnant wife about nine months before and was in a rough emotional state. I'd recently returned to my job running my family's jewelry store. So I was primed as someone ready to be taken advantage of.

"I first saw Sophie, aka Saffron, and her small daughter, Sarah, at a small café in my neighborhood. They were frequently there when I stopped by in the morning. So when I came across Saffron one day, crying outside the shop, saying her wallet had been stolen, it felt natural to ask if she needed help. She was very distressed, so I bought her and her daughter breakfast and we chatted. She told me, and this was all lies, that she'd been married to an Englishman who'd died the year before, leaving her a single mom. We regularly chatted from then on. When I heard she was struggling to find a job, offering her one at my shop felt natural.

"And Saffron was an excellent sales associate. She had the knack for figuring out what people wanted and excelled at the subtle upsell, and she was so skilled that people didn't even realize she was doing it.

"In retrospect, that should've been a clue.

"In the meanwhile, I thought we'd fallen in love. She moved into my flat with Sarah, and I was happy for the first time in ages. It wasn't the family I thought I'd have a few years before, but it felt right. I didn't know it was a façade of false dreams created by someone spinning tales I wanted to hear.

"The store had negotiated a large shipment of diamonds and precious stones, and it's a complicated process when we get deliveries like that, with security and a ton of logistics. But I felt relieved when they were all locked in the workroom safe. And honestly, it felt like just another day, even if it was a slightly larger order than usual. I didn't know it would be momentous in retrospect.

"Saffron must have recorded my assistant manager and me getting into the safe, along with the frequently changed security codes of the workshop and store. I didn't think to hide it from her, and she'd seemed enthusiastic to learn about how our products went from raw materials to completed jewelry.

"The delivery went fine, and I had an evening meeting afterward. When I came home late, Sophie, I mean Saffron, and Sarah were gone.

"I was reeling, wondering what had happened and what I'd done wrong when my assistant manager called. He told me the store had been burglarized. The thieves had focused on the diamond shipment, although they'd also stolen a few vintage gold pieces.

"The theft almost sunk the store, but we regained our footing, despite the substantial financial loss. I had to make employees redundant, which hurt even worse than losing the diamonds. But I was able to offer them their jobs back eventually, and a few returned. We're doing well now."

Rose's voice asked, "How'd they know to target the store?"

Michael maintained his even keel, and I wondered how long it had taken him to come to terms with everything. "It turned out they'd had intel from someone on the seller's side who'd given them the logistics in return for a share of the profits. He lived and worked in Antwerp, which is a key city in the diamond trade. He was arrested and served jail time for his part in the scheme. But Saffron Jones and others in her crew were never found."

Rose asked, "What about you personally? How did you recover from having your trust violated?"

"It took me ages to even consider trusting anyone again. It's still difficult, to be honest. I've never created the family I wanted, although that might not have happened if I'd gotten married again. But I've found other ways to bring meaning to my life." There was a sense of finality in Michael's voice.

Rose clearly wanted more details. "You mentioned that Saffron Jones had a child with her?"

"Yes, a small girl, whom she said was five years old, although the child seemed younger, maybe four. She was a darling child. Very vibrant and inquisitive, and rather obsessed with cheese."

I laughed to myself, wondering why that was the detail he remembered. Or maybe, it was the detail he was willing to share.

Rose's tone was gentler. "Do you think Saffron used the child to lower your defenses?"

"Presumably, yes, it helped. Especially when I saw Saffron in distress while accompanied by her daughter."

Rose's next question made me stiffen. "Have you had contact with Saffron's daughter?"

"That's not something I'm comfortable discussing, and it's unfair to someone who holds no responsibility for what happened.

Let's just say I wish the child well and hope she's built a life for herself far from, as you'd say, the ripples of her mother's crimes."

I leaned back in relief. Michael could've outed me to the world, but he'd chosen not to.

Rose's voice took on her slight newscaster note as she said, "Thank you for joining my podcast, Michael. And as a reminder, everyone, this is your host, Rose Trevino, from *Rose Investigates: Thorny Crimes and Intrepid Offshoots.* I'll be back in one week with our next episode looking into the life and crimes of notorious grifter Saffron Jones."

As I sat, trying to mentally process the interview, I sent a link of Michael's interview to Jackson.

Whenever I thought about my mother's crimes, I tried to put myself in the victim's place. This was the first time I'd gotten an authentic inside glimpse. Although Michael had sounded measured. I doubted he had been so calm back when everything went down, and his life had imploded.

But something struck me. When had Michael landed in Oregon? Had he arrived before Bianca died? Or was it just chance that he was here the same time she died holding a Ground Rules coffee cup?

Another thought pinged to the front of my brain. Antwerp. For some reason, I had a flash of a statue of a large man with small people in front of him. Belgium had to be on the list of countries I traveled through as a child, and now I wondered if I'd spent time in Antwerp. A quick online search brought me to a photo of the *Lange Wapper*, which turned out to be a statue of a Flemish folkloric legend, in front of the Het Steen castle in Antwerp. He was a trickster figure and potential water sprite, who cheated when he played games with children, and, this squigged me out, was known for stealing women's breast milk.

Had I known the person convicted in Antwerp? How close had my mother and I been to the arrest? Had he been a career criminal, or had my mother slid into his life a real-life trickster figure who'd gotten him involved in the scam, treating him like a pawn in the process? Was it a chance someone on the inside had been arrested while my mother walked free?

From what I knew of my mother, we'd probably been in Antwerp before the con while planning it.

The family of the person who'd ended up in jail was also caught in the ripples of my mother's crimes. Instead of researching this further, I closed my browser. I could spend the rest of my life investigating everyone connected to my mother, both innocent and guilty. And the knowledge made me feel heavy like I was carrying the weight of too many burdens. Intellectually I knew I wasn't responsible for my mother's crimes, but knowing I'd been a small part made me feel culpable, like it was my fault.

I felt guilty when I thought, once again, if the rumors were true and my mother had died in a car crash, my life felt a little lighter. Because she couldn't con anyone else.

But for now, I should focus on Ground Rules.

As I prepared to return to work, one of the writers from the group in the corner stopped me.

"Someone really died here a few days ago?" the writer asked.

"Yes, one of the other café owners."

"How tragic," the writer said. "You know, I'm a mystery writer. Well, almost one, not just aspiring, with my debut coming out next year."

Oh, dear Lord. First Rose and her plucky Nancy Drew act, and now a budding crime writer. But I smiled. "That's exciting."

"Yeah, it doesn't quite feel real, to be honest. But what's it been like being around an actual criminal investigation?"

This sweet summer child didn't know about Ground Rules's risk of becoming the coffee company of death. Maybe things weren't as bad as I'd feared. "Honestly, it's terrible, and it's horrible in general to know someone who died suddenly."

She nodded and looked sympathetic. "That makes sense. Fictional death is totally different."

I was about to move on when she said, "I'm in the local chapter of a national group of mystery writers. We're always looking for people to speak about topics related to real investigations. I'd love to meet an actual detective. But when I emailed the local police to ask about getting a speaker, they never responded."

"That's too bad," I said. My dad flashed through my mind. Would he want to speak to a group like this?

"Well, thanks again."

"Do you have a card? Absolutely no promises, but I know a retired detective I can hand it off to. But, like I said, he might not be interested."

Her gaze snapped to me with an excited look that reminded me of the Lab who showed up at our order window each morning on her morning walk, ready for biscuits. She dug in her bag, pulled out a pen case and a wool hat, and eventually found what she was looking for. But struggled to pull out a card case, like she was so excited she couldn't use her fingers. "I'd be thrilled if you passed my card along. Tell your friend that we're friendly and we pay a small stipend. We'll probably ask a ton of questions."

I could picture my father standing mute in front of a group as they fired questions at him, looking like he wanted to be anywhere else. But I could also see him calmly listening to the questions, enjoying it, and ending up in the acknowledgments of mystery novels. I'd pass on the card and let him decide for himself.

"I'll see you soon," I told the writer, and she left, talking about needing to walk the cat before she finished her writing goal for the day.

I blinked.

Yep, she really said walk the cat.

The woman in the gray was still at her table. Her posture radiated misery. I kept walking, but then my feet stopped.

"Are you okay?" I asked.

"I'm waiting for someone, but it looks like I've been stood up," she said. "Unless you've seen this woman?"

She fiddled with her phone and pulled up a photo of a woman in her midthirties dressed in a blue shirt with a jaunty red scarf and thick hair with blond balayage highlights.

I shook my head. "She doesn't look familiar."

"We've been dating online for months, and this was supposed to be our first in-person meeting."

Uh-oh. This rang warning bells in my mind.

"Has she contacted you today?"

The woman in gray shook her head. "Not a word. Which is very unlike Gracie. Maybe she had a car accident? Should I call the police?"

"Do the two of you ever video-chat?" I suspected where this was going.

"No, she doesn't have reliable internet access, so we email, text, and call each other every few days. But she said she'd finally make the trip into Portland today, even though I offered to drive out to her home in a little town on the Oregon Coast."

"Are you sure she, well, exists?"

"Of course she exists. We've talked. Gracie has a lovely voice. She lives with her elderly mother, who's had a lot of health scares over the past year, which is why we haven't met. We were supposed to meet a few times, but once her mother fell and had to go to the hospital, so who can blame her for canceling?"

"I bet her mother had another health issue the next time you were supposed to meet."

"Yes, and it's so tough for Gracie. She keeps calling out and missing work to care for her mom. She's barely been able to pay their mortgage a few times."

"Have you helped Gracie out with that?"

"Of course, I love her. She paid me back the first time and didn't want to ask for help when her mother broke her knee and needed around-the-clock in-home care, plus money for her mother's surgery. I was hesitant to pay the amount she needed, but when we made plans to meet today, I sent her the money."

I felt a sinking feeling, not like the way I felt when I thought of

my mother's crimes. "This isn't my business, and I could be wrong—
I hope I am—but you should make sure Gracie is real."

The woman in gray stared at me. "You think I've been conned?"

"It's called catfishing. Someone creates an elaborate fake profile
and uses it to scam people. But like I said, I could be mistaken."

The woman in gray looked angry, so I held up my hand. "Like I
said, I could be wrong. I hope I am, and Gracie walks in the door."

I brought the woman in gray another caffè latte for free.

But over the next hour, multiple people entered the shop, but
none were Gracie.

I stopped back by her table. As I commiserated with her, I
thought, you never genuinely know who people are. Although their
actions are usually a clue to the true person deep inside. In an ideal
world, the layers we find are good surprises. The sort of surprises that
make us willing to trust our friends and family.

But not always.

# Chapter 15

Bax had left work midafternoon to pick his son Niko up from school since it was now his custody time. So as I closed the shop, I texted Bax and asked if he'd like me to pick up a to-order of arroz con pollo from Laura's Fowl Play café, aka her take on Colombian chicken and rice, which is one of my personal favorite meals. Even the thought of it made my stomach growl.

Bax's one-word reply of "please!" was all I needed.

And as I walked up to the counter inside Fowl Play, I realized I could kill two birds with one stone: I could pick up dinner and see if I could finesse information from Laura.

From the reviews I've read of Fowl Play, even if our conversation was a bust, I'd be a winner since her small-but-limited menu is supposed to be fantastic.

"Hi, Sage!" Laura said. She had a woman who looked enough like her to be a younger sister working with her.

After I ordered three orders of arroz con pollo plus an avocado salad and empanadas Colombianas, I asked, "How are things? The opening and reopenings definitely didn't go as planned."

Laura shook her head. "It's been unbelievable. But we did well at lunch, and I have high hopes for the dinner rush. I can't believe it snowed."

"You're putting in some intense hours," I said. Laura had popped into Ground Rules, ordered a coffee from Colton, and then headed to her café, presumably to prep for lunch. It looked like she'd been here through dinner. That's a lengthy time to cook and handle customers. Just standing that long is exhausting.

"I got used to the long days running my food cart. At least now, my little sister helps, and our nephew will help us close several nights a week. For two years, I ran my cart solo. By the end, I was very ready for a long vacation."

"Your cart was in downtown, right?"

"Yep, Abby and I were next to each other for years downtown, which was really helpful, and we moved together to a pod in NoPo for a while."

"Having neighbors you trust is invaluable with food carts," I said.

"I've been lucky on the whole," Laura said.

I played innocent. "Didn't someone in your old downtown food cart pod get into a fight with Bianca that went viral?"

Laura blushed. "That was me."

"That must've been hard knowing strangers saw that. I know I hate seeing videos of myself."

"It could've been worse. At least I walked away. Not everyone did, you know? And if anything, Bianca looked worse in the video than I did. Unhinged."

"What do you mean, not everyone did? Do you mean people got into actual physical fights with Bianca?"

"Almost. Once, Bianca and another owner were yelling at each other, and Phillip butted in and punched the other guy. It was intense and the guy . . . what was his name . . . ended up with a broken nose. I think he pressed charges against Phillip, and Phillip had to enroll in anger management classes to avoid jail time. But even after the classes, Phillip kept saying it was the other guy's fault for talking nasty to Bianca."

"What did you think when you saw the Breakfast Bandits had a café here?"

"For as annoying as Bianca is, and even though I knew I would do my best to avoid her, at least her food is excellent so it represented the building well. Or was, I should say. It still hasn't fully sunk in that she's dead."

"I never had the chance to try anything she made."

"She had the skills to be the chef at an upscale place, like one with Michelin-star pretensions. She started in one of those places and became a sous chef, so she was second-in-command. But she packed it all in for some reason and moved out here."

"Do you remember where that was?"

"Good question. Chicago, maybe. But I know she worked making small fancy bites at a winery in Napa Valley before she landed in Portland, so it could've been there, too. She said once she wanted to move to San Francisco, but it's too expensive."

"She wasn't wrong about SF being expensive," I said. Portland isn't cheap, but compared to the other West Coast cities, like SF, LA, and Vancouver, BC, it's cheaper.

Laura looked thoughtful. "I wonder what will happen to her business. I doubt Phillip has the same talent, so we'll have to see if he can keep Breakfast Bandits going. Maybe he will sell it."

"Do you think it's worth anything?"

"Something? Yes. A lot? No idea."

"I also wonder what he'll do."

"You know that Phillip is weird. I'm not saying he's a killer. But there's something not quite right about him," Laura said.

Laura's sister brought my to-go order over, and the tantalizing scent of chicken and saffron came from the bag.

Laura smiled at me. "If you have more questions about Bianca, you can ask them, Sage. You don't have to buy food. Although I always appreciate the business. I hope you love the food."

"I can't wait to try it." I grinned and carried my food out toward my bicycle. Laura had known I was prying and hadn't seemed to care. Was that normal?

As I carefully strapped the food down in the grocery basket on the rear rack of my bicycle, I realized there was one question I wanted an answer to but didn't know how to get: Who benefited from Bianca's death? As the building had gotten ready to open, my fellow business owners had been in a watching-and-waiting mode with Bianca, waiting to see if she'd play nice. Nothing had erupted before her death, except for a few sarcastic comments. So killing Bianca to stop her from causing trouble felt like a stretch.

I tried to imagine being in Phillip's position and having a business partner who, for whatever reason, caused strife everywhere she went. Putting out her continual fires must have been exhausting.

Had he enjoyed it? Had Phillip amped up a few minor disagreements into full-fledged fights? Maybe he'd fanned the fires, making small matters take on immense significance, keeping Bianca on edge.

But as I started my bike ride home, I wondered about Laura's candor.

More importantly, I wondered what she'd hidden behind the truths she'd said. Since something told me I hadn't gotten the whole story.

Not yet, anyway.

When I came home, Niko was encased in his favorite beanbag chair, intently reading a graphic novel, while Kaldi lounged over his shoulders like a live kitty stole.

Niko's face lit up when he saw me. "What's in the bag?"

"Come follow me and find out."

"Dad!" Niko yelled as he followed me. "Dinner is here!"

Bax was already in the kitchen, and he pulled out plates and cutlery as I unloaded the bags.

"Do you like empanadas?" I asked Niko.

"If you do, I bet I do, too," Niko said.

Bax laughed behind him. Niko had never been a picky eater, but according to Bax, Niko would eat anything I handed him to impress me.

The food was a hit, and we had enough leftovers to pack lunch for Bax and me and an after-school snack for Niko since he didn't have access to a microwave at lunch.

"We'll pack you a fun bento box," Bax promised when Niko whined it being unfair that he couldn't take his leftovers to school.

As Niko and Bax cleaned the kitchen, which didn't take long, I settled down on my laptop. I didn't know much about my fellow café owners, although I knew my uncle Jimmy had run background checks. But I decided to do a deep dive into them for the heck of it.

Some of it made me smile. Laura had moved to the USA from Colombia as a child. She'd been interviewed by a local paper about her experience, how she'd ended up in the ESL program in elementary school and eventually graduated summa cum laude from a local university.

But Caleb's background made me sit up straight.

Caleb had gone to jail for embezzlement?

I clicked on the article about Caleb from the local alt-weekly. He'd once been a hotshot financial planner who'd decided to dip into client funds. Caleb was caught, pleaded guilty to multiple charges, and opened his first pizza cart not long after he was indicted since no one wanted to hire him. He'd start paying restitution even before he'd gone to jail and made the argument that he'd pay everyone back quicker if he didn't serve time. The judge disagreed although Caleb's sentence was the minimum recommended time. After serving part of his sentence, he'd been let out and restarted his pizza company.

"I'm about halfway through paying everyone back," Caleb said. "I know I will never fully be able to apologize to everyone I hurt, but at least I can try to show by my actions that I regret what I did and that I'm trying to make things as right as possible."

Was Caleb still clean? Was there any chance he was still sketchy, and Bianca had found out?

Or was I reaching for straws again?

When Niko had gone to take a bath, Bax looked at me with a serious expression. "There's something we need to do."

"Umm, okay," I said.

"By we, I mean you," he said.

"Sounds ominous."

"I need you to play *Falling Through the Shadows*. You don't have to play until the end, but you need to start the game. It's killing me that you haven't played it."

I laughed. "You know you started out this conversation in a heart-stopping way."

He hugged me. "Sorry!"

"If you insist, I'll play." Even though the thought made me feel anxious. It twirled around the different anxiety that had been plaguing me since Bianca's death.

Bax set me up to play *Shadows* on his gaming laptop, complete with his padded over-the-ear gaming headphones, then checked on Niko to make sure his son was getting ready for bed as I started the game. I was glad Bax had known to make himself scarce instead of watching me. I knew I'd have a while since reading was part of the bedtime process, and Niko always tried to get Bax to read as long as possible. Recently, he'd tried to get Bax to read more chapters on Kaldi's behalf.

Clearly, cats need bedtime stories, too.

I'd seen an earlier version of the game's intro, and I knew all the words. It was my voice reciting them. Playing this game was like reading a book I knew by heart, even if I hadn't seen all the pages in their final alignment. I played about half an hour and then saved my progress, looking forward to playing more.

Whew. I liked the game, even though it was still odd seeing, and hearing, the main character.

And Bax was relieved when I told him how much I'd enjoyed it.

"I was so worried, especially when you declined the first few times I tried to get you to play."

"I've always had faith in the game. I think I just wanted to wait until it was finished."

"Mostly finished. We're still working out a few bugs."

If only we could fix the programming in our lives to remove the flaws.

★  ★  ★

After I slid into bed, what Laura had told me about Bianca, and to a lesser extent Phillip, kept popping up in my mind. I decided to start with Phillip and picked up my phone.

My first step to check him out was simple: I searched the Breakfast Bandits's social media feed. They mainly focused on their daily specials and reminded people of their hours of operation. I scrolled back, and they'd announced where their cart was each day over the summer.

So they hadn't been in a designated food cart pod for a few years. I'd known a few carts who liked being nomadic. One mainly focused on special events and catering gigs. While another had a regular route they followed, getting permission to park at a couple of big corporations in the burbs a few days a week and also rolling into farmers markets and festivals. But the Breakfast Bandits's schedule didn't feel organized, so I wondered what was happening behind the scenes.

I scrolled back and saw a post about them leaving the well-loved pod in downtown Portland where they'd been neighbors with Laura and Abby. They'd all been one of many fantastic carts that had lost their leases and been forced to move when a new luxury hotel development bought the land. Now, the space was a five-star hotel instead of unique worldwide cuisines. I still missed the Scottish-style fish and chips, which had moved out to Beaverton in the opposite direction of my house, and the Hawaiian cart, which had gone brick-and-mortar, but also in the suburbs.

Losing their coveted spot must have hurt, and a pang of sympathy popped into my brain. But that didn't excuse Bianca's behavior. And it could explain why their schedule didn't feel organized. Maybe they hadn't found a food cart pod they wanted to commit to full-time. Finding the right spot can make or break a business, and I'd heard horror stories about disorganized lots. Like the one that charged relatively high rent, but didn't pay their contract for garbage or porta-potty service, leading to a literally smelly situation, angry food cart owners, and outraged neighbors.

I scrolled back up and checked out a few photos with Phillip. He stood by a river holding a burrito in one, and it turned out they had been a vendor at a kayaking competition. Another was of him and Bianca holding the keys to their new spot in the Button Building. Bianca glowed with happiness, and I wished I'd had the chance to see her like this.

And the petty side of my brain wondered how long her happiness had lasted.

*We've found a home!* the caption read. *Instead of being wandering breakfast bandits, you can find us in the brand-new Button Building! Grand-opening plans TBD.*

And Phillip's personal account had been tagged, so I continued down the rabbit hole.

His account was public but with minimal content. A few posts about the Breakfast Bandits. A couple of him and Bianca. One of him trying and failing to execute a kickflip on a skateboard with the caption *I swear I used to be able to do this!*

I sent a message to Rose asking what she'd found out about Phillip's background. Her response was almost immediate. *On it! I'll investigate and catch you tomorrow.*

You know, having an overeager podcaster at my beck and call as an unpaid researcher had its moments.

I turned my focus to Bianca's social media.

Bianca's personal account was focused on food. She posted a series of pretty photos of entrees she'd made at home, supporting Laura's claim that Bianca had the skills for fine dining. Even though I'd just eaten, some of her photos almost made me hungry. Perfectly poached eggs in vibrant red shakshuka. Seared scallops on a bed of salted greens drizzled with a pomegranate sauce. Beautifully broasted short ribs with chanterelle mushrooms and bone marrow butter. She'd gone through a macaron phase, with plates of colorful cookies artfully arranged around a vintage teapot. Over the summer, she'd made colorful veggie and meat skewers served alongside fresh fruit cut into fun shapes. I wished I'd seen this side of Bianca, the one willing to painstakingly craft food that I suspected tasted as good as it looked.

It's too bad this side of her wasn't what the public had seen. And I wondered what the rest of her meals looked like versus this curated view.

I bet they all tasted delicious, even something simple like scrambled eggs on toast, since she obviously cared deeply.

Bax slid into bed, and I abandoned my phone, happy to give up social media research for a personal connection.

# Chapter 16

On my way to work, I observed most of the snow had melted, although I saw a few small patches of snow in shadowy areas. After we opened, I was happy to see customers steadily trickle in.

The writers group showed up again. I enjoyed them wandering in, ordering a drink and maybe a pastry, and then sitting at the same table and ignoring each other while they tapped on their laptops.

A bark outside told me there was someone at the sidewalk order window. I slid the door open to find a black Lab with his paws on the counter. I assumed his "woof" translated to "biscuit, please!"

"You're turning into one of my most loyal customers," I told the Lab.

His human ordered an oat milk latte, and a few minutes later, I handed it to her, then gave the dog, who still stood with his front paws on the counter, a treat shaped like a heart.

"Thanks!" she said, and the dog walked down the block.

Inspiration struck, and I wrote a quick sign: IF WE DON'T SEE YOU, FEEL FREE TO BARK, I MEAN, KNOCK, ON THE WINDOW! I drew a dog bone and added a small price tag that said FREE TO OUR CUTEST CUSTOMERS on it.

But as I taped the sign in the window, I paused.

Why was Mark Jeffries skulking around the Button Building

again? He walked around the side of the building, and I wondered if he was visiting one of the restaurants.

Several dog walkers stopped by throughout the morning and raved about the sign. I hoped they told their friends about the coffee-with-a-dog-biscuit option now available in the neighborhood.

One of the group members who wrote together quietly stopped by the counter on her way out. "Is it still okay if we meet here each week?" she asked.

"Sure. Is your group always so over-the-top?" I asked.

She laughed. "The whole reason we meet is to write, and not talk, for an hour. It's a long story. Everyone knows to buy a drink."

"You're always welcome."

She left, and Nina paused by me.

"I have a very important question," Nina said. I realized the circles around her eyes were darker than usual. Her pixie cut looked messy versus purposefully hip.

"Shoot."

"What exactly is in the chai concentrate? It's like crack in liquid form. Seriously, I love it."

"It's just the usual chai spices. Fresh ginger, etc." Given what happened to Bianca, comparing anything in our shop to drugs didn't sit right with me.

"The spicy bite slays me. What is that, ginger?"

While I didn't use anything unusual in our chai concentrate, meaning there was no secret ingredient, something inside me didn't want to discuss the ingredients with Nina. "It took me a while to find the right balance of spices, so I'm glad you like it. As much as I love espresso, having solid tea options, including our matcha from a local tea maker, a small but curated selection of loose-leaf tea, and house-made chai, is important to me since not everyone likes or can drink coffee." Gosh, I sounded like a promotional robot as I tried to head off Nina's questions.

"I can tell. Can you share the chai recipe—"

"Do you have any good vegan options?" a voice boomed out.

Saved by the loud. The woman who'd just walked in the door had beautiful blue and purple hair and the sort of vocal resonance that would make an opera singer proud. "Please say yes."

"We can do all our drinks with nondairy milk. Food-wise, we have vegan energy bars from a local supplier."

"I haven't tried those." She picked up one of the bars my friend Zarek's shop made. We'd been neighbors at the Rail Yard. But he'd closed down his cart and pivoted to manufacturing vegan energy bars. Sales were strong, and he'd even hired a few employees to ramp up production. "We also have coconut and pumpkin seed cookies by the same vegan manufacturer. These are brand-new, and we're one of the few places to carry them." Although we wouldn't be the last to carry them. I could see them selling like hotcakes and even going national.

"I need both, along with a vegan vanilla latte."

"Coming right up."

I rang her up as Colton started making her latte.

She tore into the cookie packaging and took a delicate nibble. "Delicious."

After she walked out, Colton said, "We get so many characters in here. I love it."

"Hopefully, we stay busy."

"I have a good feeling about the shop," Colton said, then strode forward to greet a new group of customers, all dressed in scrubs.

Colton's confidence made me smile, but when I turned, I realized I didn't know where Nina had disappeared to. Then she popped out of the back, chugging from a coffee cup.

Nina caught my eye. "Double espresso," she said.

"The cure for everything." Before I could say anything more, a familiar customer walked in.

During the first year Ground Rules had set up at Campathon, we'd had a customer who'd taken her VIP pass seriously. She'd paid for a package that allowed her unlimited food and drinks for the entire festival. She'd taken this as permission to stop by our cart almost hourly.

I'm fairly sure she's why the festival quit offering the all-you-can-eat passes since they'd been on the hook for all her drinks.

"You're here!" I said.

"I am! I'm so excited to see your shop."

We chatted for a moment, and she handed over a coupon for a free drink to pay for a mocha.

"I've been dropping by your cart weekly for over a year. It's on the way to the medical clinic I volunteer at."

"You're a nurse-something," I said.

"Good memory. Nurse anesthetist."

She told me about the clinic where she volunteered, which provided free medical care for the destitute.

"You know, we sometimes donate to Inner City Assistance, and if you need coffee in your outreach, let us know."

"Give me your card. I bet our mobile clinic would take you up on the offer on cold days."

I gave her a couple of my cards, and she left a few minutes later.

Midmorning, two more familiar faces walked in.

My brother, Jackson, and Piper, his girlfriend whom I suspected he would propose to sometime soon, if she didn't pop the question first.

Piper is good for my brother. She counterbalances his seriousness and brings out his smile. But even though she has a naturally cheerful air, she's grounded. And she's always one of the smartest people in the room, although she never feels the need to flaunt it.

I want to be like Piper when I grow up.

Today, they were dressed in hiking pants and boots, with heavy jackets, instead of their usual attorneys-about-town style.

"Are you braving the great outdoors?" I asked.

"How did you guess?" Jackson asked. His tone was dry enough to make the final batches of melting snow outside evaporate.

Piper put a thermos with a screw-on top on the counter. "Can we get this filled along with a couple of cappuccinos to go?"

"For sure."

I wrote their names and the word "cap" on their cups, and Jackson insisted on paying for their coffees and a couple of muffins. He'd reviewed the business contracts when we founded Ground Rules but refuses to take any food on the house as a thank-you.

"Come join us if you have a moment," Piper said.

So once their coffee was ready, I carried it to where they sat in the shop. "Here you go," I said. I sat down across from them.

"How are things going with the shop?" Piper asked.

"Good, overall."

"And have you heard anything about the murder investigation?" Piper took a sip of her drink.

"Not really, but that shouldn't be a surprise."

"True, I'd be annoyed if one of my investigators shared info with a suspect," Piper said.

Ouch. I glanced at Piper; sympathy bloomed across her face when we made eye contact.

"I'm sorry if that felt mean, but from what Jackson has told me, you have to be on the detective's radar, no matter how unfair it feels," Piper said.

"My dad basically said the same thing."

A young podcaster blew into the shop like a perfectly made-up tornado. Rose's path altered when she clocked me at a table, and her eyes widened slightly when she saw who I was sitting with.

"Sage, you're here with your lawyer? Did something happen? Was anyone arrested for Bianca's death?"

"Sage's lawyer," Piper said under her breath.

"In this case, I am, but I'm here today for coffee," Jackson replied in an equally quiet voice, and then gave Piper what I'd call a "significant look."

Rose looked between Jackson and Piper with a quizzical expression that made me suspect her investigative journalism skills told her there was something here to be explored.

"You know, I don't think I got your name or your card when we met at the Tav," Rose said.

"That's right, I don't think we exchanged info," Jackson said. His voice was bland. He picked up his coffee and drank like he didn't have a care in the world.

Rose looked like she wanted to keep asking questions. But she must have felt the invisible wall Jackson had just built. She looked at me. "So, is there news? Did you tell your lawyer about Phillip having access to the drug that might have killed Bianca?"

Jackson looked at me with a sardonic eyebrow lift.

"No, I haven't had a chance." I was painfully aware of Piper's presence. While I trusted Piper, it made sense to not tell her about Rose's lawbreaking. "Rose snooped in the Breakfast Bandits shop, and it looks like Phillip has Xanax, which might have contributed to Bianca's death."

"Is there any chance this death was just an unfortunate drug interaction? The victim could've messed up her own doses," Piper asked. "It's sad, but I've seen it before."

"I assume that's one investigative path," I said.

"Or someone targeted Bianca to put pressure on Sage. But who would do that?" Rose looked at me. I knew both Piper and Jackson were eyeing me as well.

"Well, Mark Jeffries and Michael Fernsby III have both been around. And as you know, Bianca had issues with, at least, Abby and Laura." Not to mention Phillip, who still made the skin on the back of my neck crawl when I saw him.

"Maybe Bianca killed herself accidentally but was trying to set up Sage to look bad," Rose said.

"If that's true, it won't help your developing career as Nancy Drew," I said. I immediately felt guilty for sounding mean.

"I'm trying to clear both of our names," Rose snapped back.

I held up my hands in a calming gesture. "I know we're on the same side."

"Maybe you should let the professionals handle it," Piper said.

Rose looked like she wanted to argue, so I said, "Thank you, US Attorney Piper."

Rose's expression lightened. "You're a US attorney?"

"Yep."

"Are you available to answer legal questions?"

Jackson stood up. "We should go."

Piper popped up quickly. "Yes, that trail isn't going to hike itself."

I laughed and slowly stood up. "I'll see you two kids later."

They left, and Rose looked at me. "So, what's your attorney's name?"

"Sorry, Rose, I need to get back to work."

But I checked my phone on the way back to my side of the counter and saw that Jackson had texted me as they left. *Michael Fernsby III is in town? We need to talk. Dinner tonight?*

I responded, *You saw the link I sent to his interview, right?*

*I didn't realize it was recorded here in Portland. Tonight?*

*I'm up for a war council at your house or mine.*

*I'll drop by your house with dinner.*

*Okay,* I replied, happy I'd get dinner out of this at least. I returned to work.

The coffee wasn't going to make itself, after all.

And hopefully, we'd figure out what happened to Bianca so we could move forward without the shadow of her death stopping us from seeing the sunlight.

Not long after my brother and Piper left, I checked the bus bins in the communal area. Which had two Ground Rules mugs. But as I turned, I almost ran into my nemesis.

Mark Jeffries. Wearing a Left Coast Grinds hoodie, so it's not like he was trying to skulk around the Button Building incognito.

"What are you doing here, Mark? Should I ask my lawyer to send another cease-and-desist letter?" I asked. The last and only letter, which essentially banned Mark from the Rail Yard, wasn't legally binding. But Mark had almost injured me in front of multiple witnesses, including a local attorney who'd proclaimed she'd make an excellent witness in front of Mark and several customers, and he'd been smart enough to stay away.

"There's no rule that I can't drop into this building for a quick meal," Mark said. "Don't worry, I won't risk my life by ordering one of your coffees."

"Like you could appreciate the finer points of our shop." Although I knew Mark could recognize the finer points of our coffee if he didn't already have a grudge against two of his former employees striking out on their own. As much as I disliked him, he knew good coffee. It's one of the reasons he was threatened by us.

"This is a nice little scam you have going for yourself, isn't it?"

"What—"

"Your mother must be proud."

Mark walked away, and I was tempted to throw one of the mugs at his head.

But violence is never the answer.

Plus, my aim is terrible.

But then I paused. How did Mark hear about my mother? Very few people in my life, outside of relatives and Harley, knew about her. Rose was able to track me down, though. Clearly, people could find me if they knew the right terms to search.

Both Colton and Nina had seen Michael Fernsby III. Had one of them heard enough of my conversation to make them realize something deeper was at play? Had they noticed the weird vibes and decided to research why?

Which means they would've had to share the info with Mark.

Did I have a spy on staff? Was one of my new employees secretly working for Left Coast Grinds? One of Rose's videos flashed through my mind. The one where Mark said he had an inside source.

If yes, was it Nina or Colton?

And could one of them have poisoned Bianca? They'd both had access to the fatal cup. Although they would not have known if they were going to poison Rose or Bianca.

Maybe they hadn't cared. Perhaps they'd just aimed to drug one of them.

Caleb came into Ground Rules for a coffee. I glanced at the clock; it was almost time for him to start selling his world-class Detroit-style pizza.

"When you look at your menu, what do you think is the best drink you offer?" Caleb asked.

"Good question. I'm a purist, so I really like a straight shot of espresso. But that can be a little much, so a macchiato is a way to still get a lot of the espresso experience but—"

"With the espresso 'stained' by milk," Caleb said.

"Exactly. It lightens the experience but still lets the taste of the espresso come through without diluting it as much as a cappuccino, which is always a solid choice."

"What if I usually just go for a basic drip coffee?"

"Go for a pour-over. We have a pretty awesome single-origin from a family farm in Guatemala available, along with a great option from Colombia if you like a medium roast with nutty undertones."

We debated the finer points of the available beans before he settled on my first recommendation.

Caleb stood on the other side of the coffee bar as I made his pour-over, taking my time to run the spout of the gooseneck kettle clockwise at a glacial speed, letting the water seep through the fresh grounds.

"Are these a pain to make when it's busy?" Caleb asked.

"They can be a time suck, which is why I think they've fallen out of favor slightly over the past years with customers who don't want to wait. Although they're still one of the best ways to make a cup of coffee quality-wise." I glanced at Caleb, wanting to ask him about what I had read last night. But I didn't want to offend him or imply he was a crook.

Even if he'd pleaded guilty and served his time. Because if he had taken responsibility for his actions, I wanted to applaud that. Not everyone is willing to admit they made a mistake and take action to fix it.

"I don't mean to be rude, but you've had an interesting past, right?" I flinched as I heard the words. I know not to say anything like, "I don't mean to cause offense, but."

"Meaning I've been to jail? Yep, I've made some stupid mistakes. Not violent mistakes, just financial."

"I shouldn't have said anything. I'm sorry."

"It's okay. It's not a secret," Caleb said. "Jimmy Jones is your uncle, correct?"

I nodded. "Great-uncle, if you want to be technical."

"He's taking a chance on me. Technically, your uncle owns most of the equipment in my restaurant. No bank will loan me money, but Jimmy said everyone deserves a second chance. He funded my micro-restaurant at a market rate loan."

"That's a show of faith."

"It really is. Your uncle is a good guy. And the better Doughman does, the faster I can pay both my victims and Jimmy back. I've paid back almost seventy percent of what I owe my former clients, and the end is finally in sight."

"That's good."

Caleb glanced at me. "From something Bianca said, she made it sound like you've also been in trouble with the law?"

"No, never," I said. "Wait, what did Bianca say?"

"Nothing specific, but she hinted you have some sort of dark, sketchy past. But I hate gossip, so I didn't go fishing for more information, and she walked away in a huff."

"When was this?" Had Bianca been gossiping about me? Had her gossip set me up as the potential fall person for her murder?

"The day she died." Caleb's tone turned solemn.

"I've never been in legal trouble, but my mother can't say the same thing," I said.

"Just your mother?"

"Yeah, my dad and older brother are the opposite of trouble. So I've had good role models, and any mistakes I've made are definitely my own. But none have resulted in criminal charges, to my dad's relief."

"My parents were hardworking people. All of my mistakes were my own hubris and stupid decisions."

Caleb's drink was ready, so I handed it over. He said, "Cheers," before leaving.

# Chapter 17

After my run-in with Mark, I wanted to move, so I left Colton in charge, curious to see how the shop would do without me. I pedaled away on my bike, ostensibly to pick up a restock of coffee beans for our almost empty resale shelf which was selling more briskly than we'd planned. But I detoured to the Rail Yard on my way.

I locked my bicycle up to the picnic table by the Ground Rules cart, where Kendall was working alone.

"How are things?" I asked.

"Bit slow. You want a drink, boss?"

"No, but thank you. Last year at Campathon, did you have any run-ins with Bianca from the Breakfast Bandits?"

Kendall blinked. "Let's just jump straight into why you came, why don't you."

I just looked at him.

"There wasn't anything specific enough for me to complain about. I just kept my distance from their cart."

We chatted for a while, and Kendall sent in his list of cart restock items, which I promised to pull together and have Harley deliver.

Since I was going to take coffee beans back to the shop, I wrapped up the already packaged and ready-for-sale bags in canvas reusable shopping bags, then used my *Tetris* skills to safely stow them in a crate, which I bungee-corded to the rack on the back of my bicycle. Then I pulled the items Kendall needed, mostly sleeves of cups, lids, and nondairy milks. I packed those for Harley to deliver, and sent her a text letting her know.

As I worked, I listened to the newest episode of Rose's podcast, which had just dropped earlier in the day.

"Hi, my intrepid listeners. I bring you today's episode with a heavy heart. I find myself questioning if I should archive this footage and pretend I never recorded it.

"But I thought it was important to share this interview with you.

"I didn't have a chance to interview Bianca Moore as much as I'd wanted. I wanted to dig into her story through the joint lens of what I could find, record-wise, and Bianca's own words.

"But Bianca died just a few days ago. And her death feels personal to me for multiple reasons. She was on the way to becoming one of my friends. And I suspect she wasn't someone who let many people in her inner circle, so becoming her friend was meaningful.

"And because I was standing next to Bianca when she collapsed. I didn't know I'd spend her final moments with her.

"If you follow me on my social media accounts, you know I'm investigating her murder.

"But I also want to tell Bianca's story in the context of Saffron Jones.

"And forewarning, today's podcast has a lot of intrepid offshoots.

"Because Bianca was also affected by Saffron's crimes, both directly and indirectly. It dramatically altered the course of her life.

"And we have to go back into history to fully understand the whole picture of this situation.

"Bianca's father was actually Saffron's target. He inherited a petroleum-based business in Texas, but that wasn't his passion. His passion? Art. But while he loved the art world, he knew his particular talents weren't in creating masterpieces but in appreciating them. So he invested in art, both in scrappy young up-and-comers while also trying to hunt down masterpieces by the sort of artists you see in museums, including some with questionable provenance.

"This was how Saffron set her hook and caught him, claiming she had one of the missing pieces of the famed Ghent Altarpiece.

"But more on the specifics of the altarpiece later. First, I want to ask a question:

"Why would someone fall for an art scam like this? When I first heard of this crime, I wondered how someone could be so gullible. But then I remembered hearing in a class that the Second World War resulted in quite a bit of lost and stolen artwork. What I thought would be a five-minute research break turned into hours. It's estimated over thirty thousand pieces of artwork stolen during World War Two are still missing. Some of these were looted from homes and museums. Others were bartered by Jewish families trying to escape the Nazis.

"Some collectors would do anything to buy these missing pieces. And they do not want to give them up.

"While researching this, I read about a man, Diego Gradis, whose family—their last name is Deutsch de la Meurthe—was forced to flee Paris to escape Nazi forces. Part of their family escaped to Morocco and Switzerland; not all were so lucky. Their family home was used as a headquarters for the occupying Nazi forces. When Gradis's grandmother returned after Paris was liberated, all of their possessions were gone. Unknown to her family, she filed for restitution with the French government for four specific drawings, along with some other possessions. For context, Georgette Deutsch de la Meurthe died in 1987 at age ninety-two.

"The path the four drawings took from being stolen to recovered could be a podcast in and of itself. They eventually ended up in the hands of Cornelius Gurlitt, the son of a notorious Nazi art dealer. I'll summarize it by saying that Cornelius defended his right to possess the art, regardless of how it was obtained. But while his private art collection was headline news in Germany, the widower of his sister, Benita, called the police and arranged to turn in twenty-two pieces of pilfered artwork.

"The different reactions of Benita and Cornelius could also be a podcast. Because Benita saw the artwork as a dark burden, she kept it secret from the world, and it wasn't returned until after her death. While Cornelius was like a dragon protecting his hoard of pilfered art.

"In 2018, Gradis was invited to Berlin to view the collection, which was displayed with other pieces in the Gurlitt treasure trove. Gradis showed photos of the artwork to his father, then aged ninety-seven, who remembered the drawings. The artwork was returned to Gradis after the show.

"Obviously, returning four pieces of artwork won't bring back what Gradis's family lost. But it helps. To quote Gradis in an interview with *Forbes*, 'Looting artwork does not just deprive a person of a belonging with a financial worth, it deprives a person of part of their identity.'

"Doesn't most crime, at the very least, bruise someone's identity?

"And maybe for some, it does more than bruise but destroys.

"Now that I've talked about a World War Two art story that lives rent-free in my brain, let's talk about Saffron Jones.

"Given the amount of artwork still unreturned and unaccounted for, Saffron's scam made more sense to me, even though it feels even more heartless.

"Let's head to the heart of the scam.

"I visited Bianca's father, Otis Moore, at his retirement home. It's a decent, clean place, but it felt a little sad. Maybe because when I volunteered at a nursing home in high school, it felt more vibrant. More events. Colorful artwork on the walls. But the staff at Otis's retirement home seemed kind, at least. Although my entire podcast is dedicated to how we never know what goes on behind closed doors.

"Otis is physically recovering from his second battle with cancer, but his mind feels as sharp as a proverbial tack. During our interview, he sat in a brown corduroy recliner with a stack of books next to him and a pair of reading glasses. At one point in our interview, he told me he was an octogenarian, which was a new vocab word to me. It means someone in their eighties, by the way.

"Let's listen to part of our interview."

"I'm so sorry for your loss." Rose's tone was warm and sympathetic.

"I can't believe my daughter is gone."

"I'm here to talk about Saffron Jones and the impact on both your life and Bianca's."

"I don't want to talk about Saffron Jones. She already ruined my life." His bitterness came through so thick it felt like it was choking him.

"I'm curious about the Ghent Altarpiece and a few other pieces of art you had in your collection."

Rose cut away from the interview for a quick history lesson.

Her voice took on a peak-podcaster tone as she said:

"Let's pause the interview for a second so I can tell you something relevant. The Ghent Altarpiece, also called the *Adoration of the Mystic Lamb*, is a fifteenth-century polyptych altarpiece in St. Bavo's Cathedral in Ghent, Belgium. It's considered important because it shows the transition from Middle Age to Renaissance art. I'll pop a link in the notes for this episode on my website, and you can see the altarpiece for yourself.

"The story behind this piece of art could be a whole series in and of itself. There's a reason it's referred to as 'the most stolen artwork of all time.' And there's a long story behind why it was stolen by the Nazis in World War Two. It was returned by the Monuments Men, a group from the Allied forces who tracked down items looted by the Nazis and returned them to their rightful owners.

"The altarpiece is currently on display in Ghent, Belgium.

"Well, most of the altarpiece is on display. One of the panels is a re-creation to make the altarpiece look whole.

"Because in 1934, its lower left panel was stolen, and only one of the two panels was recovered. And many people would do anything to possess the missing panel."

Rose switched back to the interview.

"You once owned several pieces of artwork that were, let's say, lost during World War Two?"

"Yes, but I thought the owners sold these pieces to fund their escapes. I saw myself as keeping the artwork safe. And I paid good money for them years after World War Two ended. Decades later."

"And then Saffron Jones approached you about the missing panel from the Ghent Altarpiece?"

"There have been rumors about that panel for years. But Jones acquired a real Camille Pissarro for me, so I trusted her when she said she had an inside line. Saffron said she could acquire the missing panel from the grand-son of one of the original thieves, provided the payoff was right."

"What did you plan to do with the altarpiece once you'd acquired it?"

"I wanted to keep it, of course. It would've been the gem of my collection. But Jones took my money and skedaddled."

"So you reported her to the police?"

"She stole from me and deserved to be arrested."

Rose's voiceover resumed.

"When I talked with Otis, like Cornelius Gurlitt, he reminded me of a dragon attempting to hoard artwork. There was one fatal flaw with reporting Saffron's scam to the police. One of the detectives on the case was married to an art historian and recognized one of the pieces of artwork on display at Otis's home . . . and it also had a sketchy provenance. Meaning it was stolen during a bur-glary in New York in the 1960s, and, at some point, Otis bought it on the black market. So after a thorough investi-gation, Otis faced charges of receiving stolen goods. As I've already alluded to, multiple pieces in his collection were acquired through questionable means. Some of those paintings were returned to their rightful owners. At least two are held in museums for safekeeping because of lengthy court battles over their ownership.

"So while Saffron Jones stole from Otis Jones, the ripples of her crime brought other crimes to light, and in a roundabout, brought justice to the world.

"But back to Bianca.

"How did Bianca end up in Portland? I never received an answer to that question, although it was on my list to ask her.

"From what I've gathered, Bianca moved to Portland when it was a hip and cheap destination. And she started a food cart, which, having explored the city, feels like peak Portland. So maybe she'd moved to Portland to build her own life away from the shadow of her past.

"But the scars Saffron left on her family were practically visible on Bianca. Remember my quote earlier about looted artwork depriving a person of their identity? As I talked with Bianca, I felt the crime that shaped her teen years also bruised her identity. Bianca wore those marks like badges of honor, and I suspect they got in the way of her living her best life.

"Or maybe it was an excuse. Let's listen to Bianca so you can get your own feel."

"That grifter stole my life," Bianca said. I noted that she sounded bitter, like usual.

"How?" Rose used a sympathetic tone that clearly worked on Bianca.

"When my father lost his fortune, it included my education and trust funds. I was forced to leave the private academy I loved to attend a public high school, which I hated. Especially since my father was front-page news, and everyone bullied me about it. It also hurt my university applications because my old school was a pipeline to the Ivies. While most of my public school classmates went to community college or maybe a state school. Plus, if I wanted to go to a university, I had to take out loans and go into debt. My entire life changed in a blink of an eye, and it wasn't my fault."

"That's sad."

"And Saffron Jones's daughter is sauntering around Portland like it doesn't matter that her mother ruined lives."

"Surely, you losing your trust fund was not her daughter's fault."

"It's so unfair."

"How did you recognize Saffron Jones's daughter?"

"When I first met *bleep bleep—*"

I straightened up. Rose had bleeped out my name, thankfully.

"—I knew she looked familiar. The first time I heard her speak, it brought back the memory of meeting Saffron Jones when she came to scam my dad."

Believable as I was almost a doppelgänger of my mother.

"You knew about the plan to buy the Ghent Altarpiece?"

"I didn't know the specifics. I thought Saffron was an art dealer my father worked with, and I knew Dad had taken her out on a few dates. Then our life fell apart, and it was her fault. So I'll never forget her."

Bianca's voice continued on in a flood of words. "I knew *bleep* had to be related, so I trolled through her business records and saw she was connected to Jimmy Jones. So it was obvious she was also poisonous."

"Reports say that Saffron Jones died a few months ago."

"I hope she suffered. She deserves to die slowly and painfully."

Rose spoke in her overview voice. "You might have noticed that I bleeped out a name in that interview. I did it out of respect for the privacy of Saffron Jones's daughter, whom I hope will consent to be interviewed. But I don't want to out her.

"Thanks for listening, everyone. Again, this is Rose of

*Rose Investigates: Thorny Crimes and Intrepid Offshoots.*
Catch me next week for our next installment into the life
and times of notorious grifter Saffron Jones."

I realized Harley was waving at me, so I pulled my headphones
out of my ears.

"What's up?"

"You looked entranced. You filled your crates ages ago and were
just staring at nothing."

"I should get back to the shop."

But first, I told Harley about the podcast.

"Listening to Bianca must've been like communing with a
ghost."

"Exactly. It made me shiver."

Rose's entire podcast had brought up multiple ghosts in my life,
with Bianca's feeling like the most poignant.

After I closed down the Group Sales shop, I had a while before
my brother was supposed to come by with dinner. After tossing in a
load of laundry, instead of taking care of the sort of daily chore I
should do to keep my life flowing easily, I circled back to my ongoing question: What happened to Bianca?

I read Rose's text from a few hours before. *I did a deep dive into
Phillip, and here's what I found out.*

As I read Rose's summary, I wondered if she could have a future
as a private investigator. Or, with her love of recycled fashion and research skills, she might make a world-class dramaturge for a theater
trying to be accurate. Maybe a theater specializing in true-crime
reenactments, even though that sounded like a fast track to night-
mares.

Phillip had grown up in Arizona and moved to Portland in his
early twenties. Rose had found a handful of posts connecting Phillip
with various jobs, including one as a bouncer for a music venue on
North Mississippi and one from a local neighborhood newspaper

doing a profile on a new café opening, which included Phillip in a photo of their kitchen staff. I loved the small papers in Portland that focus on hyperlocal news affecting a quadrant of the city, although I wondered how they survived. Maybe, like Rose's podcast, they're a labor of love fueled by the hope of, somehow, making it big.

Rose had also included an audio file from earlier in the day. I popped in my earbuds so I could listen. The tone was slightly muffled.

"Hi, Phillip. I'm preparing tribute posts for Bianca. Can I ask you a few questions?"

"As long as it's quick. I'm getting ready to open and run the shop by myself." Phillip's tone was clipped, not quite angry, but like he was only a few minor annoyances away from sliding into a rage.

"I heard Bianca used to be a sous chef at a really high-end place. Like, mind-blowingly good restaurant."

"Yeah, that's right," Phillip said, and named-dropped a restaurant down in the California wine country that I'd heard people include on their bucket list.

"Why'd she leave?"

"Bianca was chased out by someone jealous of her. One of the people she managed was gunning for her job and started backstabbing Bianca. She'd tell the executive chef that Bianca made mistakes during the dinner rush. But that's not the worst part. She'd sneak extra salt or weird spices into the foods Bianca would make, so they tasted wrong. It was almost like gaslighting."

"Isn't gaslighting when you make someone doubt their lived experiences? It's from the movie?"

"This person made Bianca doubt reality and distrust her cooking skills. And poor Bianca had a mental breakdown and did in-patient therapy. When she got out, she decided to make a clean break. She quit her job and moved here."

"Is that why Bianca took Valium?"

Phillip's intake of breath sounded surprised. His tone held a borderline angry edge. "How did you know about that?"

"Bianca mentioned it once. Maybe it was a joke?"

"I sincerely doubt that. Bianca didn't like people to know she was taking any type of drugs. She grew up in a family that didn't believe in drugs for anxiety or depression, just grit, and determination. She thought she should be strong enough to deal with life without meds, but she needed them."

"Therapy for depression and stuff like that should be like getting physical therapy," Rose said. "Normal, if you need it."

"You'd wish." Phillip sounded bitter. "But what would I know? I'm just the kid who kept getting sent to anger management classes. You know the woman who backstabbed Bianca apologized a few years ago? Bit too late in my book."

"How'd you two meet?" Rose asked.

"When Bianca was getting her food cart ready, she'd sometimes do pop-ups in a little café. I worked there as a line cook and offered to help her, which made the owner feel better since I was there to ensure everything was left as it should be. Then, when she opened the cart, I worked with her in the mornings and at the café in the afternoons until I could switch to just working at the Breakfast Bandits.

"Of course, when all of us in our pod downtown were kicked out to build a fancy hotel, it almost destroyed us. I took some evening shifts at a bar to keep us afloat." Phillip droned on for a few minutes. I was sympathetic to all the carts that lost their coveted downtown spot, but it was also one of the risks of being a food cart. When real estate was cheap, leasing out empty lots to food carts made sense. But when the land value skyrocketed, those lots became more valuable and were redeveloped.

"Starting a full-time micro-restaurant spot seemed perfect since we could be open more reliable hours and not have to move the cart. That being said, all of the women with cafés here are snooty. They're no better than me, but they all have attitudes."

Phillip whined for a moment, which made my sympathy for him wither, and then Rose ended the interview.

As I soaked in the interview's aftermath, I realized Harley had been in a situation similar to Bianca's. But her older sister advocated for Harley to get the help she needed. Bianca's life might have been different if she'd had someone to look out for her.

Had one of Bianca's former coworkers really set her up? If she had, it would be on the list of reasons Bianca struggled to trust others. Or maybe the stress of a high-intensity kitchen had been too much for her, and she hadn't wanted to admit she was making mistakes. The apology Phillip mentioned could've been a simple "I'm sorry I couldn't help you while you were drowning."

And then I heard feet on the front steps, and Kaldi ran to the front door with a chirp.

It was time to shift gears.

# Chapter 18

Kaldi chirped again as I walked to the front door, which I flung open with a dramatic welcoming gesture. Jackson had arrived promptly at seven p.m. as planned with a pizza and a salad . . . and my dad.

"What's this about Michael Fernsby III?" Jackson asked as he walked in the door.

"It'd be safer to check who is at the door versus flinging it open," my dad added.

I led them back to the dining room table and decided to focus on Jackson's question. "Michael showed up at the coffee shop on the snow day, looking for Rose. Supposedly, he's in the area for a conference."

"Supposedly?"

"Michael didn't say which conference. I couldn't find anything jewelry-related in the region. Rose desperately wanted to interview him for her podcast, and he agreed to talk to her at the Button Building."

"There was also a microlending conference in town. It wasn't that big, but I heard it was pretty great," Jackson said.

"What's that?"

"The conference was held by a not-for-profit that encourages small loans, and they brought in most of their competitors," Jackson said. "I assume you don't know much about this, but please stop me if I'm mansplaining. Suppose you were a woman in a third-world country with a business idea. You don't need much to launch the idea, let's say a thousand dollars. Most big banks wouldn't be interested, but someone in the USA, for example, might see it worthwhile to loan the money. Some of the main microloan programs might even spread that thousand dollars over multiple donors, allowing someone like you to donate two hundred fifty dollars, or even less, and make a small profit of one to two percent while helping out someone who needed it."

"That sounds amazing. Now that I think of it, I had heard about them before." Maybe Ground Rules should look into microloan programs for coffee farms.

"It's a fantastic idea with the potential to do good. And like any investment, it's not a given the small investor will get their money back. But the programs are serious about vetting the potential businesses to make sure they have a realistic chance of success. So, it's possible Fernsby was in town for that. We should check the event's website and see if he's mentioned. Some conferences list attendees."

If Michael had been in town for the micro-investing conference, he'd gone up in my estimation. "You know, I looked up the website of Michael's company. They looked like they take ethics seriously, talking about why to consider lab-grown diamonds and stuff like that. Maybe they're into microlending potential suppliers?"

"Or they're smart enough to know that advertising blood diamonds is a good way to get shunned." Jackson's cynicism was on-brand.

My father hadn't said anything as he opened up the Caesar salad container and found a set of spoons to work as salad tongs. He loaded up half of his plate, then opened the pizza box and snagged a slice of Margherita with perfectly browned fresh mozzarella. We made eye contact.

"Hi, Pumpkin," he said. Even though he'd been in my house for a few minutes.

"Hiya, Dad."

"No Bax?"

"He's working late tonight. The sasquatches have a serious time crunch to get the game ready to launch. But it looks like they'll make it on time."

"That's good."

Beside me, Jackson loaded up his plate with salad. From prior experience, I knew he was a salad-first, followed-by-pizza guy.

My father spoke. "I'm concerned Fernsby is in town, but it could be a coincidence."

"For what it's worth, I don't think Michael sought me out. I only saw him because of Rose's podcast. And we don't know if he was even in the country before Bianca collapsed. He definitely wasn't near the fatal coffee cup." If he was involved with Bianca's poisoning, he'd had an accomplice.

Maybe Rose's podcast had set all of this in motion by causing different forces associated with my mother to meet in one place. Perhaps the fallout was inevitable.

Or maybe Rose had set up the meeting to see if there was an explosion. But she hadn't been there to see it. She'd been running late.

Or had she? Had she been secretly spying on us?

"After we eat, let's go over who had access to Bianca's coffee cup," my dad said.

"I can even crack out one of Bax's whiteboards," I said.

My father sat up a bit straighter. "That's a great idea!"

So about fifteen minutes later, after we'd eaten the Caesar salad and pizza, I set up one of Bax's whiteboards from the stash in his office on an easel in the living room. Bax used them when brainstorming video games. This wasn't the first time one had become an impromptu murder board.

I wrote down the timeline I'd worked out.

"So, really, the suspects are Nina, Laura, Abby, Rose, Phillip, and you," Jackson said. "At least these are enough suspects to throw doubt if you're arrested."

"Thanks," I said.

"What do you know about Abby and Laura?" my father asked.

"Not much, other than they've both run their businesses for a few years. Both were food carts before they signed up for spots in the Button Building. From what I've seen, neither had a reason to target Bianca. Although neither of them liked her, either." I told them about Laura's argument with Bianca.

My father looked deep in thought. "Bianca had a connection to your mother. Is it possible Laura or Abby also have one?"

"You know," I said slowly, "Uncle Jimmy knew about Bianca's history with my mother. So it's possible. But how many victims could my mother have locally? Do you know, Dad? Can you look it up?"

"I'm a private citizen now, so I don't have access to the information the police have. Even when I was in the police, I would need to have a reason related to an ongoing case to look info up. But I know a private investigator we could ask to investigate this. She'll have access to a few tools that will get through social media privacy settings and she can probably track down Fernby's travel itinerary. She's sharp. Both of you would like her."

"I don't know if we need that yet. Sage hasn't been charged. But it seems like a good thing to keep in our back pocket." Jackson's tone was grim, reminding me this wasn't a puzzle. Or a game.

This was my life, and there weren't any do-over cheat codes.

Hopefully, Detective Leto would solve the case and bring order back to my world without me needing to hire a PI. Although I could see the appeal. Was there anything relevant in Laura or Abby's background? For some reason, one of them had turned into a murderer.

"You know . . ." My voice trailed off.

"Don't space out on us now," Jackson said.

"Mark Jeffries has been hanging around the Button Building, and the Breakfast Bandits started carrying Left Coast Grinds products."

"Don't tell the police. That's your motive," Jackson said. I knew his sarcasm was intertwined with a small kernel of truth.

"Could he be so serious about sabotage that he set me up for murder?" Maybe with Phillip's help?

We talked for a while but didn't come up with anything helpful.

Before he left, I handed my father the business card the mystery writer had handed me a few days ago and told him about her. "So if you want to talk to a writers group, give her a ring."

My dad tucked the card into his pocket with a thoughtful expression.

Jackson laughed.

"Careful, Jackson, they might have questions about the juvenile system."

"They'd be lucky to have me as a speaker," Jackson said. And with that note, they left.

# Chapter 19

Even though I wanted to work the Ground Rules shop on the weekends, at least until we got established, I knew I shouldn't. I needed time off to recharge and explore the sides of myself that weren't Barista Sage.

And this was my first weekend off in months.

But that didn't stop me from hopping on my bicycle and heading to the shop to check on everything.

Sadly, Bax had headed to the office early but said he would return in the afternoon. He promised we'd do something fun for dinner and spend all day tomorrow together. I could work with that.

Kendall was in charge of the Ground Rules shop. He'd promised the hours, which were eight to two on the weekends, worked with his school schedule, and allowed him more time off on weekdays.

It also meant Sophie had gotten more managerial hours at the cart, which made her happy. So it was a win, on the whole, even though it was always hard for me to let go and let my competent staff do their jobs.

When I dropped in, Kendall and one of the baristas from the cart, Brooklyn, had everything in hand. Most of the tables were full, including one with the writer from the weekday group, who glared intently at her laptop like it had just insulted her mother.

"You just couldn't stay away, could you?" Kendall asked as he made my macchiato.

"This shop is just so new. I have to check in on it."

"We have everything under control, boss."

Brooklyn hummed as they carted a full dish bin back to the cleaning area. Their hair was pulled into a thick bun at the back of their head, and I was a bit envious of their Chelsea boots.

"I'm glad to see you're busy."

"We've been steady all day."

Brooklyn abandoned the dishes to help a group of teenage girls who'd walked in. One of them wore a hoodie from a local high school.

"Are lattes gluten-free?" one of the teens asked in a confident tone.

Brooklyn barely smiled, and their voice was kind. "Totes GF. Gluten is the protein found in wheat, and it's completely different from the protein found in cow's milk."

"What if I'm also allergic to cow's milk?"

I suspected the teen was messing with Brooklyn, but it didn't ruffle them.

Brooklyn answered in a voice the perfect mix of pep and unruffled calm, "Some people with celiac are hesitant to consume oats because of the risk of cross-contamination, but our oat milk is certified gluten-free. So anyone who wants to avoid gluten is safe with our coffee. Just avoid the pastries."

"I'll take an oat milk latte with vanilla syrup," the girl said.

The rest of the girls ordered mochas, although one tried to order a blended ice drink from the mermaid brand. But Brooklyn didn't have to say anything; the gluten-free teen corrected her friend.

"And I'll take a chocolate chip cookie," the chastised girl said with a snide look at her friend. The gluten-free pretended she didn't hear.

"Seriously, boss, just go," Kendall told me as he prepared to make the teens' drinks.

"Are you the owner?" the gluten-free teen asked.

"I'm the co-owner."

"Can I interview you for my business class? We're supposed to write a paper about a local business, and I want to focus on something women-owned. Wait, is your business partner female?" The teen's intensity reminded me of Rose.

"Yes, this is a women-owned-and-operated business." Except for our financial backer, but that seemed too complicated for the moment.

I gave the girl my card, wondering what I was getting into. Had I been that self-assured as a teen? I doubted it.

I was about to leave when I spotted a familiar face: my uncle Jimmy leaving Best Burgers. So I headed his way.

"One of my favorite nieces," my uncle said when he saw me.

"One of my favorite uncles," I replied.

"Your only uncle."

"Twenty-five percent of your nieces."

My uncle sat down at a table, and I joined him. We spent a while discussing Ground Rule's opening days, and I purposefully switched gears.

"Have you decided what's going to happen with Breakfast Bandits?"

"I'll tell you what I just told Abby: if Phillip wants out of the Breakfast Bandits's lease, I'm willing to let him without any penalties. While I assume that will happen, I'm not about to force the remaining owner to make any decisions. His life was just upended."

"We'll see what happens," I said. "But about that."

"Oh?"

"How many people here did you rent to because you felt sorry for them?"

"What do you mean?"

"The Breakfast Bandits have a history of not playing nice with others. They were even kicked out of a farmers market, of all places. And you loaned money to Doughman." He'd also invested in Ground

Rules when we were just a baby idea in which he'd seen the promise, so I should add myself to that list.

"Everyone here has a strong business plan and the potential to succeed," was all my uncle would say.

We chatted for a while, and I checked in the shop again, only for Kendall to shoo me away.

I bicycled home, glad to see the shop doing well without me.

Bax wasn't home yet, so I slipped my headphones on and queued up the newest episode of Rose's podcast. The one with my uncle Jimmy, so I was curious how she'd managed to spin his say-nothing-important interview.

"What leads someone to become a life-long criminal? If you talk to a sociologist, you might hear about factors like socioeconomic status, access to education, and opportunities. This makes me wonder how a sense of hope leads to criminal acts, both for people who have hope and those who don't.

"I also wondered: Is becoming a criminal genetic? Is it waiting there, under our skin, ready to emerge at any moment?

"Or did it come from the way she was raised?

"Saffron's family is hesitant to speak on the record about their wayward family member.

"But I found out a few things. According to Saffron's uncle, she had a perfectly normal upbringing. Saffron had a comfortable childhood with access to the basics that all children should have, like plenty of food, so food insecurity wasn't an issue. Safe housing, seasonally appropriate clothing, and all of that jazz.

"I talked with James Jones, known as Jimmy, a Portland, Oregon, business owner and uncle of Saffron Jones."

"Saffron was a good kid. She was as smart as a whip and did well in school. I don't think anyone who knew her as a child expected her to go the way she did."

"So she wasn't in trouble at all?"

"Not a lick."

I laughed several times as I listened to the rest of the interview. No matter which angle Rose used, my uncle didn't give an inch. It was a master class on saying nothing.

But Rose did raise a few interesting questions. Why had my mother become the woman she did? Was it a fluke? Genetics went haywire? Because everyone else in the family had at least a basic level of compassion and empathy. While those were two emotions my mother faked like a pro but didn't seem to truly feel. But when I compared her to Jackson, whose entire law practice is based on a sense of compassion and getting justice for children who can't advocate for themselves, I sometimes wonder if she was really our mother. Biologically, at least.

Bax came home, and we discussed where to head for dinner, eventually deciding on pho. Since I would have Bax all to myself for the rest of the day and tomorrow, I tried to put thoughts of my mother and Bianca aside and stay in the here and now.

# Chapter 20

On my way to work on Monday morning, I only needed a light raincoat versus the snowsuit of last week. It finally felt like March.

Getting the shop ready felt automatic. Colton arrived ten minutes before his shift, pulled a shot of espresso, and was prepared to work on time, which I appreciate as his boss.

Our morning was steady, and Nina jumped in and helped when she arrived for her shift, five minutes early and ready to go. She still looked faded around the edges, but seemed more energetic than she had last week.

We worked together well as a team, and I made the dish bin rounds when there was a lull midmorning. After dropping the almost full bin from inside the shop, swapping it for an empty bin, and handing it off for Nina to clean while Colton helped a customer, I headed to the dish zone in the communal area.

And once again saw Mark Jeffries leaving the Breakfast Bandits, with Phillip hot on his heels. Phillip reached and grabbed Mark's arm.

Mark spun around, and the two stared at each other. They were a few inches too close for comfort, even as a bystander.

Should I grab a spray bottle to break up their fight?

But Mark spoke first. "Think very carefully about your next step. This isn't going to help me change my mind."

"I'm sorry, man." Phillip took a step backward, and his posture deflated.

I tore my gaze away and pulled a couple of Ground Rules mugs out of the communal bins. We needed to develop a better method of separating our individual dishes. I made a note to work on that later. One mug clinked against another as I loaded it in my bin, and they looked at me.

"Do you mind? We're having a private conversation," Mark said.

"Yes, an absolutely realistic request while standing in a public area." I turned and pulled the final two mugs, followed by a couple of small pastry plates, from the bus bin area.

"You have my number if you decide you can agree with my offer," Mark said, and split. He gave me a dose of side-eye as he passed by.

Which I returned with interest.

As he walked out the door, I got the sense Mark had more than a series of coffee tattoos up his sleeve.

I glanced at Phillip. "What's up?"

"Why would you care?"

"I'm your neighbor."

"You just want to gloat."

"Phillip, chill. I'm just curious why Mark Jeffries has been hanging around here." The snap in my voice made Phillip blink.

"Why would it concern you?"

"I know you and Bianca wanted to cast me as a big bad villain without ever talking to me. But I'm just a small business owner wondering why a competitor who offered to buy out my company and didn't want to take no for an answer has been skulking around."

"Really? He tried to buy out Ground Rules? Mark talks about you like you're the worst coffee in town." Phillip looked at me, and, if anything, his expression made him look dead inside. Like he needed to be at home dealing with his grief. "I'm looking for a financial partner to keep the Breakfast Bandits going. I'd hoped Mark

Jeffries would be interested, but he's only interested in switching my café to revolve around coffee. And there's no way the owner of this place would lease space to a second coffee shop. You know, Bianca tried to get the Button Building owner to drop your shop, but he told us the other leaseholders weren't up for discussion. So he's not going to change his mind now."

I held in a laugh. "For real?"

"That's what Bianca told me, anyway. She thought the building owner owed her. She ranted about it for a while, but I was trying to game with my brother, so I wasn't listening."

"You weren't at the meeting?"

"Bianca handled the lease and the business arrangements, and I did what she told me to do in the cart. I do need to talk with the owner about our lease. Do you have his number? The police took Bianca's phone, and she kept all of our records."

"I have one of the owner's business cards in my shop. You can have it."

Did Phillip honestly not know about my connection to the building's owner, aka my uncle? Or was he playing dumb?

"Were things okay between you and Bianca? It looked like you were arguing at the grand opening."

Phillip looked at the polished concrete floor. "Things had been tense between us for a while, but we would've worked through it. Bianca's social media had gotten the attention of a chef who'd known her years ago when she was trying to climb the culinary ladder before striking out on her own. He asked if she'd be interested in handling the small plates for a high-end joint he's opening up in a winery between Newburg and McMinnville."

Aka Oregon's wine country.

"Was Bianca interested?"

"Yes, and no. Bianca always felt like she'd failed when she had to quit her job in San Francisco. She wanted to prove herself. The hours would've been long, but her pay would've been stable and she could've set the menu, which she would've loved. He even offered a contract so he couldn't lay her off on a whim. Which would've been comforting for her since you know that running a food cart means erratic pay. That always stressed Bianca out."

"That's one of the reasons we built up our wholesale orders," I said.

"We tried to get wholesale orders, we couldn't do that with breakfast foods, except for making breakfast burritos for a coffee shop for a while, but it didn't work out long-term."

"Left Coast Grinds downtown? About three years ago?" I remembered when they'd briefly offered small but delicious breakfast burritos.

"That's right. We thought it was our first step to build up a wholesale business, maybe to all of the Left Coast Grinds shops and hopefully grocery stores, but then Mark said the burritos weren't quite working. It wasn't the quality, but it was hard to get them heated quickly in a high-volume shop."

"I can see that. It's why we've avoided offering bagel sandwiches and have stuck to pastries."

"We did try to get into a few grocery stores, but it just didn't happen," Phillip said. "Hmm, I wonder if Bianca's chef friend would be interested in partnering? Our food gets good reviews."

"I always heard great things about your food."

"Even people that hated us had to admit our food was awesome," Phillip said. "I might need to try to sell off as much of the business as possible, even if no one wants all of it. The equipment should have some value. I wonder if I could sell the recipes? Bianca had whole files of recipes she'd developed. I told her to make a blog, but she didn't want anyone to steal her ideas. She thought maybe one day she'd be asked to write a cookbook, like a celebrity chef."

Phillip looked sad, and I wondered why he'd come to the Button Building today.

"No one would blame you if you stayed home, hopefully with a friend nearby, and let yourself grieve."

"I bet you'd like that." His eyes narrowed, and he was one sarcastic comment away from a full-on snarl.

I held my palms out in a calming gesture. "I said that from a place of compassion. Business-wise, the building is at its strongest when all our restaurants bring their A game. But I know I'd need to take time off if I lost my fiancé or business partner. I wouldn't be able to function." I had a strong Ground Rules crew, so if the worst did happen, the shop could function without me under the guidance of Sophie, Kendall, and, I suspected, Colton, even if he was still new. But Colton was proving he was an asset every day.

"I need to work," Phillip said. "I can't afford not to."

But was he earning anything by keeping the Breakfast Bandits open? Or wasting money on supplies? But I didn't ask since I suspected that was a conversational minefield. I opted for a different battle instead.

"I'm not accusing you of anything, but I'm trying to figure a timeline out since all of this has been preying on my mind. What did you give to Bianca the morning of the grand opening?"

"Why would you think I poisoned her?"

"I didn't say you poisoned her, but there's video footage of you handing her something. I'm just trying to figure out who gave Bianca stuff and when."

"'Cause you're worried you'll be arrested? You know, the cops already asked me about this. I gave Bianca her vitamins. She needs—needed—them to function."

"Vitamins?"

"Iron, vitamins C, D, calcium, some herbal pill with elderberry or something. It sounds silly, but she always forgot to take them. Then she'd get exhausted. So I parceled them out on Sundays into those goofy plastic containers with days of the week, and made sure she took them. If the pills were still in the container after breakfast, I'd bring them to her."

Phillip's words rang partially true to me, but something told me he wasn't telling the whole story.

He must have read the skepticism on my face. "I gave the cops her vitamins to test, so if you have a problem with that, take it up with them." He looked down. "It's not like she needs the vitamins I put together for the rest of the week."

"You guys looked like you were arguing. Was it just because of the job offer?" I kept my tone light so Phillip knew I wasn't judging him.

"At that exact moment, she was annoyed at me for interrupting her, especially when she wanted me to focus on shredding up potatoes for the hash brown special while she talked with Rose. It was one of her comfort foods, and she thought making it for the grand opening would bring us luck," Phillip said. "I will miss coming home and finding her frying potatoes with bell peppers and onions, then covering them in white cheddar. I teased her about it, but it was so good."

"She didn't offer it all of the time on your menu? It sounds delicious."

"She said she didn't want to dilute the power of potato and white cheddar." Phillip half-smiled at the memory, and I could practically taste the grief around him. He'd loved her deeply, in his own unique way.

"I truly am sorry for your loss," I said.

"Thank you." Phillip glanced at his phone. "I need to go. But if you hear of anyone looking to buy a restaurant or a decked-out food cart, let me know."

He left, and when he entered his restaurant, he stopped and tore down the WE SERVE LEFT COAST GRINDS sign.

I realized this was the least antagonistic I'd seen Phillip. He wasn't warm and fuzzy, but it was nice to glimpse the person underneath. But something still made me suspect him.

As I walked back to my shop, I worked through our conversation.

Would Bianca have accepted a different job and closed Breakfast Bandits shortly after opening it? Or was it just a pleasant dream? In addition to losing the money they'd sunk into getting the Breakfast Bandits café up and running, if Bianca had left and taken a more stable position, Phillip would've been out of a job.

And Bianca dying would cause Breakfast Bandits to fold since Phillip needed Bianca to handle both the business side of their operation and the day-to-day planning. I wondered what Phillip brought to the table. Maybe he'd handled customers and the grunt tasks. But if Bianca had been annoyed with Phillip for leaving a mundane task to bring her vitamins, perhaps that had been a common complaint in her world.

We always talk about how you never know what goes on behind closed doors, and it turns out you also never know what's going on inside food carts. And micro-restaurants.

Phillip was in deep trouble without Bianca. Unless he could sell the business for a decent chunk of change, which he clearly hoped to do. But I doubted it was worth that much. Maybe enough to repay the loans they'd taken out while getting the shop ready with perhaps a tiny buffer to help him stay afloat as he found a new job, but I doubted he'd end up that far ahead.

Plus, he still had the working food cart, which isn't cheap and should resell for a decent amount. But would it be worth killing someone over?

Maybe Phillip hadn't meant to harm Bianca by giving her ketamine. Perhaps he'd just wanted to make her doubt herself. Make her rely on him more. Manipulate her to make him the only person she could trust.

Or maybe he'd brought Bianca the regular vitamins she took daily, and it was just chance she'd also ingested something deadly.

Did anyone else know about her stash of vitamins? Could someone else have swapped out one of the pills?

If he had drugged her during the grand opening, why?

Unless he wanted proof on video to keep her dependent on him. Maybe he thought Rose would be too kind to air an embarrassing video, but he could use it behind the scenes to keep Bianca under his control.

Or maybe I was overthinking this. Maybe Phillip was innocent, and Bianca's death had blown up his life. He was scrambling around, trying to find a small foothold of normalcy, and failing.

If you'd asked me last week if I'd feel sympathetic for Phillip, I would've said no. Never. But now, part of me wished I could do something for him. But I also knew he was like an injured dog who would bite the hand of someone trying to help him.

"Sage, I need to talk to you," Rose hissed as she approached the counter. She glanced behind my shoulder at Nina, then back at me. "Privately."

"Nina, watch the shop for a moment, please."

I followed Rose to the communal seating area.

Rose turned to face me. "You can't trust Nina."

"What?"

"Nina. You can't trust her. I worked in Hoptimal Pint yesterday evening, and she came in with that Mark guy. The one who is friendly with Phillip. And they looked awfully cozy."

"Nina used to work for Mark before she left and moved out to the gorge for a few years," I said.

"The gorge?"

"Columbia River Gorge. You know, I keep forgetting you're not local."

Rose held up her phone, so I could see the screen. She showed me a video of Mark and Nina standing at the counter in Hoptimal Pint like they were ordering drinks. I'd run into Mark there before, which made me suspect he lived in the neighborhood.

Mark reached out and slid his hand into Nina's back pocket. She turned into him slightly, and his hand slid to her hip as her body rotated.

He leaned over and whispered something in her ear, and she pushed his hand away gently.

Then the video stopped.

"I quit recording and ducked down after they got their drinks. But I couldn't get close enough to hear what they discussed."

"They're going to revoke your Nancy Drew street cred," I joked. But I also felt sick inside.

Nina and Mark?

And I didn't feel sick just because Nina was married to someone else.

"What are you going to do about this?" Rose asked.

"For now? I need to think. Can you send that to me?"

"I'll add it to the shared folder." Rose typed something on her phone.

"Thanks. I'm going to get back to work." I walked back into the shop and tried to focus on work.

After closing down Ground Rules and dropping by the roastery for a while, I had just got home when Kendall texted me. *Did you see Rose's latest?*

I clicked on the link he'd sent, which took me to one of Rose's social media accounts.

"Okay, Thorny Offshoots fans, guess what? I think I've cracked the case." Rose pointed her finger at the camera and smiled brightly.

"Yes, I'm saying that I'm going to put on my best Poirot hat—wait, did he wear a hat, or was he just known for his mustache? Anyway, I will put on my best Poirot persona and crack the case tomorrow."

Rose leaned toward the camera and looked even more smug. "So be sure to tune in."

She stood up straight. "Watch out, world. Rose is about to solve her first case!"

Hmm. I watched the video a second time. Rose sounded confident. Did she really know who'd killed Bianca?

She was too savvy to talk herself up only to disappoint her followers so maybe she had cracked the case.

*Wow,* I texted Kendall back. And I wondered if Kendall followed Rose and what the story was there.

*Do you need me at the shop? It sounds way more exciting than the cart.*

*Sorry, no.*

*Take notes on the drama, if there is any. Better yet, film it for me!*

I sent him a rolling eye emoji.

Did the video Rose sent me earlier tie into who had killed Bianca? Could Mark or Nina be the culprit? Could they have worked together?

Or had she found out more about Phillip?

My thoughts buzzed all night, and I hoped Rose was right.

I hoped she knew who had killed Bianca and that this nightmare would end tomorrow.

# Chapter 21

The next morning was clear as I bicycled to work, and I looked forward to seeing the sunrise. It's the small things, after all, that I like to focus on for pockets of happiness. The snow had finally melted. The streets were quiet, but it felt normal, versus empty for an ominous reason.

But I still felt anxiety in the pit of my stomach as I set about opening the Ground Rules shop, quickly joined by Colton and then Nina. I glanced at Nina several times, wondering what she was doing here. Corporate espionage?

Or was she actively trying to sabotage us?

I'd met Nina's husband briefly. He definitely wasn't Mark. He seemed kind and wicked smart. I'd liked him; more importantly, Nina and her husband seemed to fit together.

So why was she cuddled up to Mark in a taproom?

I tried to focus on work. Between the two order windows, we almost had enough work for all three of us. But switching to two people on shift was the way to go unless we got swamped, aka the goal.

I should check in with the Ground Rules lawyer. I'd never had to fire someone, and did I have cause? Or just suspicion? Or maybe I could lay Nina off. I could claim we didn't need her. That we only needed Colton.

But I didn't want to lie.

And I wanted to know what was going on.

Plus, Rose's claim that she'd solved the case.

Would she really reveal the murderer? Would today really end this whole saga and allow everyone at the Button Building to move forward with our businesses without being suspected of a horrible crime?

I hoped so. And if it launched Rose's nascent podcasting career, she'd deserve it.

My body followed my usual opening-the-shop pattern, and I recognized the shop's new regulars. Colton bantered with a woman customer who was giving off plenty of "why yes, I am interested" signals.

"You interested?" I nodded my head in her direction as she walked outside.

"Nah. But I'm not opposed to mild flirting to increase my tips."

I looked at him skeptically, holding in a smile.

"What? You should try it. Or maybe you should read their futures since I heard you like to do that?"

"Who told you that?" I laughed.

"You're well known as the oracle of Portland coffee," Colton said.

"Kendall?" I asked. I'd scheduled Kendall and Colton to work together in the cart a few times before the shop opened. Kendall had given Colton a thumbs-up as a fellow barista.

"Yep. How come you haven't told anyone's fortune here?"

"It's just a game."

"Show me."

I turned and studied Colton intently. His undercut was freshly shorn, and his beard looked groomed, and I'd already noted a very light woodsy scent when I reached past him for a coffee cup. The smell, cedar and pine with a citrus finish, wasn't too strong, and I suspected it was from beard oil. He'd been in a good mood all day, like he was anticipating something fun, and nothing would get him down. He'd even hummed a few times.

"This is getting weird."

"Quiet, my child, I'm not finished analyzing your aura," I said. He was dressed in dark brown corduroy jeans and a brown-and-blue flannel turned up to his elbows. And his bag had looked heavier than usual like he brought extra clothes in case he spilled coffee on himself. "The spirits are telling me that you have a date with someone you have high hopes for this evening. This isn't your first date, but it's still early days."

Colton blinked at me. "Did I tell you about this yesterday?"

"Nope, you keep your personal life private, which I'm a-okay with," I said, and explained my rationale. "I could've been wrong, of course."

"And you can do this to people you've never seen?"

"A lot of it is guesswork, but I can also tell by people's body language if I'm on the right track. You'd be surprised at the little signals people give if you know to look for them. It's not always perfect since everyone is unique, but the longer you talk to someone, the more you can glean as you figure out their quirks."

"I want to learn more."

I laughed. "Just watch people closely."

A few customers trickled in, and as we made their drinks, Colton asked me, "How did you learn to read people? Or is it an innate skill?"

Why was Colton so curious about this? Could he be working with Mark and not Nina?

Or were both of my new baristas spies?

"Good question. I might be naturally observant, but you can train yourself to watch for the tiny tells that hint at the truth. I'm fairly decent at telling when someone is lying, but that doesn't always mean anything. People lie for various reasons, including to be kind or avoid subjects they don't want to casually chat about." All of Colton's tells told me he was interested, but not abnormally. He felt honest.

But I'm not infallible, even if my batting average would make me an all-star.

A regular knocked on the street order window, so I turned to take her order for a large drip coffee and her black Lab's request for a biscuit. Like always, the Lab stood with his paws on the windowsill the whole time, watching intently. They both looked happy as I handed over their treats.

Nina screeched into the shop two minutes before her shift, rushed into the back, and emerged with her apron on exactly when she was supposed to clock in.

"What did I miss?" Nina joked with a smile.

"Just the biggest tip of our lives. I'm going to buy a car with it," Colton said with a deadpan look as Nina looked at him with wide eyes, then he laughed. "Just kidding."

She swatted him with a bar towel, and we settled into our usual rhythm as customers streamed in. We were never slammed, but our traffic was steady.

Every time the door jangled, I glanced at it, wondering if it was Rose.

Finally, the podcaster came in a few minutes after ten thirty. She looked like peak Rose: her favorite trendy blazer, cute boots, and dark jeans. Her makeup was slightly heavier, with darker lipstick than usual, like she usually did when she planned to be on camera.

Like I told Colton, it's the small things. Rose's makeup was like armor for her, and I could make a guess at her plans for the day based on her style choices. While there was plenty about the podcaster I didn't know, I was starting to understand part of the core character hidden inside her glossy façade.

Nina was working the order counter while I pulled espresso shots for a waiting customer. Colton was on his break, sitting in the corner of the shop on his phone with a dopey look as he texted.

The boy was definitely smitten. Fingers crossed, his date tonight met his hopes.

"I'd like a large coffee, please," Rose said.

"Okay, Princess."

Nina's snarky tone made my gaze snap to her.

Rose purposefully rolled her eyes, like a queen bee middle schooler putting down a less popular classmate. She held up her credit card. "I'm ready to pay."

Nina handed me a cup, then took care of Rose's payment on the shop's tablet. I poured a cup of our house coffee, which I gave Rose.

"Thank you, Sage. I've been looking forward to this all day! Come join me in a few minutes once I've set up my equipment." Rose carried the coffee to the condiment station, doctored it with cream and sugar, then took a big sip.

"Heaven in a cup!" Rose said. "You know, that could be the name of your next roast."

I smiled. "I'll put that on the list."

Rose walked out to the communal area, put her coffee cup down, and swung her heavy pink backpack onto a bench. Abby and Laura joined her, and Rose ignored them as she fumbled in her bag.

I glanced at Nina, who was standing with one hip against the counter, watching Rose.

"Nina, you need to treat customers politely." My voice was quiet, but Nina reacted to its intense undertone by crossing her arms over her chest.

"I'm sorry, she just bugs me. How can you stand her? She's so fake," Nina said.

"You don't need to like someone to be polite." I needed to have a serious conversation with Nina, but a few more customers came in, so I put the thought aside.

But my eyes kept glancing in Rose's direction. At one point, Phillip walked up to her, and even Caleb dropped by the podcaster slash social media star.

Colton returned from his break, still smiling. He motioned toward Rose. "She's acting like she's on top of the world."

"Rose claims she's solved Bianca's murder, and she's going to announce it today," I said. "Hmm, I wonder if she'll do a podcast series on Bianca's murder?" If she'd solve the case, she'd have plenty of material, and I bet listeners would flock to it.

"Being on the front lines of a real investigation is definitely on a true-crime podcaster's bucket list," Colton said.

"Have you listened to *Rose Investigates*?" I asked.

"Once she started hanging around, I listened to one of her episodes from last year. True crime isn't for me. And I don't get why she's in Portland, to be honest. I know she's focused on a criminal who grew up here, but it's not like Rose needs to be in town to produce her podcast."

I nodded. "Maybe Rose wanted the Keep Portland Weird ambiance."

"Yeah, your city stole that from Austin."

"Ha, your city since you live in Portland now."

Rose looked ready to record, so I took my break, leaving Colton in charge.

I thought about how I'd never been in a real-life Poirot moment, wowing a group of people with the answer to a tricky murder, as I joined the crowd behind Rose's phone on a tripod.

Abby leaned closer to me. "It's like a reality TV show."

Laura snorted on the other side of her. Phillip joined us, standing apart from everyone even though Caleb said hi.

"It's showtime," Rose said, then held up a small black remote.

I could see the back of her phone and noticed it started recording.

"Thank you for joining me today," Rose said. She looked straight into the camera. "I'm ready to answer a question you've all been asking yourselves: Who killed Bianca Moore?

"As you know, I've been researching this tirelessly alongside a friend. A mentor, of sorts, who's reminded me to be careful. We'll give her the code name of Oma." Rose smiled at the camera. She took a sip of coffee.

"I finally—" Rose coughed, then choked a few more times. She fell to her knees.

"Help me," Rose gasped. Rose fell over onto her side.

I felt sick as I called 911 while Abby rushed to Rose.

This felt like a déjà vu nightmare.

# Chapter 22

A fire truck, an ambulance, and police car all responded to Rose's collapse. Abby had put Rose into the recovery position. Everyone else had stood around, not sure what to do but clearly wanting to take action.

I stood with Abby and Laura as Rose was wheeled away on a stretcher.

"At least she's alive," Abby said. "I heard one of the paramedics say her vital signs are stable."

"I can't believe it happened again," Laura said.

"It looks like Rose got too close to Bianca's murderer." Abby looked grim. "One murder was bad enough, and a second poisoning?"

Detective Leto walked up and asked to speak with me. Her face was grim, and I got a sense of the steely determination I'd seen from her a few times. We headed to a quiet corner.

"Take me through today," the detective said. Her tone was clipped.

I told her about the video Rose had posted last night.

The detective looked annoyed. "She didn't think to call me?"

"Give Rose a break. She's young and saw this as her ticket to stardom. I can send you a link if you want to see it yourself."

I told the detective about what I'd seen after Rose came in and how we were all ready for her to solve the case when she collapsed.

"If you give me a minute, I can pull together the security footage starting from Rose entering the Button Building," I said.

"Did you put anything in Rose's coffee?" the detective asked.

"Of course not."

At the detective's request, I recounted my morning, leading up to pouring a cup of coffee for Rose.

"Rose stopped by the condiment stand, and I noticed she didn't put a lid on her coffee. And multiple people approached her as she set up her gear to record."

"Did she have her coffee with her the whole time?"

I shook my head, realizing Rose had violated the rule that every woman who has gone to a bar or club should know: never leave your drink unattended.

"I assume your video footage will back up your story?"

"Yes, and I know you'll check for yourself."

Her eyes crinkled slightly like they were smiling even though her mouth wasn't. "Your help acquiring the footage will be appreciated, of course."

I went and grabbed my tablet and logged into the security account to compile footage for the detective. As I did, I didn't see anything overly suspicious. But I didn't have a chance to review every second of it.

I told the detective I'd sent over the footage, then asked, "So we won't be forced to shut down?"

"You're okay for now."

"Are you going to tell me to not leave town?"

"That's something you only see detectives saying in fiction, and I don't have that authority. But you have my card if you think of anything I should know."

She left, and I stood, taking deep breaths, trying to center myself. Then I realized I should tell the Ground Rules team about the day.

So I texted Harley about what happened.

Her response was in all caps. *ARE YOU SERIOUS?*

*Sadly, yes.*

After a moment, I added, *But we haven't been asked to close down for the day. So that might be good?* Provided Rose's collapse didn't scare off customers.

Harley responded, *I might need to stop by.*

So I texted back. *You're my co-owner. You're always welcome.*

Harley showed up about an hour later. Detective Leto was still on-site, along with a uniformed officer, but our shop was still open.

Harley handed me a burrito wrapped in foil. "I thought you'd need the power of carnitas."

"You're a goddess."

Harley handed over a bag to Colton. "There are two more carnitas burritos in there, one for each of you."

"Drats, I could've eaten both." From his tone, I could tell Colton was joking. He pulled one of the burritos out, along with a container of green hot sauce, and handed the bag to Nina. "Okay if I take a quick lunch break?"

"I'm hungry, too," Nina said.

"Both of you can eat. I can handle the shop."

"Call me if you need me, and I'll stop stuffing my face long enough to help," Colton said.

They walked into the customer side of the shop with their burritos and sat at different tables.

Harley glanced at Nina. "How is Nina working out?"

I needed to tell Harley about my Nina concerns, especially before talking about my options with our business lawyer. "She pulls a good shot of espresso." When she wants to, anyway.

"Of course she does. I trained her at Left Coast Grinds."

"Wait, you did?" I knew they'd overlapped, but hadn't realized they'd worked together.

"Nina was one of the last people I trained before I fully transitioned into the roastery. I always liked her and was sad about how she left the company."

"Oh?" I asked.

"Nina and Mark were pretty close, and, to be honest, I always wondered about them. You know how Mark was always too flirty with the younger girls on staff, but Nina seemed to let him in more than the others. I was working in the roastery by this point, but from what I understand, when Nina got engaged, things at work got hella awkward when Mark was around."

"Mark's been spotted around the Button Building, although he hasn't ventured inside our shop. At least not while I've been working." Given Harley's comments, I should show her Rose's video of Nina and Mark, even though this already felt too gossipy. But I decided to wait until we were alone versus standing in the middle of the Ground Rules shop.

Harley frowned. "That's weird. You'd think he'd be too busy with his own company to sniff around here."

"The Breakfast Bandits had a 'We Serve Left Coast Grinds' sign in their window until yesterday."

Harley shook her head. "Talk about loyalty to your neighbors. We decided against bagel sandwiches so we wouldn't compete with them."

"Should we revisit that decision? Or add the toast bar we talked about?"

Part of me wanted to add a simple toast bar with nut butters, jams, honey, and cream cheese for people to make their own toast. We could carry a couple of different types of bread and English muffins, including a few gluten-free options, along with their own dedicated toaster.

"It still sounds too messy," Harley said. "Imagine all of the time you'd have to spend prepping little containers of peanut butter because you know people would double-dip and do all sorts of gross stuff if you handed them a full jar."

"I know it's unrealistic, and if we made the toast to order, we'd have to charge more for labor. People will just need to make their own toast at home."

We curtailed our toast debate, which was a foregone no anyway, when a couple of customers came in. Harley jumped behind the counter to pull a few espresso shots while Colton offered to help, but I waved him back to his burrito.

Nina had disappeared, along with her Harley-provided lunch.

Once we'd served our brief rush of customers, Harley said, "It's good to be back behind the counter occasionally. It reminds me why we do this."

"Perspective is always key," I said, and the words nudged at my brain, letting me know I'd seen a few connections that I hadn't put together.

Colton pulled his apron over his head and washed his hands. "Seeing the big bosses grinding it out in the trenches is inspiring."

"Grinding it out! Good one!" I praised his pun, intentional or not.

Colton went and grabbed the mostly full dish bin from underneath the condiment stand and started loading the dishwasher with the dirty mugs and a handful of pastry plates.

Nina entered the shop, looking awkward.

"It's good to see you, Nina," Harley said. "It's been a few years. Maybe since your wedding? Your reception was lovely."

"Yeah, we moved right after the wedding. I'm happy to be back. I missed the city."

I paused and studied Nina briefly as they chatted, then returned to my supply list even though my mind wasn't focused on it. While Mark had been handsy in the video, she'd subtly rebuked him, but not in a way to cause an immediate explosion. Harley had said things had gotten awkward with Mark before Nina quit Left Coast Grinds.

Had Nina cheated on her then-fiancé, now husband, with Mark?

Or at least hard-core flirted. I remembered, years ago, Mark's attempts to flirt with me and his persistence even when I'd shot him down. But he'd known to stop, at least with me. Until the day I'd packed it in, quit because of Mark, and gone to work as a barback at the Tav. Where I knew my fellow employees would have my back, and not just because my cousin Miles ran the place. But because working as a team and looking out for each other was part of the Tav culture.

And that was my biggest concern with Nina, even without my worry about her and Mark. When she wanted to be, she was a good barista. I suspected she was generally a nice person. But for whatever reason, she wasn't a team player here. I didn't expect everyone to devote themselves to the job, but she held a part of her employee self back.

And I was starting to suspect why.

"Harley, before you go, I'd like to briefly chat with you and Nina. Colton, please handle the shop but call if you need me."

Colton's eyebrows rose slightly. "Okay, boss."

Nina bit her lip as she followed Harley and me into the small back area of the shop, which was a tight fit for the three of us.

"Nina, are you spying on Ground Rules for Mark Jeffries?" I asked.

Nina's voice was shriller than usual. "How do you know?"

With Mark hovering around the Button Building, subtle clues based on Nina's behavior, and Rose's videos, it'd been a puzzle that looked like a Monet painting up close but made a clear picture when viewed from a distance. I settled for saying, "I've noticed a few things, and it's the only thing that makes sense."

"I didn't want to, but Mark made me," Nina said.

"How?" Skepticism shaded my words. Nina was an adult.

"When I moved back to town and got the job here, Mark heard about it from a mutual friend. He threatened to tell my husband that I'd, umm, dated Mark when I was also dating my husband. And my husband thought we were exclusive."

"You thought your husband would believe Mark's claims?" Harley asked.

"Mark has video proof," Nina said. She blushed dark red. "It seemed sexy at the time. But I was young and stupid, and I've regretted it ever since. Mark threatened to release the videos online if I didn't help him."

A sliver of sympathy flowed through me, but I quashed it down. We needed to get all of the truth into the light before we could move forward. "What has Mark asked you to do? Did you poison Bianca's cup?"

"Poison? What? Absolutely not. No, Mark asked me to, like, engage in corporate espionage. Find out your recipes and what makes customers like your coffee. The cease-and-desist letter really pissed him off and he's out to get you. He said the letter wasn't legally binding, but he doesn't want the publicity of a lawsuit."

"So he sent in a spy instead. So, no sabotage? Just trying to steal our ideas. Recipes he could've replicated with time in his own kitchen."

"He brought sabotage up, and it's a hard no from me, but then he mentioned releasing the video, so I've been figuring out how to get out of this situation. I just want to live my life." She put her hand on her stomach.

Another puzzle piece clicked together. "You're also pregnant?" I asked.

Her gaze snapped to me. "How'd you know?"

"You just put your hand on your stomach, and you've been a bit off in the mornings."

"I'm barely three months along. If Mark blows up my marriage, my child will grow up in a broken home."

"You could always quit," Harley said. "Then you can't spy for Mark."

"But what if he releases the footage?" Nina had curled her arms in on herself like she was making herself into a small ball.

"Let's not make any decisions now," I said. "But Nina, how about you take a few days off, and we'll reassess everything in a few days."

"What should I tell Mark?"

"Tell him I sent you home, and I'm not sure I need two baristas. Make him think you're worried that we're not as busy as we'd hoped and you're afraid you're about to get laid off, and that should buy us some time."

Harley glanced between us. "Mark knows if he releases those videos, he's also putting footage of himself online, right?"

Nina snorted. "I brought that up, and he said it's not embarrassing when you're 'batting out of your league.' Or something like that. And the videos are way more explicit on my side than his."

I didn't even want to think about what she meant. But I realized there was something important to ask.

"Nina, do you have proof of Mark's blackmail?" I asked.

She nodded. "I saved some texts and a voicemail Mark sent me."

"Good. Back those up someplace safe and lie low for a few days, and we'll figure a way out of this."

"Will you want to fire me?"

"Honestly? I don't know. Would you even want to stay?"

"Coming here has been agony, and it makes me guilty, but I also like all of you." Nina glanced from me to Harley and back. "I really wanted to work here when I took the job. I didn't know Mark would show up and ruin everything."

"You could have told us," I said.

Nina bit her lip and looked away.

"I think Sage is right. Let's take some time and then figure things out," Harley said.

"Okay." Nina took off her apron and tossed it in the dirty bin, then pulled her jacket and bag out of one of the lockers. "Will one of you call me?"

"Of course."

"At least this happened without that annoying girl filming us," Nina said.

"What do you have against Rose?"

"She's always watching, and I don't trust her."

"I thought maybe you were afraid she'd caught you doing something embarrassing on video."

Nina flushed, and I knew my words were on target.

"I hate being recorded, and she's always sneakily recording everyone, even you," Nina muttered, and left.

Harley looked at me. "This has been an exciting day."

"Tell me about it." I stretched, wishing I could curl up for a nap.

"Hey, boss, I can use some help!" Colton called out, and I joined him behind the counter. We took care of a brief rush of customers.

As I worked, I wondered. Had Mark—and Nina—wanted to take the spying a step further? Could Nina have tried to sabotage Rose's coffee by adding ketamine, leading to a terrible tragedy when Bianca ingested it instead? Or had Rose recorded a conversation she shouldn't have, and someone was trying to attack her and missed? Then tried again today since while they'd poisoned Bianca by accident, their first attempt was successful in a terrifying way.

Or had Nina somehow known that Rose was buying coffee for Bianca? Could Nina have wanted to target Bianca? She knew that Bianca had it out for me. Did she assume Bianca would flip out if she was drugged? Because Bianca would've flipped. And if she could've proved she'd been drugged by Ground Rules coffee, she could've ruined us.

But how would Nina be able to poison the correct cup? Or did she just poison one of them, hoping to shine a nasty light on Ground Rules to help out Mark in some twisted way?

Or maybe Phillip and Mark were working together? Was it one of the ways Phillip tried to keep Bianca working with him?

Had Bianca been in on it? Had she taken ketamine and then added it to her own coffee cup so she could point the finger at us?

And then I froze.

That was it.

I mentally replayed the security camera footage leading up to Bianca's collapse.

I knew who was responsible for Bianca's death.

Now I just needed to decide what to do with the information.

# Chapter 23

Last night, I'd told Bax about what I'd figured out, and he insisted we "loop" Jackson in, so we'd video-called him for a strategy session. Piper had chimed in. Eventually, we had an official plan.

Now, nerves made it impossible for me to eat as I prepared to leave for work. From the outside, I looked the same in my usual coffee shop uniform of jeans and a long-sleeved Ground Rules T-shirt.

I paused as I left the house. It'd started raining again in a slow, steady drizzle. But that's not what caught my eye.

The first daffodils were pushing their way up into the world. A reminder that no matter how long the winter, cheerful yellow flowers are just waiting for spring to come so they can be the first to say hi to the world and remind everyone that summer is coming.

I metaphorically braced my shoulders as I prepped my bicycle for the ride to work. I reminded myself of the Arthur Conan Doyle quote from one of the Sherlock Holmes books: "When you have eliminated all which is impossible, then whatever remains, however improbable, must be the truth."

And today, I was going to confront a killer.

My motions were practiced as I opened the shop alongside Colton. "So, no Nina?" Colton asked, and I told him why as we worked, although I just told him Mark was blackmailing Nina to spy on us without getting into why.

"So now, I must figure out what to do and how to move forward. Nina is taking a few days off while we figure everything out," I said.

"Do you want my two cents?" Colton asked.

"Go for it."

"She's a decent barista. But I think you could find someone equally good or better without the baggage. Knowing she was here to spy for Mark, I'm not sure I can trust her again. It would've been different if she'd been up front about that and turned into a double agent."

"Do you like spy fiction?"

"My dad is like the biggest Bond fan. But about Nina. She could have been a better worker, too. I know we don't need to sprint all shift, but she didn't even want to hustle when it was busy. And especially if you weren't here and it was just the two of us."

"When you say she didn't hustle, do you mean she was slow but purposeful, or. . . ?"

"I mean, she slacked off. She'd go on her phone in the back or ignore customers while pretending to be busy when they came in, so I'd have to finesse things. Even if I was already making drinks or had my hands full." Colton's tone had an unusually somber note.

"Thanks for telling me." Colton was the sort of employee whom, when he said something, I instinctively knew to take it seriously. He didn't complain just to have something to say.

"Honestly, I think she's never been comfortable here. Knowing about Mark makes me think she didn't want to spy on you. Maybe she wanted to be fired?"

Colton's charitable analysis made me realize how happy I was that we'd hired him.

And I suspected he was right and that we needed to cut ties with Nina, even if she wanted to stay.

Colton and I handled the morning rush. I kept glancing at the door when it jingled, wondering if it was time to put my plan into place.

I was debating texting Jackson to let him know today was a no-go, plan-wise, when the murderer walked in the door in a jaunty walk like she didn't have a care in the world.

I said, "It's go time," and ignored Colton's quizzical look. I slid my phone out of my apron pocket and clicked record, then slid it back inside, where it would take an audio recording. I stepped around the counter and into the shop.

"Hi, Sage. Top of the morning to you," Rose said. She sounded peppy.

"You're out of the hospital?" I resisted the urge to cross my arms over my chest. I tried to look concerned.

"Yeah, I didn't even have to spend the night after my overdose, thankfully. Want to record a video with me to celebrate?" She held up her phone. Her nails were freshly manicured with a glittery overlay over pink polish.

Like sparkles on a unicorn, provided the unicorn was based on a carnivorous Shadhavar myth.

"Instead of going online, I'd like you to answer a question."

"Oh? Well, as long as I can also order a mocha."

I motioned for Rose to follow me into the corner of the shop, so we had some privacy, but she still faced one of the shop's security cameras.

"Why did you kill Bianca?" I asked.

Some, but not all, of Rose's pep slid off her face. "Why would you say that?"

"Stop lying to me, Rose. I know you did it. I just don't know why." I looked straight into her hazel eyes.

She looked away first. Her voice was soft. "It was an accident."

"You accidentally dosed her with ketamine?" My voice hadn't been this thick with sarcasm since my middle school days.

"How did you figure it out?" Rose asked.

"When I handed over the cups, you quickly took a sip and left a thick lipstick smudge. It was the only time I have seen you sip black coffee. I realized you did that to mark your cup. So you knew which cup to put ketamine in. I kept looking at who had access to Bianca's cup, which made me overcomplicate everything."

"Like I said, it wasn't supposed to be deadly," Rose said. "I've taken ketamine before. It only lasted about thirty minutes, and it never harmed me. I never imagined Bianca would react to it."

"Why did you give it to her, to begin with?"

"Bianca was always so vicious about you. I wanted to show the world what a fool she was, so people wouldn't think badly about you. I thought if she acted loopy and erratic on film, and I posted it online, no one would take her seriously. She wanted to call you out publicly and shame you into closing."

"So you mixed ketamine into her coffee?"

Rose nodded. "It tastes like nothing, so I knew Bianca wouldn't notice."

"Where'd you acquire the drugs? Please tell me you don't carry ketamine around with you all of the time."

"Of course not, Oma," Rose said.

I gave her a glare that told her the buddy-buddy, "call me Grandmother" attitude wouldn't fly with me.

"I bought it at a club downtown. I bought it for myself but never used it. I threw the packaging away in the trash, which must be how the police found the dealer's fingerprints."

Some of the answers were so simple in context.

Rose locked eyes with me with a pleading look, like she was seeking absolution. "From the research I've done into ketamine overdoses, I'm guessing Bianca was taking other drugs, and that's what caused her death. How was I supposed to know that?"

"That's why you don't give drugs to people without their consent." I studied Rose's face. "Why did you fake your own attack?"

"I wanted to muddle everything up and create so many suspects that Bianca's death would never be solved or put down as an accident."

"I mostly believe you, but I don't understand why you were trying to protect me from Bianca? She wasn't a threat to me, except for a few possible moments of embarrassment."

Rose looked down for a moment. When she looked up, a vulnerable expression crossed her face. "I think we're related," she said. Her voice was barely more than a whisper.

"Related? How?" I visualized my family tree, wondering where a thorny Rose offshoot would fit.

"Umm, I'm pretty sure I'm your younger sister."

What? I stared at her, not sure what to say.

"I was raised by my dad until he went to jail. Then I couch-surfed for a while, shuffling between my grandmother's and aunt's houses. But no one had space for me. Or time."

I made my sound soft and understanding. "Why do you think we're related?"

"When I turned eighteen, I visited my dad in the big house. He told me about the job he did with your mother that resulted in both a nest egg in an offshore bank account and me. Saffron didn't want me, so he took me in. Then he did another job with her when I was ten. Something went wrong, and he took the fall. She walked away and never looked back."

Of course she did. A few answers to questions I hadn't known to ask clicked into place. "So the podcast was a way for you to figure out your past?" Provided it was true, and Rose was also part of Saffron's tainted legacy, like Jackson and me.

Rose nodded. "Exactly. I was already interested in true crime 'cause of my dad and how it affected the victims. Then finding out my mother was still out in the world, living life large without me, made me want to explore the question even more."

"Are you even in college? Or is that part of your façade?"

"No, I am. Despite everything, I did well in high school and got a full ride to Santa Cruz. I've been taking classes remotely while doing my podcast. I'd only planned to be here a few weeks but decided to stay longer, even though I'm about to run out of money.

I've been renting a tiny room in a house and desperately need to change things up." Rose looked at me, and I could see she was planning something.

But her following words shook me slightly.

"I was ready to hate you when I came to Portland. You had a much easier life than me. I wanted the opportunities you had. But then I met you, and I liked you a lot. I wanted to get to know you better."

"You should've been honest with me from the start."

"What would you have said if I'd popped up and claimed from the get-go that we were sisters?"

"I would've had questions, but I wouldn't have immediately discounted you. My brother would've asked for a DNA test."

"Brother?" Rose looked at me with wide eyes.

"In your deep dives into Saffron's past, you didn't find out she had a son while she was in high school?" Maybe I should give Rose a small break since she wasn't a professional investigator. She was a kid in a lot of ways.

But an adult in the eyes of the law.

"And you didn't tell me? He would be a good interview source for the podcast. And I'd like to meet him."

"You have met him," I said. "And there's no way he would ever consent to be interviewed."

"I've met him?" Rose looked thoughtful. Her gaze shifted back to Colton, who was making drinks for customers who'd walked in while I talked with Rose.

"Not him. You didn't mention our potential relationship to Uncle Jimmy, either."

Rose clenched her jaw, and her tone was sharp. "That is one of the worst interviews I've ever done. Would it have helped if he'd known?"

"With the interview? No. But he would've done something if you'd told him who you were before drugging and killing Bianca.

Helped you with school or something. Invited you over for Christmas. Treated you like a niece."

"Hmm." I could read speculation in Rose's eyes and realized we'd gone way off subject. "But back to the matter at hand: you need to confess, Rose."

"I can't."

"You know those ripples you talked about in your podcast? If you don't, those ripples will be stains on everyone here at the Button Building. We will all be under suspicion for something we didn't do."

"I can't go to jail. I just can't."

"All of this research into true crime, and you're refusing to take responsibility for your own actions?"

"What must I do to convince you to keep this quiet?" Rose sounded desperate.

"There's nothing you can do, Rose. But I will do what I can to support you after you confess."

Rose turned and walked toward the door, then stopped. "No, I'm leaving. And it won't matter if you call the police because it's not like you have proof. It's your word against mine."

I held up my phone and showed her the screen.

"I can't believe you recorded me," Rose said.

"That's hypocritical. You've been recording people for weeks, whether they knew it or not."

"I recorded conversations for my podcast. This is different. This is my life."

"Did you notice the signs by the door about the on-site cameras?" I asked.

Rose's eyes flicked toward the door and then up at the closest camera.

Another puzzle piece clicked into place. "You did know about the cameras. You were careful to avoid being filmed adding the drugs to Bianca's coffee. It wasn't just luck."

"Sage, don't turn me in."

"Rose, I'm sorry, but I have to do what's right." Even if my heart was telling me to let her flee.

Rose turned and rushed toward the door to the communal area as I said, "Incoming."

The detective appeared in the doorway, and Rose wilted.

As Detective Leto arrested Rose and made her sit on one of the chairs in the communal area, I felt like a traitor.

But as I looked around at the other micro-restaurants, I knew I'd made the right decision since they all deserved to live life free of suspicion.

But that didn't stop another layer of guilt from building around my heart.

# Chapter 24

A short while later, I watched as the police led Rose away. I was quickly joined by Laura, Abby, and a few other micro-restaurant owners.

"Okay, what happened?" Laura asked. "Why did they arrest little Rose?"

My fellow business owners turned toward me, making me feel like I was getting the Poirot moment that Rose had promised her followers. I told them what Rose had done.

"Really? I suspected Phillip," Abby said.

Everyone turned and looked at her.

"C'mon, I'm sure I'm not the only one," Abby said.

Laura nodded. "I suspected him as well. I must confess, I didn't suspect Rose, although I thought her running around here recording all of us was odd."

"She definitely felt sketchy," Abby agreed.

"Although I also wondered if Bianca had tried to target Rose and chose the wrong cup," Laura said. "Rose was so nosy, after all."

I barely kept myself from openly scoffing at them. They'd been happy to let Rose film them, seeing the value in a bubbly young influencer promoting them.

I should feel guilty about suspecting Phillip. But while he wasn't responsible, legally, I wondered how guilty Phillip would feel since he'd given Bianca the Xanax that contributed to her fatal interaction. But he'd given it to her with her permission and full knowledge. If I were him, it's the sort of accident that would haunt me for years to come, even if it wasn't my fault.

"So when Rose collapsed the other day, that was fake?" Laura asked.

"Yep. Rose added a small dose of ketamine to her own coffee. But she'd taken it before and knew what to expect. She faked the overdose."

"She had me fooled. I thought Rose was dying," Abby said. "That was unforgivable."

"I can't argue with you there," I said. That was one of the worst of all of Rose's acts because it had been calculated. I believed she hadn't intended to seriously harm Bianca. But Rose had made me think a second cup of my coffee had turned deadly. She'd let Abby panic while trying to help her. She'd fooled all of us.

"So, how did you figure this out, Sage?"

"Logic. I kept looking for zebras when trying to figure out what happened to Bianca, but it was straightforward." Rose using her lipstick to mark her coffee cup was a stroke of genius, and I realized earlier that Rose never drank black coffee. She always added cream first.

"Thank goodness this is over," Laura said.

"Mostly over," Abby said. "Will there be a trial and all of that jazz?"

"I'm not an expert, but I'd guess Rose will plead to something versus this going to trial. But we'll have to see."

A few minutes later, I took a quick moment to text Jackson. *Rose confessed. Also, she might be our younger sister.*

Jackson called me. "What, now?"

"You sure responded quickly."

"I've been waiting to hear from you. Now, what do you mean about Rose?"

"Let me put it into context," I said. I stepped to a quiet spot and told Jackson how everything played out and then shared Rose's reason.

"So, in a misguided way, Rose was trying to help me, or so she claims."

"Because she thinks she's related to us."

Jackson was clearly stuck on this claim.

"It's possible," I said. Rose didn't look like me, and she also didn't look like Jackson. Rose could've taken after her father's half of her genetics. Like how Jackson resembled his paternal side.

"We should do a DNA test."

"I think she has other issues to deal with now."

"I'll rephrase. If Rose returns to Portland once her legal issues are dealt with, and she finishes the terms of whatever plea agreement she gets, then we should."

I laughed.

"What?"

"Remember when you first met Rose, and you said she was almost as annoying as I was at that age?"

Jackson chuckled. "I lied. She's more annoying. And foolish since you were smarter at her age. Listen, I need to go to get ready for a hearing later today in juvenile court. But we need to meet up and talk this through. Chicken and jojos sound good for dinner?"

"It's a plan."

"Bring Bax."

"As long as you invite Piper!"

We hung up, and as I walked back to my shop, I ran into Detective Leto.

"You trying to steal my job, Caplin?" Detective Leto asked. Her tone was serious, but her eyes crinkled like she was smiling.

"If there's an opening at your department for someone to serve espresso with a side of crime solving, sign me up."

"I'll keep that in mind."

"So, the drug dealer you asked me about? Did he sell Rose the ketamine she bought in a club downtown?" I asked.

"You're the hotshot detective of the hour, you tell me." Ah, so she wasn't going to answer.

One half of Detective Leto's mouth lifted in a smile. "Don't quote me, but I was looking at Rose. But she didn't really have a motive that we could find."

I tugged at my ponytail and then dropped my hands. "I had no idea that I was her motive. It never even crossed my mind." I'd fallen for Rose's amateur sleuth act, which told me one thing: I'm decent at reading people and knowing when they're lying, but I'm not infallible.

"I'll need to take a statement from you, but I can do that later today."

I sensed the goodbye-for-now in the detective's voice, and I remembered there was something else I wanted to ask her. "Can I ask your professional opinion about something else? Something unrelated."

She raised her eyebrows slightly. "Okay."

I told her about the Nina situation and how Mark had threatened to send the videos of him and Nina to her husband or even release them online.

"That falls on the wrong side of revenge porn laws, right?"

"Yep, there's a good chance that falls on the wrong side of ORS 163.472. I looked it up recently for a different case," Detective Leto said. "Under Oregon's revenge porn law, you can't disseminate videos of this nature to harass, humiliate, or injure another person financially or emotionally. There's some language in there about videos that can only be disseminated with the approval of both parties, and there could be an argument in there for blackmail, too. But I'm not a prosecutor, so I can't make any promises. And you'd be surprised by the results good defense attorneys can get, especially if the accused can afford a quality law firm."

"What should Nina do now? She's terrified he will release the videos and blow up her life," I said.

The detective glanced at the ceiling, and I practically saw her brain whirling behind her eyes. "Does she have proof of the alleged crimes?"

"Nina said she saved some texts and voicemails."

"Good. Tell Nina to contact me, and I'll see what I can do," the detective said. "Stuff like this angers me so much, I can't even verbalize it."

I could tell Detective Leto was telling the truth, and part of me wondered why but knew not to ask. Like Rose liked to say, we all carry around damage, after all, ripples from the good and bad events in our life.

# Chapter 25

Two weeks later, we held our second launch party. Really, it felt like a third grand opening. But it also felt like a celebration, even if there was a bittersweet edge.

Colton and I handled the crowd, and I still debated if we should hire a third barista. Nina was officially an ex-Ground Rules employee by mutual decision. She told me she'd had a heart-to-heart with her husband. Something told me she'd given him a truncated version of the truth, but that wasn't my problem, just like how Mark Jeffries's ongoing legal problem for trying to blackmail Nina wasn't my problem. But I hoped the local district attorney threw the book at him.

And I hoped he hired a terrible defense attorney versus being able to worm his way out of the situation.

Midday, I noticed the You're My Everything Boiled Bagels COMING SOON sign on what used to be the Breakfast Bandits. They'd be open similar hours to Ground Rules. I'd met the owners, and they seemed fantastic, so hopefully, we'd be good neighbors.

And I always love a good bagel sandwich, even if it wasn't the toast bar of my dreams.

Phillip had dropped by and said a polite goodbye a few days ago, and I'd made him a cappuccino.

"This is good," he said, sounding surprised. He told me how

he'd been able to sell the equipment inside the Breakfast Bandits shop and their food cart. He would use the proceeds to fund a new start for himself outside of Portland.

"I want a fresh start," he said, and I wished him luck.

Caleb came in for a coffee close to lunchtime.

"Do you think you'll have a busy day selling pizza?" I asked him.

"Thankfully, yes, and I bet I didn't even need to run any re-grand opening specials, although I did," Caleb said. "After everything that happened, a party feels right."

"We all worked so hard to open our restaurants that we should take a moment to celebrate," I said.

"This has been roughest on you, right?" Caleb said.

"I don't think it's been easy on any of us."

"But you felt targeted, and we all wondered why your coffee was drugged. And then you're the one who figured out what was going on. Even if you made the right choice, turning in Rose must weigh on you, at least a little bit."

Caleb had no idea. "But I couldn't have lived with knowing what happened and not taking action." It's the sort of slippery slope I had to avoid.

"On the bright side, Rose is young. She'll end up doing, what, maybe five years of a ten-year sentence at the worst? She'll have time to make amends and start over," Caleb said. "Rose will deserve a second chance."

"Fingers crossed she makes the best of it."

Caleb left with his coffee.

We served a decent number of free drinks, most of them to regulars at the coffee cart since we'd passed out coupons there. I loved seeing them visit the store.

"Although the Rail Yard Ground Rules cart would also have the number-one place in my heart," one man joked.

"Tell me about it. I will always love that cart wholeheartedly," I said.

"It's also directly on my route to work."

A while later, a familiar face walked in. He'd ditched his wool coat for a tan jacket that I would bet was a Burberry.

"Hi, Michael," I said. "Are you in the market for another London fog?"

"Oh, my, no. But I'd love a cappuccino."

After I made the drink and handed it over, Michael asked, "Can we speak for a moment?"

We were in a lull, so I nodded yes. "Colton, please watch the shop while I step to the side."

"Sure thing, boss."

I grabbed my water bottle and walked around the counter to join Michael at one of the tables. He'd folded his jacket over the back of the chair before sitting down. His blue sweater looked fancy casual.

"I'm flying back to London tomorrow morning, and I wanted to say goodbye," he said. "I truly mean it when I said I'm happy to see you again, and I'm glad to see you're doing well."

"I enjoyed meeting you again, too." Should I apologize for my mother's actions?

But Michael slid something across the table. "I'd like to give you this."

"You don't need to—" But I still opened the small box to find a dainty star sapphire pendant inside.

"I thought that would go with your ring."

"I love it." I really did. It was my style.

"It's a lab-grown sapphire since I have issues with the environmental cost of mining for precious stones."

"Interesting stance for a jeweler," I said.

"When I inherited my family's company, I decided we needed to look at how we were impacting the world."

"I have a similar ethos for Ground Rules, but on a different scale. It's one of the reasons we highlight the family-owned farms we acquire beans from."

"I noticed. I subscribed to your newsletter and like the one that just came out."

I motioned to the necklace. "I feel awkward accepting this. You should hate me."

"But I don't because I know you're a victim, too. And as angry as I was about your mother over the years, I always wondered what happened to you. I'm relieved that you seem to be flourishing with your own small business instead of following in your mother's footsteps."

"Taking my mother's path was never an option."

Michael studied my face, and I steeled myself for a difficult question.

"Back then, what did you think was happening? Like when your mother had you go by a different name?" Michael asked.

His question pointed toward the well of guilt inside me. "Honestly, I thought it was a game. And my mother spent time working with me, so I'd respond to the name she chose for the moment, like Sarah, and never say the name Sage. I didn't understand what she was doing, and when I was getting old enough to understand, she dumped me off in Portland. But I ended up with my dad, which was the best end result."

"Your father lives locally?"

"Yes," I said. "My dad put a lot of time into making sure I had support to, I guess, have a normal life. Along with my older half brother."

And now it might be our turn to give our younger, wayward sister support. I thought of Caleb's words and how, if she made amends, Rose would eventually deserve a second chance.

In the next few years, I'd have to decide how involved to be with Rose. Especially if she was correct and she was my little sister.

My sister. I'd wanted one as a child, but then I'd found a brother.

Something told me her childhood had been harder than the little snippets she'd shared. She hadn't had my father or Jackson in her corner. Or Miles or Uncle Jimmy.

I remembered a saying I heard once: learn to bloom where you plant yourself. Rose needed to figure out how to find a spot to bloom, pun not intended.

Michael and I talked for a few minutes until he left. I felt a small sliver of relief, knowing that one chapter in my life had been closed with a bittersweet yet happy ending.

As I got back to work, I felt grateful that, despite hardship, life had led me here.

Kaldi sat in the front window as I walked up the front steps after dropping my bike off in the garage. I still buzzed from the overwhelming success of the second and hopefully final Button Building launch.

I halted with my foot on the final step.

A tall, skinny box with a ribbon wrapped around it was sitting on the front porch, right in front of the front door. It didn't have a shipping label, but a gift tag was hanging from the ribbon, along with a sage green envelope tucked underneath.

I knelt and looked at the tag.

*To Sage Caplin & Lukas Evans Baxter.*

I slid the envelope out from underneath the box and opened it to find a card inside. The front showed clinking champagne glasses with the word "congratulations" in a calligraphy-style script. Very simple and elegant, printed on heavy paper, like it was from a chichi stationery shop. I looked inside, and the note was written in looping writing that reminded me of my own, except more polished.

> *Rumors of my death have been greatly exaggerated. Enjoy this belated engagement gift!*
> *—SJ.*

Saffron Jones.

My mother.

My very alive mother.

I carefully opened the box and pulled a bottle of champagne out.

A very expensive bottle of champagne.

I sighed and took a photo of everything, then carried it inside and left it on the entry table on the side wall. I headed straight to our home office with Kaldi on my heels, where I flipped through the small box on my desk and pulled out the card of the FBI agent who'd contacted me a few months ago. As I held my phone, I pondered what to say. I decided to go simple. I tapped out a text message and added the photos.

*My mother made contact.*

I pressed send.

So my mother was out there, somewhere in the world. No one would've known to look for her if she'd laid low. She could've lived a peaceful life as whomever she'd chosen to be that day.

But, of course, she couldn't go the easy route.

Knowing my mother was out there, somewhere, would invariably cause ripples throughout my life.

I texted Jackson about the champagne, wondering if she'd also contacted him. Then I texted my dad and Uncle Jimmy. Might as well keep everyone in the Saffron drama loop. Because one thing I'd learned was to not keep this a secret, at least not from my family, who are also involved, no matter how tangentially.

And did Mother know about Rose's predicament? Was she a fan of the podcast? Would she consider it her greatest-hits show?

I guess I had to have faith that justice would be served someday. Maybe even in an unexpected way.

Meanwhile, I had my own life to lead, with my own decisions to make and stand by. I'd done a decent job planting myself in the spot I'd chosen, and I just needed to continue tending to the roots alongside the blooms.

And everything looked golden.

# Acknowledgments

I'm lucky to know wonderful people with interesting careers who are also willing to answer questions about their specialties. All mistakes are my own.

I'll start by saying thank you to Frank Zafiro for his insight into police procedure and for making some fun plot suggestions (I'm resisting the urge to say "thanks, Opa" to him). On the legal flipside, thank you to Rankin Johnson for answering legal questions from a defense attorney's perspective. I owe Dr. Sarita Heer a coffee for her art history help and Bryant Ramirez a pint of beer at a soccer game for his help with Spanish. And giant thanks to my pharmacist, who trusted my questions about drug interactions were for fictional reasons and sent me helpful materials.

On the publishing side, thanks again to Joshua Bilmes and JABberwocky for seeing my potential back when I was in the slush pile.

Thank you, too, to the crew at Kensington Books. I'm excited to keep working with all of you. Artist Tsukushi drew yet another fantastic Ground Rules cover. She deserves a lifetime supply of her favorite brew for her adorable coffee cart illustrations.

My Portland writing community continues to impress me with its warmth and support. Writing is always solitary, but having friends to discuss the intersections of craft, business, and luck makes the journey more enjoyable. Thank you, friends.

# RECIPES

## Ground Rules Blondies

One of the joys of this blondie recipe is that it's naturally gluten-free, but you'd never guess that based on the taste. The almond flour gives these a chewy deliciousness that's almost addictive. Mixing in oat flour (versus one hundred percent almond) gives the blondies lighter, airier texture. If you want to serve this to a GF friend, make sure your oat flour is certified gluten-free.

This recipe is also naturally dairy-free, but again, you can't tell based on taste!

### Ingredients

1 cup almond flour & oat flour mix (either ¾ cup almond flour and ¼ cup GF oat flour; or ½ and ½)

1 cup brown sugar

1 teaspoon baking powder

½ teaspoon salt

1 large egg

⅓ cup canola oil

1 teaspoon vanilla extract

### Preparation

Preheat your oven to 350° F.

Line an 8-by-8-inch pan with parchment paper (or grease the pan well, but honestly, use parchment paper; the cleanup is much easier).

Mix the brown sugar, flour, salt, and baking powder in a large mixing bowl. Using a fork, make sure to blend the dry ingredients.

Add the oil, egg, and vanilla extract to the dry ingredients and stir with a wooden spoon (or similar). The batter will feel more like cookie dough than brownie or cake batter.

Pour the dough into the waiting 8-by-8-inch pan and use the wooden spoon to spread it out.

Bake for 25–30 minutes. One way to check if the blondies are done: insert a toothpick into the blondie; you want it to be mostly crumb-free when you pull the toothpick back out.

Cool in the pan for about 5 minutes, then cool on a wire rack. Slice into squares once the blondies are fully cooled off.

**Note:**

You can use all-purpose flour, but then your blondies won't have the chewy, nutty taste.

# Vanilla Simple Syrup

## Ingredients

½ cup water
½ cup sugar
1 teaspoon vanilla extract

## Preparation

Mix the water and sugar together in a saucepan. Bring to boil, then remove the pan from heat and stir in the vanilla extract. Let it cool. Pour the syrup into a mason jar or other container and store in your fridge.

## Note:

You can easily cut this recipe in half to make a smaller amount of syrup, or double it for a larger batch. It's forgiving—and delicious.

You can make this a "bourbon vanilla" simple syrup by adding a shot of bourbon to the water and sugar mix. Make sure the bourbon boils for a few minutes to remove the alcohol. Or add it at the end with the vanilla if you want it to be a boozy simple syrup.

## Vanilla Coffee Soda

**Ingredients**
- ¾ cup cold brew concentrate
- 1 tablespoon vanilla simple syrup
- ¾ cup club soda
- Ice

**Preparation**

Mix the cold brew concentrate and vanilla simple syrup in a wide-mouth, pint-sized mason jar (or glass of your choosing). Add ice to the top of the glass, then slowly pour in the club soda. Lightly mix, and your soda is ready.

# Ground Rules Chai Concentrate

If you're a fan of chai, you're in luck: it's very easy to make your own chai concentrate at home.

### Ingredients
    1 inch of fresh peeled ginger, chopped finely or crushed
    3 cinnamon sticks
    5 cardamom pods, lightly crushed
    10 black peppercorns
    1 star anise, lightly crushed
    3 whole cloves, lightly crushed
    ⅓ cup sugar
    5 cups water
    5 teaspoons of black tea leaves
    milk of your choice

### Preparation
Mix the spices and water together in a saucepan, and bring to a boil. Let them simmer for five minutes, then add the sugar. Once the sugar is dissolved, remove the mixture from the heat and add the black tea leaves.

Let the tea steep for four to five minutes, then strain the concentrate into a glass jar or bottle.

Let it cool, then store the concentrate in your refrigerator.


To serve:
Warm up ½ cup of milk with ½ cup of concentrate. You want a 1:1 ratio of milk to tea.

### Notes:
If you want to avoid caffeine, make the concentrate with rooibos. Just adapt the brewing time based on the tea you choose.

You can substitute bagged tea for tea leaves. Use five tea bags (one cup of water = one tea bag or a teaspoon of tea).

You can add or eliminate spices to get the flavor that speaks most to you. Some people might prefer less cinnamon; other people might add fresh nutmeg. You could even add vanilla or orange zest.

A mortar and pestle works great for preparing the spices. You can also use the back of a spoon to crush them.

# London Fog Tea Latte

### Ingredients

black tea (Earl Grey is standard but you can sub in a different
black tea, if desired)
milk/cream (oat milk and nondairy milk work great!)
vanilla simple syrup

### Preparation

Brew your tea and be sure to leave room for the milk and
simple syrup. It's okay to brew the tea a little strong, meaning,
slightly less water than a usual cup since you're adding milk.
Most black teas have a brewing time of 3–5 minutes; do not
overbrew, or your tea will turn bitter.

Once your tea is brewed, add a teaspoon of simple syrup (or
to taste—if you want a sweeter drink, add more) along with
your milk of choice.

Stir, and enjoy! If you want to feel fancy, sprinkle your tea
with dried lavender, which you can buy as a dried spice for
culinary uses. Just be sure to use a small pinch because it's
potent.

## Tomato-Orange–Coconut Milk Soup

This recipe was inspired by the iconic tomato-orange soup at Elephant's Deli in Portland, Oregon. But this version is dairy-free and has a spicy kick.

### *Ingredients*
    canola oil
    1 onion, diced
    1 jalapeño, diced
    1 28-ounce can crushed tomatoes
    1 tablespoon voodoo spice mix
    1 cup orange juice
    2 crushed garlic cubes (optional)
    1 14-ounce can of coconut milk (Note: you want a can of real
       coconut milk.)

If you don't already have a favorite voodoo spice mix, here's a starter DIY voodoo spice recipe that you should tweak to your personal taste:

### *Ingredients*
    1 teaspoon celery salt (or regular salt)
    2 tablespoons brown sugar
    2 teaspoons paprika
    1 teaspoon granulated or dried garlic
    1 teaspoon granulated or dried onion
    3 teaspoons red chili powder
    1 teaspoon dried basil
    1 teaspoon ground pepper

Mix together thoroughly; store the extra in a jar or closed container.

## Preparation

Add canola or other oil to your favorite soup making pot; Dutch ovens work great here! Put over medium heat, and once the oil is warm, add the onion and cook it until it's starting to get translucent. Add the jalapeños and cook for a minute, then add the crushed tomatoes and spices. Bring the heat up slightly until the tomatoes come to a boil, then cover, reduce heat, and let it simmer for twenty minutes.

After twenty minutes, add the can of coconut milk and bring the mixture back to a boil. Simmer it for a moment.

Turn off the heat and blend the soup. An immersion blender is useful here. Be careful if you use a regular blender or other method, and remember the soup is hot.

Once the soup is blended, return it to the pan if necessary, turn the heat back on, and stir in the orange juice.

Now your soup is ready to eat! Serve with toast, grilled cheese sandwiches, etc.

## Note:

If you decide to use real dairy instead of coconut milk, add ¼ teaspoon of baking soda at the same time you add the voodoo spice mix. This will neutralize the acid in the tomatoes and keep it from curdling the cream.

## Quinoa and Roasted Vegetable Salad

**Ingredients**
Vegetables:
1 red bell pepper, cut into bite-sized pieces
2 carrots, cut into bite-sized pieces
1 cauliflower, cut into bite-sized pieces
2 cups of Brussels sprouts, cleaned and quartered
Additional:
olive oil
2 cups cooked quinoa, prepared based on the package's directions
salt and black pepper
Optional:
chickpeas (1 16-ounce can, drained and rinsed)
leftover roasted chicken or cooked chicken, shredded
For the dressing:
⅓ cup fresh lemon juice
⅔ cup olive oil
sea salt
fresh ground pepper to taste

**Preparation**
Preheat your oven to 425° F. Add the prepared vegetables to a mixing bowl and drizzle with olive oil. Toss them, then add a sprinkle of salt and black pepper and toss again.

Spread the vegetables out on a lightly greased cookie sheet. Be sure to give them room and use a second cookie sheet if needed.

Put the cookie sheets in the oven and roast for about 30 minutes (if you're worried, start checking about 15 minutes in). You want the vegetables to be fork tender and look toasted and even a tad bit charred around the edges.

If you decide to add a root vegetable (like potatoes, sweet

potatoes, etc.), consider baking it on a different sheet than a vegetable that takes less time.

Meanwhile, cook the quinoa according to the package's directions, then set aside.

Make the dressing by squeezing the lemon juice and then whisking the juice with the olive oil. Add sea salt and pepper to taste.

When the vegetables are done, add them to a large bowl along with the quinoa and optional chickpeas, drizzle the dressing over the top, and mix.

Your salad is now ready to serve! If you're using chicken, add it to each serving of salad.

You can store the salad in a large bowl or parcel it out into meal prep containers for a quick grab-and-go lunch.

**Notes:**

The fun part about this salad is you can sub in whichever vegetables you have available. If you don't like one of the vegetables, just leave it out! Or substitute with something else.

This is a great recipe for leftover roast chicken. Alternatively, you can also boil or bake chicken breasts to go with this!

While quinoa works well in this, you can substitute any grain you'd like. Bulgar works well, as does rice or couscous. You can make this naturally GF depending upon the grain you choose.

Fresh cherry tomatoes also make a fun addition! Add them when you're ready to eat.

Visit our website at
**KensingtonBooks.com**
to sign up for our newsletters, read
more from your favorite authors, see
books by series, view reading group
guides, and more!

BOOK ||||/|| CLUB
# BETWEEN THE CHAPTERS

Become a Part of Our
**Between the Chapters Book Club**
Community and Join the Conversation

**Betweenthechapters.net**